THE WILDWATER WALKING CLUB: BACK ON TRACK

Book 2 of The Wildwater Walking Club series

CLAIRE COOK

MARSHBURY
BEACH
BOOKS

Books by Claire Cook

Publisher's Note: This is a work of fiction. Names, characters, places, and incidents are a product of the author's imagination. Locales and public names are sometimes used for atmospheric purposes. Any resemblance to actual people, living of dead, or to businesses, companies, events, institutions, or locales is completely coincidental.

Marshbury Beach Books
Cover Photo: StevanZZ
The Wildwater Walking Club: Back on Track/ClaireCook
Paperback ISBN: 978-1-942671-20-6
ISBN: 978-1-942671-21-3

Praise for The Wildwater Walking Club

"*The Wildwater Walking Club* is a quick smart read that will get you thinking about walking, friendship, and making time for the things you love."—*Book Reporter*

"A great feel-good story."—*Philadelphia Examiner*

"Readers who enjoy a celebration of friendship will want to walk alongside the Wildwater trio."—*Midwest Book Review*

"A beach tote couldn't ask for more."—*Kirkus*

"*The Wildwater Walking Club* reminds us of what's important in life—the joy of friendship, the power of a brisk walk, and of course the importance of a good book. I couldn't put it down."—*Anisha Lakhani*

"The women of *The Wildwater Walking Club* are a delightful trio, full of heart and determination. As they—literally—put one foot in front of the other, the three new friends find unlikely paths that point them toward more fulfilling lives. Their journey left me genuinely inspired (and with the curious urge to go out and buy a clothesline)."—*Jean Reynolds Page*

"Claire Cook's wisdom, candor, and effervescent enthusiasm shine on in every word she writes."—*Book Perfume*

"Charming, engagingly quirky, and full of fun, Claire Cook just gets it."—*Meg Cabot*

"Claire Cook is wicked good."—*Jacquelyn Mitchard*

THE WILDWATER WALKING CLUB: BACK ON TRACK

"We're all just walking each other home."

Ram Dass

Under the Boardwalk (Revisited)

Oh, when the sun shines down and turns your hair into a poof
And your sneakers get so wet you wish they were waterproof
Under the boardwalk, over hot sand and to the sea
Walkin' at the edge of the water, that's where we'll be

(Under the boardwalk) slathered in sunscreen
(Under the boardwalk) walkin' toward the dream
(Under the boardwalk) picking up the pace
(Under the boardwalk) making it a race
Under the boardwalk, boardwalk!

Day 1

198 steps

LAVENDER WATER

2 cups distilled water
2 ounces (4 tablespoons) isopropyl alcohol or vodka
15 drops lavender essential oil

Mix all ingredients and pour into a glass container you've sterilized by placing it in boiling water for 4 to 5 minutes. Fill a small spray bottle and shake before spritzing sheets and pillowcases to release tension and encourage calm.

On the one-year anniversary of the day I became redundant, I woke up between crisp white sheets I'd sprayed with a new batch of homemade lavender water before hanging them out to dry on my backyard clothesline. I took a moment to inhale the invigorating fragrance of fresh summer air mixed with the soothing caress of lavender.

"It's okay," I whispered to the dark blur of my ceiling. "I still have six months of base pay and benefits left. I don't need to panic. Yet."

As a positive affirmation designed to get my morning off on the right foot, even I knew it could use some work.

"Every day in every way I'm getting better all the time," I whispered.

I gave the sheets another reassuring sniff. "Amazing opportunities exist for me in every avenue of my life," I tried.

"Every little thing is going to be all right," I whisper-sang in my best Bob Marley imitation.

My best Bob Marley imitation wasn't much, so I lip-synched to an imaginary version of Bobby McFerrin's "Don't Worry, Be Happy" playing in my head.

I'd completely forgotten I wasn't alone until Rick rolled over in my bed. I chose to see this not as proof of my lack of focus on our relationship, but as evidence that I was getting comfortable in said relationship. I wiped an index finger across the corners of my lips in case I was getting so comfortable that I'd inadvertently drooled in my sleep. I cupped the palm of one hand and blew into it to assess my level of morning breath.

"Hey," I whispered.

A small screen glowed softly as he held his phone above us.

I got ready to pull the sheets over my head in case just-woke-up selfies were a new thing.

Rick swung both legs over the side of the bed and reached for his clothes. He put his phone down on the bedside table and pulled on his boxer briefs and jeans.

Rick and I had met at a series of small group outplacement counseling classes offered by a company called Fresh Horizons that had been a part of our buyout packages. The classes had seemed helpful at the time, but I also had to admit that almost a year later, we were both still unemployed, or at least underemployed.

Before we'd taken our respective buyouts, I'd been a Senior Manager of Brand Identity at Balancing Act Shoes. Rick had been some kind of IT ethical hacking wizard at a company that helped financial institutions, as well as the occasional political party, identify their website vulnerabilities. Because the word *wizard* had actually been in his official job title, I always pictured him sitting at his computer behind a red velvet curtain, shirtless and wearing a pointy white wizard hat with Senior Overlord of Ethical Hacking emblazoned across the brim in gold letters. It was sexy, in a geeky kind of way.

You could say that Rick's and my former companies had unwittingly played cupid and brought us together. Or because we'd both taken buyouts, you could say that maybe like really did attract like. But then again, you could also say that two people as messed up as we were right now had absolutely no business attempting a relationship until they got their rebound career paths figured out.

A shadowy Rick slid into his flip-flops and yanked his T-shirt over his head.

"Hey," I said again. I was romantic like that. "What's up?"

He didn't seem to hear me. Maybe he was sleepwalking. Or at least sleepdressing.

Rick picked up his phone again and held it arm's distance away. He gazed at it as if it were some kind of magic orb. Or as if someone really important was on the other end, and he didn't want to chance losing his phone before he could take the call privately.

Then he flip-flopped out of the bedroom without even glancing in my direction. A long moment later, my front door clicked shut.

"This can't be good," I whispered.

I stood on my front steps and watched puffy white clouds and soft blue sky jostle for territory above picture perfect green trees. I swatted a mosquito.

I did a time check: 8:05. The deal was that if my walking partners hadn't joined me by now, I'd head out on our regular route without them. I'd start off slowly to give them a chance to catch up, in case one or both was running late instead of simply blowing me off.

I sat down on the top step and retied one of my laces. I was wearing a pair of the sneakers I'd bought just in the nick of time before my employee discount expired. This particular model was called the Walk On By. It was strictly a women's model, and I'd been part of the team that had positioned it as the shoe every woman needed to walk away from the things that were holding her back and toward the next exciting phase of her life. *Shed the Outgrown. Embrace Your Next Horizon. Walk On By.*

I'd logged lots of miles in these sneakers, but I wasn't sure I'd gotten much closer to that next exciting phase of my life.

After I'd been tricked into taking a buyout from Balancing Act Shoes and dumped by the guy who'd tricked me in one fell swoop, I'd wallowed for a while. But even rock bottom doesn't last forever, and eventually I was all wallowed out. At that point I'd somehow managed to get back up on my feet and start walking. Before long two of my neighbors, Tess and Rosie, joined me.

My house was the smallest of five houses built on the grounds of a working lavender farm when the owners decided to sell off some of their property. As my realtor had explained it to me, if you imagined a pie, the original house still owned half, and the five newer houses each had a pie-shaped slice of the other half.

Rosie lived directly behind me on the original lavender

farm. I lived on the middle pie slice. Tess lived on a slightly larger slice next to me. The street Tess and I lived on was called Wildwater Way, although there was neither any noticeable wildness nor water in the immediate vicinity. The three of us called ourselves The Wildwater Walking Club, which was a little goofy, but so what.

I took a moment to retie my other shoelace, even though it didn't actually need it.

Walking solo today would make me feel virtuous. Perhaps even a tad superior. I'd head for the beach and fill my lungs with great big gulps of life-affirming salt air. I thought about how good I'd feel once I found my rhythm and the endorphins started to kick in. How I'd be strengthening my bones and muscles. Preventing heart disease, high blood pressure, type 2 diabetes. Improving my balance, my coordination, even my mood.

I extended my non-dominant wrist, the one wearing my Fitbit. I twisted my arm back and forth, and back and forth some more, for as long as I could take it.

My faux walk complete, I swore softly and went back to bed.

Day 2

231 steps

I'm not going to think about Rick. I'm not going to think, period.

Apparently I'm not going to walk either.

Just when I thought I was doing so well.

Day 3

54 steps

Why is it that my life is always two steps forward and one long pathetic slide back?

Day 4

132 steps

I know what I'll do. I'll create a lavender ice cream flavor for Ben & Jerry. I'll call it Lavender Fields Forever. They'll love it. They'll love me. The three of us will live happily ever after.

But first I have to try all their other ice cream flavors. Research.

Day 5

1179 steps

I contemplated the weeds in my garden as I circled my spoon around and around in a pint of Ben & Jerry's Hazed & Confused. Then I took a massive bite and let the hazelnut and chocolate iciness melt in my mouth while I checked my Fitbit. 38 steps without moving a foot. Not bad.

I contemplated the weeds some more. They appeared to be coexisting happily with all three varieties of my lavender—Grosso, Hidcote and Munstead. When Rosie had started my lavender garden for me, she'd told me that the trick to taking care of lavender is not to overlove it. Not much danger of that happening.

I stroked Grosso's foliage to release its feisty fragrance, which was laced with a hint of camphor. I loved its tall, brave, pointy stems and the way the whole plant stretched gracefully and unapologetically, not afraid to take its full space in the world. I widened my own stance and tried to access my inner Grosso.

I racked up 23 additional steps of ice cream-stirring

mileage. I sighed a time or two, checked to see if sighing registered on my Fitbit. No such luck.

As soon as I heard Tess's car pulling into her driveway, I bent over and yanked a weed just so she wouldn't think I'd noticed her. I stayed low until the whirring sound of her garage door closing stopped.

Tess and I had been doing a lot of this kind of ignoring lately. Waiting until the other one brought in her mail before checking our own mailbox. Making sure the coast was clear before we headed out to our adjacent backyards. Rosie was easier to avoid since a buffer of woods separated us, but I was pretty sure Rosie and I had both pretended not to see each other at the grocery store late one afternoon.

Dodging one another had turned into almost as much of a workout as walking together every day had been.

When I was vertical again, I juggled the ice cream I was holding and spoon-fed myself some Chocolate Therapy. I tried to separate the taste of the chocolate ice cream from the tastes of the other ingredients, chocolate cookies and chocolate pudding. As if somehow this level of discernment might lead me to a deeper understanding of my life, or lack thereof.

One arm was freezing from hugging three pints of ice cream and the other was getting tired from all that twisting. I put the Ben & Jerry's down on a grassy spot while I switched my Fitbit to my other wrist.

I racked up some more mileage by twisting my fresh arm back and forth.

"Why, Noreen Kelly," Tess's voice said behind me.

I jumped.

"Are you actually cheating your Fitbit *and* eating ice cream for breakfast at the same time?"

I ignored her and pulled another weed.

Tess put on her reading glasses so she could get a closer look at the Ben & Jerry's on the ground. "Ooh, Empower Mint—I don't think I've tried that one yet."

Three chickens emerged from the wooded path that connected Rosie's and my properties. They cut across my backyard in a well-choreographed row. I was pretty sure they were making a beeline for my ice cream.

"Yikes," I yelled. "The Supremes."

"Rod Stewart's right behind them," Tess yelled.

I scooped up the Ben & Jerry's containers from the ground and held them over my head.

The hens surrounded us. Rod, their rooster, stood off to one side for reinforcement.

"Come on, you guys," Tess said. "Cluck off."

The chickens kept circling.

Even chicken decisions were beyond me right now. "What do you think?" I asked Tess. "Should I let them split one pint, and then you and I can have the other two? Although I'm pretty sure I've read that dairy is bad for chickens."

Tess shrugged. "And then there's always the issue of ice cream headaches."

"Good point. Although maybe we could just warn them to eat slowly."

"There you are," Rosie yelled as she jogged our way shaking a box of Kashi Good Friends. As soon as they heard the sound of their favorite cereal, The Supremes ditched Tess and me and Ben & Jerry and headed for their owner.

"I'll be right back," Rosie yelled, still shaking the cereal box. The Supremes followed her in a single file, Rod Stewart hot on their heels. "And thank you for not giving them any of that. Poultry diarrhea is not a pretty sight."

Tess and I looked at each other. "Eww," Tess said. "Thank you for that lovely image."

I nodded. "Yeah, I know. It's almost enough to make me throw away the rest of this ice cream."

And then I dug back into the Hazed and Confused.

"Hey," Tess said. "You're not going to hog all that to yourself, are you?"

"Oh, cluck off," I said.

Rosie, Tess and I sat around my kitchen table, each with a pint of Ben & Jerry's and a big spoon. Tess had pulled her blond-streaked hair back in a ponytail so it wouldn't end up in the ice cream. Rosie must have just finished taking a shower right before The Supremes and Rod Stewart escaped, because her red hair was getting shorter and curlier as it dried. My dark brown hair was pretty much doing what it always did—just hanging around looking as ordinary as the rest of me.

We were all wearing the perfect ice cream binge outfits: yoga pants and baggy T-shirts.

"Okay, switch," Rosie said.

We rotated the ice cream counterclockwise.

"You both better be germ-free," Tess said. "I like to keep my summers healthy so I can build up my strength for another school year." Tess was a third grade teacher. Even though I'd never seen her in action, I knew she was awesome at her job. And if I ever doubted it, I was pretty sure she'd tell me. I wondered if it was possible to catch self-confidence instead of a virus from an ice cream spoon.

Rosie sampled her new flavor. Rosie was a landscape designer. She had her own clients and also drew plans for her contractor husband's clients. Her designs were gorgeous. Maybe I could catch some of Rosie's talent while I was catching Tess's self-confidence.

Rosie closed her eyes. "Hmm. I'd have to say Empower Mint, Chocolate Therapy, Hazed and Confused. In that order."

I closed my eyes. "Hazed and Confused, Empower Mint, Chocolate Therapy."

"No way," Tess said. "Empower Mint, Hazed and

Confused, Chocolate Therapy. But maybe we should do one more round just to be sure."

We passed our pints again.

"Listen," I said. "I'm really sorry you caught me cheating my Fitbit, Tess." The truth was I was probably more sorry about the getting caught part than the cheating part. "And I'm sorry I haven't been walking lately. I just can't seem to get my act together."

"Shit," Tess said. "You can't seem to get your *shit* together. It's stronger that way."

"Act is classier," Rosie said.

"Shit is more real," Tess said.

"No shit," I said.

Even though it wasn't that funny, we all laughed anyway, in that laid-back way of friends who have passed the trying-to-impress stage and genuinely like one another.

"Well, it's not like Tess and I have been showing up to walk either," Rosie said.

"Speak for yourself," Tess said. "You have no idea if I've been showing up if you're not showing up. I could be walking every single morning without you."

"Sure you could," Rosie said.

We all sighed, one sigh overlapping the next, kind of like a wave at a ballgame.

"Okay," Rosie said. "So I tied my Fitbit to the ceiling fan in my office the other day. Just long enough to get caught up on some landscape plans."

"Genius," I said.

Rosie dug into the Empower Mint. "Not if you have two tweens in the house. Connor and Nick saw it spinning around and totally fitness-shamed me."

"One of the teachers at school," Tess said, "lets the kids take turns wearing her Fitbit at recess. But personally I prefer the dryer."

"Seriously?" I said. "You put your Fitbit in the dryer? You're not afraid it'll melt?"

Tess shrugged. "You just use the air fluff setting and add some clothes to cushion it."

"Excuse me," Rosie said. "But I thought we were all supposed to be practically dryer-free now. You certainly made us work hard enough to get the town of Marshbury clothesline ban lifted."

"It's called upcycling," Tess said. "I mean, if we're not going to use our dryers for towels—"

"Or sheets," I said.

"Then we might as well find a good use for them," Tess said. "Plus the energy savings are tremendous on air fluff."

"Just FYI," Rosie said, "Dogs wearing a fitness tracker can rack up 7,000 to 35,000 steps per day."

"But," Tess said, "dogs really hate it when you put them in the dryer."

I looked from Tess to Rosie and then back to Tess again. "Not to get all mushy, but I really missed you two."

"Right," Tess said. "When you weren't dodging me out by the mailboxes."

"I loved it when the three of us were walking together every day," Rosie said. "But you miss one day, and then it's so much easier to miss the next one, and before you know it, the entire walking ritual falls apart. Just like family dinner at the dining room table."

"Maybe it's because things are so much easier to start than they are to maintain," I said. I took a quick bite of ice cream so I didn't have to think about how this might apply to the rest of my life.

"I hate, hate, hate maintenance," Tess said. She ran one hand through her freshly highlighted hair. "I mean, look at hair color. You should be able to dye your hair once and be done with it until you decide you want another color. Nails, too."

"Gardens, too," Rosie said. "People always want me to design and install these elaborate gardens for them, but they're totally unrealistic about how much work they'll have to put in to keep them up, even though I warn them."

"Don't look at me," I said. "I pulled three weeds today."

"So we just have to get back on track with walking then," Tess said. "Easy peasy lemon squeezy."

"I think it's easy peasy chocolate freezy," Rosie said.

"Potato-potahto," Tess said.

"I can start Monday morning," I said. "I've got that health coach certificate thing all weekend."

Tess eyed the empty ice cream containers. "Now I get the extreme ice cream binge. You needed to get it out of your system before you turn all healthy on us and become one of those obnoxious nutritionally superior people."

"It's research." I reached for her ice cream container. "I was thinking I might pitch a flavor to Ben & Jerry's. It could set me on a new career path."

"Good luck with that," Tess said. "Hannah pitched them a flavor for a school project one year, and she had to sign a waiver saying that if they used her idea, she understood that she might only get compensated in ice cream and/or promotional items."

"They must get inundated with flavor ideas," Rosie said. "Their lawyer probably makes them do that to protect themselves."

Getting paid in ice cream was probably not the kind of growth I was looking for. Disappointment rose in my chest as one more career door closed in my face.

I cleared my throat. "So how is Hannah anyway?"

"Hannah?" Tess said. "Hannah? Oh, right, you mean my daughter who finished her freshman year at college and then found a paid internship and a place to stay so she didn't have to come home for the summer. It took us years to get her brother completely out of the house, so I have to say I didn't see that one coming. And once again I didn't schedule any tutoring jobs over the summer because I wanted to have time to spend with her, so I can blame my reduced income on her, too. I think our best bet is to sell the house and buy one of those tiny houses we can hitch to the back of the car and hit the road before the next major holiday. Let our darling daughter see what it's like to try to track *us* down for a change the next time she needs mon—"

"I'd love to start walking again," Rosie said, interrupting Tess mid-rant. "But I keep thinking I'll never get all the work I have piled up finished before we go away. I mean, this trip sounded like such a good idea at the time. Plus, with the lavender angle, I can totally write it off."

Tess dug into the Empower Mint. "And I thought I was beyond brilliant getting a cultural enrichment grant. I just have to document the trip and bring back a bunch of cultural crap to share at school."

I shrugged. "And I figured I was going to be broke soon anyway, so I might as well go for it while I still could."

"I've been wondering when to bring this up," Rosie said. "And I know there's not much time left, but the truth is I'm not sure I should go after all—"

"Don't you dare back out," I said. "If anyone backs out, it should be me. No way should I be spending that kind of money right now."

"I'm kind of over the whole trip idea, too," Tess said. "I kept meaning and meaning to look into the refund policy. Maybe I can find a way to use the cultural enrichment grant for something closer to home. Or even online—I mean, it's not like the Internet isn't a boundless source of culture."

"You don't want to go with us?" Rosie opened her eyes wide. "Gee, thanks a lot, Tess."

Tess put her spoon back in the Chocolate Therapy and slid the container to the center of the table. "It's not so much that I don't want to go. But at least you two get to be roommates. It's really hitting me that I'm about to spend eight nights sharing a stateroom with someone I haven't seen since high school."

"Oh, you know those old friendships," Rosie said. "Five minutes in and the years will melt away and the two of you will be just as immature as you used to be. Plus Noreen and I will be there."

"What's her name again?" I said.

Tess rolled her eyes. "Joy."

"See," Rosie said. "How can we possibly have a bad time with someone named Joy?"

I grabbed three water bottles from the fridge to balance out the ice cream. "What's she like anyway? Will she want to walk with us?"

Tess took a long slug of her water before she answered.

"So the weird thing is," she finally said, "the more I think about it, the more I'm pretty sure we never even hung out together in high school."

"Not at all?" I said.

Tess shook her head. "I'm not sure we had a single conversation in all four years."

"Really?" Rosie said.

"Really," Tess said.

Rosie and I looked at Tess.

"Damn Facebook," Tess said.

Day 6

10, 001 steps

It was early enough on Saturday morning that traffic was almost light the whole way from Marshbury to the Braintree split. I stayed right on Route 3. By the time I pulled off the highway, I even had time to do a quick coffee shop drive-through. Just in case further caffeinating turned out not to be an option today, it seemed like a good idea to try to get ahead of the curve. It was hard to know just how healthy health coaches-in-training were expected to be.

Since I might need to order broccoli at lunch to look good, I woofed down a lemon scone along with my coffee on the way to campus. I stopped just inside the parking garage to dispose of the evidence in a big trash barrel.

I pulled into a vacant parking space directly across from the elevator. It hit me that this particular parking spot might be a trap, some kind of fitness *gotcha* with a video camera monitoring it. Just to be on the safe side, I backed out again and found another spot a nice, healthy walk across the garage.

I put my car into park and looked around. It seemed that just about every other car in the parking lot was a Honda Fit, ranging in color from sunshine yellow to eggplant purple to ocean blue. Apparently I'd missed the memo that a perky little car in a motivating color was a health coach prerequisite. My boring old gray Camry felt as oversized and clunky as I did.

I gave my car a pat on the steering wheel. "We are beautiful inside and out," I reassured us both, "and we are growing more attractive each and every day."

There are well over fifty universities, colleges, and community colleges in and around Boston and its neighboring cities and towns, many of them oozing with charm. Lush green quadrangles, gorgeous ivy-covered buildings, elegant stone towers and columns and chapels and statues.

This university leaned more in the direction of a prison, kind of sparse and monochromatic, heavy on the concrete blocks. I took the elevator up and followed the signs for the continuing education program. The lobby was brightly lit and freshly painted, which seemed encouraging. I scanned a list of classes and room assignments on a big whiteboard and wondered for a moment if I should have signed up for Understanding Your Digital Camera instead.

The health coach certificate training began this weekend with two nine-hour days on campus. Intensive distance training would follow, including live and recorded online classes, quizzes, writing assignments, and practice coaching. Twelve weeks later, another long weekend on campus, including a final assessment, would wrap things up.

When I'd first read about the field of health coaching, I was immediately drawn to it. It was a relatively new field, and it seemed hip and cutting edge. The overall health care field was booming, and with the current tsunami of aging baby boomers, health care appeared to be an arena that would continue to grow along with the median age of the population.

In a way, it seemed like an almost logical step to go from

designing campaigns for athletic shoes to designing health programs for the people who wore them. Practically a shoe-in.

But now, as I stood with my hand on the doorknob to the health coach certificate classroom, I wondered what the hell I'd been thinking.

The head health coach honcho, whose name was Kim, seemed nice enough. She was about my age, give or take. She had kind of a crunchy vibe—long straight hair, flowy bohemian dress, Birkenstocks. She rattled off an impressive list of credentials.

She told us how lucky she felt to have found this career, how it was her passion, how challenging our program would be, and how much she was looking forward to sending another group of well-trained health coaches out into the world, because the world needed us.

The other students and I sat facing each other at desks pushed together in groups of four. I checked everybody out as casually as I could. I'd expected them all to be midlife career reinventors like me, but a disheartening number of them seemed young, or at least youngish. Or maybe I just felt old, or at least oldish.

I was wearing skinny ankle-length navy pants with a summer-weight white sweater over a sea foam green T-shirt. I thought the sea foam complemented my pale skin and mossy green eyes, and also worked well with the teal band on my Fitbit. My hair was still at that good place between touch-ups when the graying roots hadn't even started to show yet.

The T-shirt had a V-neck and nice flattering drape that floated away from any potential midsection imperfections I might be in denial about. I'd gone back and forth trying to decide whether to wear strappy sandals, or sneakers in case there was some kind of fitness test. I finally settled on a pair of denim blue Jambu walking shoes that I hoped were the appropriate blend of fitness fashion and functionality.

I smiled at the woman seated directly across from me. She gave me a dismissive smile back, then took a prim sip from her stainless steel water bottle. Okay then, so the two of us were probably not going to be new best friends.

The woman next to the woman who'd just dissed me reached for her own water bottle, which was made of glass that was sheathed in a green protective silicone sleeve. The woman across from her and next to me had a serious-looking water bottle, too. Hers was made of plastic that I knew beyond a shadow of a doubt was BPA-free. It even had a carabiner hanging from it that she could use to clip the water bottle to a belt loop, just in case she had a sudden urge to go climb a mountain and needed both hands free.

Great. My own water bottle was a disposable. Not even a hip, overpriced throwaway like Evian or Fiji or Smeraldina, but a cheap, flimsy supermarket brand. Health coach training had barely begun and already I didn't fit in.

I flashed back to my first day of first grade. I was so proud of the cute plaid book bag I'd talked my mother into buying for me. It even had a little matching plaid umbrella attached to the front flap. And then the third grade girl who had been assigned to help me slid the umbrella out through the loops that held it to the bag. She walked the umbrella all the way down to the end of the hallway and put it in a big wooden umbrella stand. On this brilliantly sunny day, my plaid umbrella stood alone like the cheese at the end of "The Farmer in the Dell."

It was a huge first grade faux pas. *I know it's not raining out,* I wanted to scream at the top of my lungs. *I'm not an idiot. It's supposed to be DECORATIVE!*

All these years later, I fought a nearly identical urge to yell, *I was in a rush this morning! I have plenty of high-end water bottles at home. No phthalates! Lead-free! Ecofriendly!*

When I tuned back in, I realized the students were going around the room introducing themselves. There was a fair amount of letter-dropping happening. MS, MA, MEd, RN, RD, LD, as well as several personal trainers certified by ACE, AFFA, ACSM. I tried to pull together a joke about how my own completely unrelated Bachelor's probably sounded like BS, but it fell flat even in my head.

A cardiac nurse introduced herself and started going on and on about how frustrating it was when patients ignored her instructions.

Kim nodded. "Fifty percent noncompliance with medical treatment is typical."

"My brother-in-law," another woman said, "has type 2 diabetes and thinks as long as he takes his meds, he can drink soda and eat cookies all day long."

Kim nodded again. "Seven out of ten deaths are caused by chronic diseases, and lifestyle is responsible for a full fifty percent of chronic diseases."

"Exactly," the woman said. "I tell him that all the time, but he doesn't listen to me. And you should see the gut on him—"

Kim held out a palm like a crossing guard. "I'm going to stop you right there."

Then she turned and looked right at me. "Next?"

"Um," I said. "I'm, uh, Noreen Kelly and I worked at Balancing Act Shoes for eighteen years, most recently as a Senior Manager of Brand Identity. I thought one of the perks of working there would be staying in shape—you know, they had a state-of-the-art fitness center, outdoor fitness trails, the whole bit. But once I climbed my way up to management, I spent most of my time in a never-ending series of meetings. And then I took a buyout, which essentially gave me eighteen months to figure out what I wanted to do with my life. I've only got about six months left, and I still don't have a clue. I've been helping a friend of mine with a website for her lavender farm and I even make a few things to sell at the store and online."

I gulped down some air. "But the truth is it's mostly just more sitting, and I don't think that's how I want to spend my life. And for a while there I was eating so well and walking every day. And now I'm not even doing that. I've actually been cheating my Fitbit."

The woman sitting across from me gave me a look that said she'd totally pegged me as a Fitbit cheater.

I ignored her. "So when I happened to read about the health coach certificate, it somehow just called out to me. I figured maybe it could help me figure out what I needed to do to get back on track. And if I managed to figure that out, maybe I could figure out a way to help other people figure out what they needed to figure out."

Even to my ears, this sounded like an insurmountable amount of figuring out. "And I want you to know I have better water bottles at home," I couldn't stop myself from adding.

Then I bit my lower lip so I wouldn't burst into tears.

Kim gestured to two chairs at the front of the room. "Perfect. Why don't you come up and join me, Noreen. You can help me demonstrate a health coaching session."

Kim sat up straight in her chair. I made every effort to do the same, even though I was dying to crawl under my own chair and hide.

"There's quite a bit of overlap between life coaching and health coaching," Kim said, "but in health coaching, we see everything through the lens of our primary goal, which is health. Bearing that in mind, what is your question, goal or problem?"

"How much time have you got?" I said.

A few people in the class actually laughed. These would be my friends if I ever made any.

Kim nodded slowly, almost as if her head were a pendulum and she was trying to hypnotize me. Although I guessed if her head were a pendulum, it would be swinging side to side, not up and down.

An awkward silence filled the room. Kim didn't jump in to fill it, which pretty much left me out there hanging. I hated that.

"Okay," I said. "If I had to pick one thing, I'd like to find a way to start walking again every day."

Kim did her pendulum thing again. I waited her out.

"So," she finally said. "You'd like to find a way to start walking again."

I fought off a very un-future-health-coach-like urge to say *duh.*

"Yes," I said instead. "I was doing so well for a while, but now I'm not really walking at all. And the whole time I'm not doing it, I'm thinking of a gazillion reasons why I *should* be doing it."

"So," Kim said slowly. "You're not walking."

A hand shot up across from us. Kim gave a quick nod. "Should you tell her about all the health benefits of walking?" a woman said.

"I bet Noreen already knows all the reasons she should walk," Kim said. She looked at me.

"Oh, yeah," I said. "I recently recited them all to myself right before I went back to bed."

Kim started her long slow nod again. "So. What's standing in your way now?"

I considered this. "Well, I used to think that the hardest part of any workout was just putting on your sneakers. And that once you did that, all you had to do was keep placing one foot in front of the other. But now I think there might be this crucial gap between the sneakers and that first step."

"What do you think you could try?" Kim said.

"Well," I said, "maybe as soon as I get my sneakers on, I should start walking right away instead of waiting to see if my walking partners show up." As I heard the words come out of my mouth, they seemed unintentionally profound. Had I also been waiting for someone to show up before I started living my life?

"So, walking right away instead of waiting." Kim's pendulum head went up and down slowly. "How does that look?"

"Hmm, I guess I'd wake up, maybe even set my alarm to make sure. Then I'd put on my sneakers before I did anything else. Well, maybe I'd go to the bathroom first. But then I'd walk right out the door. Just keep walking if no one else is there. Head for the beach."

"Sounds like a nice peaceful way to start the day. What else would you need to make this happen?"

I thought for a moment. "Nothing."

Another hand shot up. "Are you ever allowed to tell her all the bad things that will happen to her if she doesn't walk?"

Kim smiled. "Most of us already know why we should be doing what we're not doing. But when you tell people what to do, they shut down. It's always better if the client comes up with the goal as well as the reason behind it. Our job is to help the client envision it and figure out how to get there. And then give the client the time and space to achieve her or his goal in her or his own way."

Day 7

10, 013 steps

I lay in bed and waited for the sound of the alarm going off. I'd listened to that aggravating beep at the same crazy time every morning for the entire eighteen years I'd worked at Balancing Act. After so much alarm-free time, I'd kind of enjoyed hearing it go off yesterday. And I had to admit that a part of me was almost looking forward to hearing it again today.

I stared up at a serious crack, which I liked to think of as the Mason-Dixon line of my ceiling. With an entire year off, wouldn't you think I would have gotten around to fixing that crack by now? But all I'd managed to do was watch a YouTube video and make a list of the stuff I needed to buy— utility knife, mesh tape, joint compound, ceiling paint. It seemed that the more time I had, the less I managed to accomplish with it.

My alarm erupted with the beep-beep-beep I'd never thought I'd miss, the sound that told me I had things to do and places to go, that I actually had at least some semblance of a life.

"Have a good day, crack," I said to my ceiling. I hit the alarm, rolled out of bed, swung by the bathroom on the way to the kitchen. I put the coffee on, then I scrounged up an ancient frozen breakfast burrito and zapped it in the microwave.

For better or worse I'd already made a first fashion impression with my health coach cohorts, so I just threw on some clean exercise clothes and a pair of sneakers.

Yesterday I'd been so excited after my front-of-the-class coaching session with Kim that I'd started walking during our lunch break. First my Camry and I had followed a couple of classmates and their Honda Fits as they exited the parking garage. Sure enough, they'd driven right to the nearest Whole Foods. I grabbed a bottle of green juice and a bag of kale chips and circled back to campus.

I ate my lunch while I looped around and around the continuing education building. The kale chips turned out to be a serious mistake in both taste and texture. The green juice was better, but the combination of the two left me quietly burping what I could only imagine was chlorophyll. Two of the other students joined me for my last loop around the building. We all checked our Fitbits on our way back to the classroom.

The afternoon session had been a blur of information— the components of health, the mechanics of coaching, our first practice coaching sessions. I picked up a sandwich at Marshbury Provisions on my way home.

When I finally pulled into my driveway again, I was exhausted. But I changed out of my Jambu shoes and put on my Walk on By sneakers and walked to the beach and back anyway. For the first time in a long time I managed to get my 10,000 steps in, on one of my busiest days in forever, no less. I ate my sandwich, crawled into bed and conked out.

So now my dilemma was whether or not I had time to start the day with another quick walk to the beach before I left for class. I checked the time. Rather than risk a Sunday morning on-the-way-to-breakfast-or-church traffic jam, I decided I'd get the drive out of the way and loop around the building a few times before class started.

I opened a kitchen cabinet and scanned the water bottle possibilities, ruling out the ones whose tops were missing in action. I finally settled on a clear BPA-free plastic bottle with a blue built-in carbon filter designed to trap contaminates with each sip. No more water bottle shame for me.

I imagined the entire health coach class gathered around the bottle-filling station in the lobby, which dispensed chilled and sanitary water with touchless activation, only to discover that it was out of order. They'd have to, *gasp*, use the regular water bubbler instead. While everybody else was wringing their hands and wondering if continued hydration was worth the risk of bubbler germs, I'd whip out my water bottle with its very own built-in filtration system. *Take that*, I'd be too polite to say as I executed a worry-free refill from the bubbler.

I blinked myself back from make-believe water bottle competitiveness. I grabbed my stuff and jumped in the car, began winding through the tree-lined streets on my way out to the highway.

A solitary car was parked at the Marshbury town common. It looked so familiar that I slowed down.

I have a theory that the odds of having a successful relationship with someone can be accurately predicted by the bumper stickers, or lack thereof, on the back of the car of the person in question. Bumper stickers speak volumes. Not privately, or at least semi-privately, like tattoos, but right out there for all the world to see.

A guy who has a bumper sticker that says STILL CRAZY AFTER ALL THESE BEERS is just asking to be pulled over by the cops, and you could be with him. A guy whose bumper sticker says HORN BROKEN WATCH FOR FINGER will grow even less funny as time goes by.

If a guy has those stick people decals across the back window with the gummy outlines of the mom and kids and dog and cat still visible where he's peeled them off, this does not scream adult male available for loving relationship. If a guy's car is covered with bumper stickers all telling you what to do, who to vote for, what to legalize, what to eat or not eat, then he's marking his territory—he might as well be peeing on the bumper—and it's just a matter of time before he'll be infringing on your space, too.

BUMPER STICKERS ARE NOT THE ANSWER, one bumper sticker proclaims. That might well be true, but it's quite possible that bumper stickers are underrated as a reliable relationship early warning signal.

I pulled in behind Rick's empty blue Civic, close enough to read his bumper stickers: THE COMPUTER WHIS-PERER, WIZARD ON BOARD, THE PARTY DOESN'T START UNTIL THE FLYING MONKEYS SHOW UP, NOT ALL WHO WANDER ARE LOST, WHAT WOULD YODA DO?

Not for the first time, I took a moment to analyze Rick's need to inform other drivers on the road of his affinity for *Lord of the Rings, Star Wars, The Wizard of Oz.* Maybe I could buy him a *Peter Pan* bumper sticker to add to his collection: I WON'T GROW UP.

Movement caught my eye. Halfway across the town common, three enormous verdigris elephants were standing on their hind legs in the center of a huge fountain, water spewing out of their trunks. A barefoot Rick was splashing around the elephants, waving his phone in front of him.

I slammed my car door.

"*What* are you doing?" I yelled as soon as I was within earshot. The closer I got, the more disheveled he looked in his wet T-shirt and shorts. And where were his shoes, or at least his flip-flops? He didn't even live in Marshbury, but all the way over in the next town. I didn't have time for this.

He looked up from his phone. "Oh, hey. Did we have plans this morning?"

I squinted at him.

"Or last night? If I missed anything, I'm sorry. I guess I got caught up."

I tilted my head and squinted at him some more.

Rick crossed the distance between us. He put his non-cell-phone hand on my shoulder and leaned in for a kiss. Despite myself, and also the fact that he hadn't shaved in recent history, I felt that same jolt I always did.

He smiled at me, his green cat eyes crinkling at the edges. "How about tonight? Pizza and a game of mini-golf? I'll come by around 6:30?"

I had to admit that Rick and I were at our best on the miniature golf course.

"Okay," I said. "Listen, I have to go. I've got that health coach thing this weekend. Remember?"

"Oh, right," he said as if he'd really remembered. "Hey, good luck with that."

When I was back in my car, I sat for a moment, hands on steering wheel. "We're fine," I reassured my Camry and me. "The world is a kind and gentle place, and we are surrounded by love and serenity."

I tried not to look, but I couldn't help glancing over before I pulled away from the curb. Rick was jabbing his phone around in front of him as he walked barefoot across the green grass of the common. Maybe in his head he was off to see the wizard, or even off to *be* the wizard, as he walked an imaginary yellow brick road.

I didn't even need to take another look at his bumper stickers to know the odds of this relationship working out.

Apparently I'd become the official health coach class guinea pig. Once again Kim and I were sitting on adjacent chairs. I noticed that everybody else had dressed way more casually today than yesterday, too. I took a sip of water. Not that I'd ever admit it, but I'd brought my water bottle with me to the front of the room just to be sure nobody missed seeing it.

"So," Kim said. "How did this morning look?"

I closed my eyes to shut out the vision of Rick prancing barefoot through the fountain with the elephants.

"Walking was your goal," Kim prompted.

"Oh, right," I said. "Walking. Well, I walked on our lunch break yesterday, and then I walked to the beach when I got home last night. It's been a while since I've hit 10,000 steps, so I was proud of that."

Kim was doing her pendulum nod.

"But then this morning I was afraid if I walked I might be late for class."

"So," Kim said. "Getting to class on time today was an obstacle. Were there other obstacles?"

"Yes," came out of my mouth before I could stop it. "Actually, there's this guy I've been seeing. He took a buyout, too, and we met at a career counseling class that was part of our buyout packages. Not a class to *become* career counselors, but to *get* career counseling, and boyohboy did we need it. Anyway, he's a really nice guy, but we're both, well, kind of a mess right now, so I know we're not good for each other."

Kim nodded slowly. I'd never been to a therapist, but I had to admit now I sort of got the whole thing. It was kind of nice to have someone just nod her head and listen instead of trying to break in with her half of the conversation. A couch to stretch out on might have added to the ambiance though.

"So," I said, "that was another reason I didn't walk this morning. I mean, I'm not making excuses or anything. His car was pulled over on the side of the road at the town common, and he doesn't even live in the same town as I do, so I didn't feel like I could just keep driving. And then I saw that he wasn't in his car. He was splashing in the fountain barefoot and waving his phone around—"

"Pokémon Go," somebody yelled.

"Ohmigod," one of the classmates who'd walked with me at lunch yesterday said. "My husband ran right into a metal post while he was playing Pokémon Go. Twelve freakin' stitches on his forehead."

"Did you see that story on the news," somebody else said, "about that guy hitting a police cruiser because he was playing Pokémon Go while he was driving? Like all those idiots who *text* while driving aren't bad enough."

A few more people jumped in with their Pokémon Go stories.

"Thanks," I said. "I feel so much better now. And I think I vaguely remember Pokémon. Wasn't that the video game that came out around the same time as slap bracelets?"

"Slap bracelets were the '80s," the woman whose husband had collided with the metal post said. "The original Pokémon came out in the late '90s. Pokémon Go is completely different though. It uses your phone's GPS, and you have to run around all over the place capturing virtual creatures."

"Well," I said, "playing Pokémon Go seems a lot better than being certifiably insane, which was the other possibility I was considering. At least I think it's better, right?"

Kim was nodding her head again, which I chose to take as a yes.

"So," Kim said, "this is a good example of the way health coaching often overlaps with life coaching. And by the way, Pokémon Go, when played safely and on foot, is a fun and effective form of exercise, so keep that in mind. Anything that entices people away from the computer and gets them moving is a good thing."

I practiced my own pendulum nod.

Kim nodded back. "And never underestimate the transformative impact of one caring person. Simply listening to your health-coaching clients is huge. Sometimes it's the biggest thing of all."

"Thanks for listening," I said.

Kim smiled. "So let's review your goal and action plan, Noreen. Your goal is . . ."

"To walk every day," I said.

"Good," she said. "That's very specific. And how far will you walk?"

"10,000 steps," I said, "without cheating my Fitbit."

Kim nodded. "That's measurable. And it's action-oriented and it's important to you. Is 10,000 steps a day realistic for you? And since there were obstacles today, will first thing tomorrow be a good day to make a fresh start?"

"Absolutely," I said.

Kim nodded. "So, your goal is to walk first thing in the morning and to achieve 10,000 steps every day. This is a good example of SMART goal setting, S-M-A-R-T, a mnemonic acronym that originated in the field of organizational management in the '80s. SMART has quite a few similar meanings but for our purposes we'll say it stands for specific, measurable, achievable, relevant, and time-based."

"Cool," I said. "It's been a while since I felt smart."

The feeling stayed with me for the rest of the day. My classmates were loosening up and getting friendlier—maybe I was, too. A bunch of us even carpooled to Whole Foods. I grabbed a kale chip-free lunch, and then we all ate while we circled around the continuing education building.

We spent the afternoon learning about mindfulness and meditation and stress reduction. Kim went over the requirements for the course again. We divided into groups and did some more coaching practice.

When I finally pulled into my driveway at the end of a long busy day, a pizza box and a six-pack of Rick's favorite beer, Audacity of Hops, were sitting on my front steps. The fact that Rick was wandering around in my front yard waving his phone wasn't even that stressful. Maybe because I knew what he was doing now. Or maybe because I'd spent half the afternoon meditating. Maybe both.

I checked my Fitbit for my step count.

"Hey," I yelled as I got out of my car. "How about we have a quick picnic and then play some Pokémon Go?"

Rick's eyes lit up.

Day 8

10, 198 steps

"Wait for us," Tess yelled when I'd made it about halfway down Wildwater Way."

"Yeah," Rosie yelled. "Wait up, Noreen."

I turned around and walked in place, swinging my arms so they could catch up to me. Not cheat-your-Fitbit arm swinging, but that good kind of arm-pumping action that gets your heart going and makes you realize what a beautiful day it is.

"Gorgeous day," I yelled.

"Don't be such a Pollyanna," Tess yelled. Her blond-streaked hair was up in a high ponytail and she was wearing capri-length exercise pants and big diva-like sunglasses. Her turquoise reading glasses, which she'd probably forgotten about, were hooked on the front of her T-shirt. The T-shirt was white with traffic cone-orange letters that said TRUST ME, I NEED THE WHOLE SUMMER OFF.

"I like your ponytail," I said when she got closer.

"Crap," Tess said. "It's supposed to be a cute messy bun, which according to the daughter I never hear from is totally on point right now." She dipped her head upside down, gave her hair elastic another twist, pulled her ponytail halfway through the opening she'd created. When she was upright again, a big bouncy loop of hair stuck straight up.

"You look just like Pebbles," Rosie said. Rosie did a little skip and a hop to reach us. "All you need is a big stegosaurus bone poking through that."

I shook my head. "What was Pebbles thinking marrying Bamm-Bamm anyway? She needed to step outside her comfort zone, grow a little, see who else was out there and what kind of growth-oriented life they could build together."

"And that, girlfriend," Tess said, "is called projection. Or maybe it's transference—I always get them mixed up. Anyway, I wasn't shooting for a Pebbles look. I was going more for Wilma's ageless sophistication."

"Of course you were," I said. I took another look at the hunk of hair standing on top of her head. It was good to know it was intentional. Hardly anything I ever did was intentional. I just seemed to float along on my indecision, ebbing and flowing with the tide, covering the same rocky shoreline over and over again.

Rosie was wearing a purple bandanna, rolled and tied like a headband, over her curly red hair. Apparently she'd done this on purpose, too. Maybe I needed to up my hair fashion. Or at least start brushing it again on a regular basis.

I ran the fingers of both hands through my hair. It was a start.

The three of us were walking in place, facing each other in a little triangle. Tess turned around and headed off. "Come on," she yelled as she picked up her pace. "I don't have all day. Oh, wait, I do. It's still summer."

"Not to get competitive," I yelled, "but as of right now, I have the rest of my life off."

"I hate you both," Rosie yelled. "I don't even remember what a free nanosecond feels like."

Tess liked to walk on the outside of the sidewalk. Rosie

and I both had a tendency to hang back and let the other one walk beside Tess, since we couldn't fit three across on the sidewalk.

Today Rosie and I hung back at the same time, which meant the two of us ended up walking together.

Tess looked over her shoulder to make sure we were still behind her. "No problem," she yelled. "I love me a little elbow room."

We reached North Beach in no time. We reconfigured to walk single file through a narrow opening in the seawall, then spread out again to walk the beach. It was getting close to high tide, so Tess claimed what was left of the hard-packed sand, and Rosie and I had to walk on the loose, dry sand at the top of the beach, occasionally crunching over some dehydrated seaweed at the high tide line.

Walking on dry sand was actually a better workout. Because your feet move around more on loose sand, the tendons and muscles of your legs have to work harder. My Fitbit might not register the difference, but I knew. I swung my arms a little harder, paid attention to the rhythm of my breathing, tried to put my weekend mindfulness training to work and keep my head in the here and now.

The beach was as spectacular as it always is, especially so early in the morning when we had it practically to ourselves. In an hour or so, it would become a maze of beach chairs and towels, coolers and sand castles, bursting with hordes of sunscreen-slathered, bathing suit-wearing people throwing Frisbees or baking in the sun.

Oops. So much for the here and now. I yanked myself back to the present. The wind whipped the still-cool salt air in our faces. Rosie took another skip and hop to catch up with our longer legs. Tess's cute messy bun morphed into a ponytail once again.

Out of the blue, Rosie started to sing "Under the Boardwalk." Tess and I joined in. We didn't really remember the words, so we just kept making them up as we went along.

Two women in designer exercise clothes were walking in our direction, their gold jewelry sparkling even at a distance. When they got close enough to hear us singing, one leaned toward the other and whispered something. They both looked at us and giggled.

"Wait till we start a midlife girl group and get famous," Rosie said. "They'll be sorry they made fun of us."

"Right," Tess said. "All we have to do is learn to carry a tune first."

"Women like that always make me feel so judged," I said. "Like I'll never measure up."

"Maybe the only way they can feel better about themselves is to put us down," Rosie said. "They could have deep-seated self-esteem issues."

"I am so freakin' sick of everybody else's issues," Tess said. "Do I take my deep-seated issues out on them? I mean, how old are you? Get over your dysfunctional childhood already."

Just before the women passed us, Tess started another made-up verse at the top of her lungs. She added some dance moves as we walked, two scoops to the right, then two scoops to the left, a marginally more graceful version of Elaine's classic dance on *Seinfeld*.

The two women gave us matching snooty looks.

We laughed and sang and scooped and left the not-so-nice women in the dust.

"So," Rosie said once we'd settled down again. "How did the health coaching thing go over the weekend?"

"Okay, I think," I said. "I'm still trying to wrap my brain around how much coursework is involved and whether or not I'll ever actually use it in the real world. I mean—"

"Yeah, yeah, yeah," Tess said. "You'll figure it out. At the very least you'll get healthier. Come on, let's get to the important stuff. What the hell were you and that hot boyfriend of yours doing wandering the street last night waving your cell-phones around and laughing like idiots?"

"Oh. That." I sighed. "We were playing Pokémon Go."

"Never mind," Tess said. "I don't want to hear about it. It sounds way too kinky for my delicate sensibilities."

"Ha," I said.

"Connor and Nick can't get enough of Pokémon Go," Rosie said. "They've spent half their summer so far playing it with their friends at the mall. The malls haven't had this much action since back in the pre-Amazonian era."

"It's a lot more age-appropriate for Connor and Nick." I shrugged. "I guess it was kind of fun though. But I have to tell you, walking is a much better workout. There's too much standing around trying to catch virtual characters and—"

"Wait, wait," Tess said. "I knew there was something I had to tell you both. I finally called to see what kind of refund we could get on our trip, you know, if we decided to go that route. We missed the deadline by like three months."

"Really?" I said. I couldn't tell if I was happy or sad.

"Really," Tess said. "What were we *thinking* booking this trip?"

All three of us shook our heads.

"We should have gone back to Sequim, Washington," I said. "We had such a great time there last year. Or how about that lavender farm on Prince Edward Island we talked about visiting. Remember? The Five Sisters of Lavender Lane?"

"I'm just so crazy busy," Rosie said. "About the only thing I really have time for is a quick visit to Cape Cod Lavender Farm in Harwich."

"Whoa," Tess said. "When did this turn into Our Lavender Life?"

Tess sighed. Then Rosie sighed. Then I sighed.

"I think what happened," I said, "is that we were fresh off the high of our Sequim trip. I mean, the lavender festival, the wineries. That walk on the Dungeness Spit out to the lighthouse was epic. So it just made sense to try to top it with another trip."

"It was those damn commercials on PBS," Tess said. "They're so seductive, they just suck you right in. Long sexy riverboats, Scandinavian design, sparkling glasses of wine on white tablecloths, hunky smiling waiters, majestic castles, pink sunsets. And that narrator's sexy voice: *Paris, Budapest, St. Petersburg, Beijing.*"

"Good accent," I said.

"I know," Tess said. "I sound just like that guy, don't I?"

"River cruising looks so elegant," Rosie said. "Plus, I don't think I've ever taken a trip without having to figure out all the details myself."

"Me either," Tess said. "It would be so great not to have to do all the thinking and planning for a change. And it would feel like taking a road trip, but you don't have to keep packing up because your hotel room travels with you. I swore I would never do another ocean cruise after we took one for our anniversary and I spent every second I wasn't eating hanging over the railing trying not to puke my guts out. But supposedly being able to see the horizon on a river cruise makes all the difference."

"I have to admit," I said, "they had me at the ship-top walking track. Can you imagine getting the last of our daily mileage in by circling around and around under a sky full of stars?"

"They had me at Provence," Rosie said. She put the back of her hand to her forehead and made a swooning sound. "Not only is it the ultimate lavender trip, but the lavender will be at peak bloom when we're there."

"Then why were we all trying to get out of it if we really want to go?" I said.

"Buyer's remorse," Tess said. "I do this to myself every single damn time. As soon as I commit to something, I try to find an excuse so I can wiggle out of it."

"I think I do that, too," Rosie said. "I mean it's always so much easier not to go than to go."

Somehow we were back in my driveway already. Time really did fly when you had someone to walk with.

"Okay," I said. "Here's the deal. Our goal is to have another adventure together. It's essentially paid for, or at least it's on our credit cards. So we're doing it. We'll be taking the Lyon and Provence trip on the second week of July. We'll be gone for eight days, plus travel from Boston to France. We'll be sailing on the Viking Buri, and to earn this trip we have to walk 10,000 steps a day from now until we get back. It's a SMART goal—specific, measurable, achievable, relevant, and time-based. Technically I'm supposed to let you come up with the goal yourselves, but in a way we've already done that, so I think it's okay."

"Well, well, well," Tess said. "I think we've just been health coached."

Day 9

11, 222 steps

I tried to line up my golf ball with the tunnel at the bottom of the miniature Cape Cod shingled lighthouse. I stepped away, executed a promising practice swing, then stepped back and attempted to line up my ball again. I visualized the hot pink golf ball dancing across the whale-shaped expanse of Astro-turf, tearing through the dark tunnel, circling around the hole, dropping in. I pictured being one with the ball, whatever that meant.

I swung. The ball missed the lighthouse entirely and landed in an adjacent shipwreck surrounded by a school of sharks.

"Bummer," I said.

Rick looked up. He was straddling a lobster pot and trying to catch some kind of virtual creature with his phone.

"Tough break," he said. And then instead of coming to my rescue—maybe fishing for my golf ball or even jumping in to discuss strategy for my next shot with me—he went back to his phone.

My golf club was just long enough to flick my hot pink golf ball from the jaws of a shark with yellowed teeth and a serious overbite. Four shots later the ball circled around the hole and dropped in, just like I'd visualized it.

I picked up the ball and looked around for Rick. He'd crossed a wooden gangplank to a pirate ship and was attempting to shimmy up the mast while keeping his phone hand free.

A perfect little family—perky parents, adorable kids—was trying not to crowd me while they waited for their turn at this hole.

I picked up Rick's club and ball. "It's all yours," I said as I faked a smile in the direction of the family.

In a shady patch of real dune grass, I sat down on a seawall made out of some kind of fake rock substance. A tall statue of a pirate that looked a little bit like Johnny Depp stared down at me.

"I know," I said to the statue. "It's pathetic. I'm too old for this ship. I mean shit."

Johnny Depp didn't say anything, but he didn't have to. We both knew.

I flashed back to the first time Rick and I had been alone together. We'd skipped our Fresh Horizons small group career counseling class to sneak into the senior center lounge in the same building.

We'd stretched out side-by-side in red leatherette chairs, physical attraction like a power surge between us. Rick had looked up at the ceiling and said, "Divorced, two grown kids, homeowner, nonsmoker, Virgo, buyout."

I'd looked up at the ceiling, too. "Single, no kids, home-owner, nonsmoker, Libra, buyout."

"Movies, Indian over Chinese, everything but anchovies, no idea what's next," he'd said.

"Long walks, Thai over Indian, plain cheese, ditto."

He'd turned to look at me with his cat green eyes. I liked the way his forehead wrinkled when he was thinking about something. His thick hair, pale brown with paler strands of gray, could have used a good cut.

"Are you sure we haven't already dated?" he'd asked.

"It's a possibility," I'd answered.

"I've never been more messed up in my life," he'd said.

"That would be another ditto," I'd said.

An entire year later, it was astonishing how little had changed.

"It's not that we're in a rut," I said to Johnny Depp.

His weathered brown-black eyes didn't look away.

"We haven't even made it to the rut-worthy stage," I said. "I mean, to get stuck in a rut you have to actually climb into the rut in the first place. We're pre-rut."

Johnny Depp stood there, solid, grounded. He wasn't going anywhere. He probably didn't even play Pokémon Go.

"For a while there, it was looking so good," I said. "He was trying. I was trying. I honestly don't know what happened. And now here I am talking to you, even though I know you're not real. And that's the least of my problems. By a long shot."

Rick sat down beside me on the fake seawall. "What did you just say?"

For a split second I considered introducing Johnny Depp to him.

"Nothing," I said instead. I handed Rick his club and his ball.

"Thanks," he said. There was a small frayed hole in the hem of his shorts, but his knees were still in good shape.

We both stared straight ahead.

"Listen," I said.

"I know," he said. "I don't even know why I opened the Pokémon Go app on my phone. It's not like there are any good hot spots around here anyway."

I didn't say anything.

Rick jiggled his knee up and down, as if a part of him wanted to run, and the energy had to escape his body somehow. He smelled like Mitchum deodorant battling a humid summer day.

As soon as his right knee stopped jiggling, his left knee took over.

"How about this?" he said. "You hold on to my phone, and we finish our nine holes. And then maybe, I don't know. What do you want to do?"

"Listen," I said again. "I don't think things are going very well between us."

Now it was his turn not to say anything.

I stood up, handed him my golf stuff. His eyes didn't quite meet mine.

"If at any time you want to have an actual conversation, let me know. In the meantime, I'm going to walk home." I checked my Fitbit. "I still have 5,312 steps to get in today."

I scrambled some eggs and ate a solitary dinner at the little table in my kitchen while I started today's health coach certificate assignment. Fortunately, the required reading was about positivity and not about downward spirals leading to depression kicked off by possible breakups at miniature golf courses.

As I read, I learned that positivity can change your life by making you more receptive and more creative. That people who are positive live up to ten years longer than people who are negative. That positivity helps us grow, and negativity makes us shrink. That it's not just negativity that's damaging —even neutrality can hold us back in our lives.

Neutrality. That was it. Rick and I were in neutral. We didn't have a big scene at the mini golf course. I didn't stomp off. He didn't chase after me. Johnny Depp had shown more emotion than both of us put together. And Johnny Depp was made of wood. Or at least fake wood.

I kept reading. So apparently positive emotions, like love and joy and gratitude and interest, ebb and flow and that's okay. Negative emotions are important, too. Horrible and heartbreaking things happen, and that's how we grow. But we should aim for a positivity to negativity ratio of at least three to one. And pushing beyond our neutrality can put us on an upward spiral toward being more positive.

Rick called just after I'd brushed my teeth and crawled into bed with my laptop to finish my homework. I was so tired I almost didn't answer. But not answering didn't seem like the most positive thing to do.

I reached for my phone on the bedside table. "Hi."

"Listen," he said. "I can do better. I want to do better. I think what I need to do is go back to Fresh Horizons for a while."

"What?" I said.

"Why not? I mean, you've got that health coach thing, so it might be good for me to do a small group career counseling refresher course. It's probably still covered under my buyout package."

"It was only covered for 90 days." I said. "Remember? We compared our buyout packages and it was the same for both of us."

"Well, maybe it would be worth paying for out of pocket then. I was really starting to feel good when I was going all the time. And I miss those other guys. They knew where I was coming from. We had something to talk about, even if it was unemployment. It would be good to catch up with them."

"Rick," I said. "It's been almost a year. Those guys aren't there anymore. They've moved on."

A sad silence hung between us.

"Do you have any of their email addresses?" I said. "Or phone numbers?"

"Nope. I never even thought of it. But there must be some new guys there now."

"You can't stay in small group career counseling forever," I said, even though I wasn't really sure that it was true. "Maybe instead of trying to go back, it would make more sense to try to think of something that would move you forward."

"The thing is . . ." Rick said. His voice turned low and scratchy like he hadn't used it in a while. "When I took my buyout I kept thinking the guy I reported to was going to try to talk me out of it. To say that I couldn't leave, that they needed me, that they wouldn't be able to function without me. And he never said it. I mean, I know it wasn't like I got fired or anything, but that's how it felt. Like a kick in the gut."

I wanted to cover my ears and sing *lalalala* so I didn't have to hear this. Instead I did a long slow pendulum nod, even though Rick couldn't see me.

"And back when my marriage broke up . . ." His voice cracked like an adolescent.

I closed my eyes.

". . . I kept thinking the same thing. That there was going to be some kind of last minute save. That my wife, my ex, was going to say that she couldn't live without me, that our kids needed us to be together, to work it out. And of course it never happened. It was like I didn't measure up. By the end, it was all so damn civilized, as if it was no big deal, like *I* was no big deal. And our friends became her friends, at least I think they did. And even my old friends, I mean, who wants to talk to anyone when . . ."

"I'm sorry," I said.

"I mean, my kids are all kinds of awesome, but they've got their own lives. And I've got plenty of friends online, even if they're all gamers. I know I can make a good living—I'm doing some contract work right now. I guess I want you to know that I'm trying to get it together. At least trying to try. But what if I put myself out there again and I'm not good enough? And then I have to face the fact that the reason I keep failing is because I'm a failure. I'm not sure I can handle that."

When he laughed, it was an ugly sound. "So I have to admit it's pretty compelling to get lost in a game or two, maybe slay a dragon or rescue a damsel in distress."

Hot salty tears surprised me by rolling down my cheeks. I pictured Rick, the hole in his shorts and his hair that needed a good cut. How could he get a life when he couldn't even manage to get a haircut?

"So listen," Rick said. "I can understand if you don't want to see me anymore, but if you could maybe give me a little more time, I'd really appreciate it."

I slowed my breathing down, tried to stay in the moment instead of drifting away to somewhere safer, anywhere really.

"It's just," I said, "sometimes it feels like you and I are on a sinking ship and each of us only has enough energy left to save ourselves. And it's the saddest thing ever, but that's the way it is."

"Bingo. There's the optimism I was looking for."

I laughed.

"Dinner on Thursday? I'll leave my phone in the car?"

"Okay," I said. "Will one of us be in charge of remembering which day is Thursday?"

"Maybe we could job share it," Rick said.

I tossed and turned all night, awash in a salty sea of sweat and regret, my sheets tangling around my legs like seaweed. In some ways Rick's buyout story was my buyout story. Eighteen years of working my butt off at Balancing Act, mistaking a job description for a life, and in the end nobody had told me I was indispensable either. Nobody had tried to talk me out of leaving, nobody had attempted to pull me into the inner circle that would reemerge, triumphant, after the takeover and buyouts and reconfiguring and getting rid of redundancies and establishing synergies and all the rest of the corporate gobbledygook finished going down.

But in another way, my buyout story was so much worse than Rick's. I'd been a total sap. Michael, the guy I'd started seeing on the down low when he came in with the company that took over Balancing Act, was the one who'd talked me into taking the buyout. He'd promised he'd be right behind me, dangling fantasies of cross-country road trips and entrepreneurial adventures. I'd fallen for it hook, line and sinker. And then it turned out he was just stringing me along to get me to take the buyout. I'd been used and abused, end of story.

Michael had been simply the latest in a lifelong series of relationships that somehow imploded. Men had been drawn to me in sufficient numbers over the years, so I knew I wasn't completely repulsive or anything. I knew how to date. I even knew how to live together. But even if the guy didn't end up betraying me by tricking me into taking a buyout, somehow I didn't know what to do next. Eventually, things just went flat, and the guy moved on. Or things went flat, and I'd think, hey, I'm not going to be one of those women who settle, and I'd move on. And then six months later, I'd look back and think, was that it? Was that *the guy*? Should I have tried harder to make it work? I mean, what was so fatally wrong with him? Why didn't life come with an instruction manual?

Even if Rick's marriage hadn't ultimately worked out, at least he had a failed marriage, real grown kids. I'd missed the husband and kid boat completely. Somewhere in my tossing and turning I uncovered the rest of what I was thinking deep down inside: If Rick was a failure, that meant I was a massively bigger failure.

Maybe it was like those two women making fun of Tess and Rosie and me on the beach to make themselves feel better. Maybe Rick had latched on to me because I was the only one he could find who was worse off than he was.

I sure knew how to pick 'em.

Day 10

12, 555 steps

My doorbell rang. *Duh-duh-duh-Duh-duh. Duh-Duh.*

I pulled the covers over my head.

My doorbell rang again, long and obnoxious. *Duuuuuuuuu-uuuuuuuh.*

I yanked the covers down to my chin so I could breathe. "Noooooo," I whispered to the crack in my ceiling.

My doorbell moved on to telegraphing S.O.S. in Morse Code. *Duh-duh-duh. Duuuuuh-duuuuuh-duuuuuh. Duh-duh-duh.*

"Seriously?" I said to my ceiling crack.

I waited for the noise to stop, for whoever was ringing my doorbell to go away. Beyond that, I didn't have a plan. Pretty much for the rest of my life.

I heard my front door creak open.

"We have a commitment," Tess yelled from my hallway."

"Come on, Tess," Rosie said. "What if she's not alone?"

"If you're having sex in there, hurry up and finish and get your butt out here," Tess yelled.

"Unfreakin' believable," I said. I rolled out of bed, pulled on a pair of yoga pants and a sports bra, put my sleep T-shirt back on.

Tess was leaning back against the wall in my hallway, both arms crossed over her chest. Rosie was hovering in the open doorway, one foot in and one foot out.

"Well, good morning, Mary Sunshine," Tess said.

"How the hell did you get in?" I said.

"Oh, puh-lease," she said. "It wasn't even a challenge. The last time you locked yourself out of your house, you went right for the spare key under the front mat. Not the most original or even the brightest place to leave a key, by the way, if you want my humble opinion."

I started moving in the direction of caffeine. "Like you've ever had a humble opinion. In my next life, I'm going to have a neighbor who's not the least bit nosy."

Tess cut me off. "I'll make the coffee while you put your sneakers on. You can bring a cup with you. We don't have all day—at least Rosie doesn't."

"Don't remind me," Rosie said. She stepped into the house and pulled my front door closed behind her. "Sorry about the breaking and entering, Noreen. It was you-know-who's idea."

"Wimp," Tess said.

"It's okay," I said. "Now that I'm vertical, I can almost see the wisdom of not staying in bed for the rest of my natural life."

In no time at all we'd hit the beach, the caffeine and my endorphins kicking in simultaneously. The waves were splashing and the gulls were squawking and the wind was whipping our hair around. I drained the last of my coffee and ran to put my mug on the seawall so I could pick it up again on the way back.

I angled my face toward the sun and took a deep, rejuvenating gulp of salt air. Then I caught up to Rosie and Tess and matched my steps to theirs.

"Thanks for saving me from myself," I said.

"Do you want to talk about it?" Rosie said.

"No thanks," I said.

"Cracking under the health coach certification pressure?" Tess said. "If you want, I can quiz you or help you make flashcards or something. Of course you'll have to pay my exorbitant tutoring rate or vacuum my house or something. I'm okay with bartering, but I don't work for free."

A piece of cobalt blue sea glass twinkled up at me. I bent down to grab it, took my time catching up to them again.

"Boyfriend issues?" Tess said. "If he's cheating on you, Rosie and I could beat the crapola out of him for you."

"Come on, Tess," Rosie said. "Noreen said she doesn't want to talk about it."

"The pathetic thing," I said, "is that the only goal I've committed to, basically the only thing I really have to do right now, besides homework, is to walk 10,000 steps a day. And if you two hadn't dragged me out of bed today, I would have messed up even that. I probably would have stayed in bed all day, or at least until I worked up enough ambition for another Ben & Jerry's run."

"You're welcome." Tess put one hand on her hip and the other behind her head. "Best looking accountability partners you'll ever have."

"I couldn't wait to get out of the house this morning," Rosie said. "But then again, I'm procrastinating on the landscape plans I should be drawing right now."

"I couldn't wait to get out of the house either," Tess said. "Because what I really should be doing is organizing and purging and getting ready to downsize."

"Don't say that," I said. "If you downsized, who'd break in and invade my personal space?"

"Don't look at me," Rosie said. "I don't do break ins. I'm classier than that. But I could probably call you repeatedly on your cell in a can't-get-out-of-bed emergency."

"That could work," I said. "Okay, you can downsize, Tess."

"Thanks," Tess said. "I'll send you a postcard from my tiny house."

"Great," I said. "Just make sure it's a tiny postcard and you write really, really small so I get the full effect."

"Done," Tess said. "Okay, I think we should start plotting our combined daily steps on a map in Noreen's garage again. Using a large visual like that and having to earn our miles to take the trip to Sequim really helped us stay on track last time. I'm sure I must have an extra world map kicking around somewhere. I mean, what elementary school teacher doesn't?"

"So, what," Rosie said. "We plot our steps walking across the ocean from Marshbury to France?"

"That would certainly give new meaning to going overseas," I said.

"Walking on water is not an issue," Tess said. "After all, we *are* The Wildwater Walking Club."

"This is true," I said. Just talking about recording our mileage on a map had caused us all to start swinging our arms and picking up our pace.

"There's a time crunch though," Tess said. "Since we're leaving so soon, we might have to scale it up. Maybe one step equals ten miles or a hundred miles or something like that. We'll have to do the math."

"You do the math," Rosie said. "I hate math."

"Me, too," I said. "And I hate that I hate math even more than I actually hate math. Females not liking math is probably the worst gender-based stereotype."

"No," Tess said. "Females being afraid of mice and spiders is worse."

"Check and check," I said. "Great, I'm a walking talking female cliché. At least I don't think that finding the right man will magically solve all my problems and I'll live happily ever after."

"Phew," Rosie said. "I sure would have hated to have to break that one to you."

"But," Tess said, "finding the right man can take care of the mice and spider issues. Once you get past the happy horse-shit honeymoon phase, this becomes one of a marriage's most treasured commodities. And if you really play your cards right, you might be able to get the math thing rolled in, too. And car washing and snow shoveling. Just because something is a sexist cliché doesn't mean we can't choose to take full advantage of it."

"I'm just going to pretend I'm still in bed and missed all that," I said. "Even to a possible future health coach, you're irredeemable."

"Thank you," Tess said. "I resemble that remark."

"Maybe," Rosie said, "we should dig up our old purple pedometers, too. There was something so low tech about them. No apps, no virtual challenges. Like a throwback to a kinder, simpler time when all that mattered was putting one foot in front of the other."

"No way." Tess held up her wrist so we could see the tangerine band on it. "I chose my Fitbit, which by the way is not a real Fitbit, but saying *fitness tracker* somehow doesn't have the same oomph—"

"Yeah," Rosie said. "It's like always saying Kleenex even though I buy whatever generic tissues are on sale."

Tess was still talking right over Rosie. "—because I found a dirt cheap deal online for interchangeable wristbands in twelve stylish colors to go with it. I can't even see the step count or the time on mine—just these little dots to tell me how close I am to 10,000 steps—but I love waking up every morning and deciding which color band to wear. I haven't had this much fun since I used to dress up to match my Barbie. It's totally motivating."

"I ignore most of the features on my Fitbit," I said. "I have to admit I don't like to be judged on the quality of my sleep. I mean, there's enough pressure in my life without adding sleep evaluation to it."

"I know, right?" Rosie said. "My Fitbit was turning me into a total insomniac, so now I take it off at night and leave it in the bathroom. It's none of its business how well I sleep or don't sleep."

"Okay," Tess said. "Map on the wall in the garage, fitness trackers of choice on our wrists at all times, or unless we choose to take them off while sleeping. And if one of us doesn't show up to walk between now and when we leave for France, we've got to pinky swear that the other two will go in and drag her out."

The three of us looped pinkies.

"Okay, swear," Tess said.

S#%*," Rosie yelled.

"F*#@," I yelled.

"M@&#-F&$%-C*&^-S@#%&," Tess yelled.

"That felt great," Rosie said. "Swearing can be so cathartic."

"I know," I said. "My favorite part of *Inside the Actors Studio* is when James Lipton asks what's your favorite curse word."

"I like that, too," Tess said. "Though I have to admit I'm a little bit disappointed it hasn't added anything new to my extensive swear repertoire."

"You know, I was just thinking, Tess," Rosie said. "Maybe you should reach out to Joy and invite her to count mileage with us so she doesn't feel left out."

"That's a great idea," I said. "She could email us her step count and we could add it to the map. And maybe we could even Skype together, just so we've met before we spend all that time together."

"No way," Tess said. "I mean, we don't even know if she walks."

"Of course she walks," Rosie said. "Everybody knows how to walk by the time they get to be our age."

"Don't be a smart ass," Tess said. "It's enough that I have to be her roommate for a week. I have no intention of compounding the burden."

"I know you, Tess," I said. "After all this we're going to end up loving Joy, and we'll look back and laugh about the whole thing. Is she meeting us at Logan or at the airport in Paris? Where does she live anyway?"

Tess shrugged. "I don't remember. San Diego? Or maybe it was San Francisco. San something or other. Whatever."

"So," I said. "I think it would be a good idea to try to keep every aspect of this trip as positive as possible. I've been doing lots of reading for class about how important positivity is, and apparently a three-to-one positivity to negativity ratio is optimal for—"

"Wait," Tess said. "Let me get this straight. You're in the middle of a health coach training unit about *positivity*, and we had to drag you out of bed this morning?"

I shrugged. "I was doing so well there for a while."

Somehow we were back in my driveway already.

"I have something positive for both of you," Rosie said. "Wait right here while I go get it."

Rosie's Loveliest Lavender Moisturizer

¼ cup coconut oil
¼ cup Shea butter
¼ cup olive oil
6-10 drops lavender essential oil

Fill small jar with equal amounts coconut oil, Shea butter and olive oil, about ¼ cup of each. Place jar in small saucepan filled with an inch or two of water. Over medium heat, stir with Popsicle stick or wooden kebab stick until melted and mixed. Remove from heat and add lavender essential oil.

Continue to stir occasionally as mixture cools. Store at room temperature or in refrigerator, depending on desired consistency and temperature. To use, apply liberally wherever your skin is dry.

Day 11

10, 955 steps

Fog hung in the air and shielded us from the sun like a big beach umbrella.

"Thank you again for the moisturizer," I said to Rosie as the three of us walked side-by-side across the wide expanse of beach parking lot. "I love how easily it spreads, and of course you can't beat that awesome lavender smell."

"I don't know," Tess said. "It was really oily. I'm not sure I liked that."

"Gee, Tess," I said. "Tell her what you really think. What's that old saying about not looking a gift moisturizer in the mouth?"

"It's okay," Rosie said. "I'm used to her. Anyway, you can play around with the ingredient proportions to make it thicker if you want. And you can also leave out the olive oil entirely, although it's really good for your skin."

"Yeah," Tess said. "Olive oil's great for your skin. If you're a chicken."

"Shh." Rosie looked over her shoulder. "Don't let The Supremes hear you saying that. They're very sensitive about that kind of comment. Anyway, you can also substitute beeswax for the olive oil and pour the mixture into molds to make Loveliest Lavender Moisturizing Bars. You just rub the bars wherever you're dry and the heat of your skin dissolves them enough to moisturize."

Tess had been walking in the middle of our pack. I hung back and then stepped to the other side, so I could talk to Rosie without going through Tess. "I'd love to try making those with you sometime. And by the way, I'm really sorry that I haven't done more for your lavender farm website since I got it up and running. I mean, I know it has lots of potential but I just can't seem to . . ."

"I get it," Rosie said, "and I really appreciate what you've done. I have to admit that I haven't put much energy into the lavender fields or the shop either lately. It's kind of hard to get into it when my dad's not here."

Rosie's parents had been the original owners of the lavender farm. When her mother died, Rosie had been the dutiful daughter who'd stepped up to move in with her father and help him with the farm, dragging Rosie's contractor husband and their two sons kicking and screaming with her.

When my widowed mother had showed up unexpectedly to visit me, The Supremes and Rod Stewart just happened to break into my house looking for a snack. My mother had climbed up on a chair and started screaming to protect herself from poultry invasion. Rosie's dad came to her rescue and it sparked a whopping romance. Rosie's dad Kent had red hair softened with white, freckles like Rosie, and he was sweet and totally charming. My mom had morphed from whiny Lois who called me every Sunday to tell me how much better than me my sister and two brothers were doing to a hot mama named Lo with spiky black hair. On the one hand, it was mortifying that my mother had better underwear and more of a life than I did. On the other hand, it gave me hope.

"Have you heard from your dad lately?" I asked Rosie.

Rosie shook her head. "Not a word. Do you remember how long they've been gone?"

I shrugged. "Maybe a month? My mom hasn't called me either. I mean, how long does it take to drive to Florida and show someone off at your condo community?"

"I just hope he shows up in time to help watch the boys while I'm gone like he promised," Rosie said.

"Hel-*lo*," Tess said. "Feeling seriously left out over here."

The three of us walked single file through the opening in the seawall. When we spread out to walk the beach, Tess took over the middle spot again.

"So where were we?" Tess said.

"I think you were insulting Rosie's moisturizer and objectifying her chickens," I said. "And Rosie was sharing her secret recipes."

"Let's see," Rosie said, "You can also pour the beeswax mixture into empty Chapstick containers, or their generic equivalent, and, *voila*, you have Loveliest Lavender Lip Balm."

"*Voila*," Tess said. "I hope that's not the sum total of your French vocabulary."

"Pretty much," Rosie said. "Although I also know how to say baguette, and I sing a mean 'Frere Jacques.' When I start my midlife girl band, it'll be one of our most-requested songs. That and "Came In Like a Wrecking Ball."

"Remember," I said, "when we first decided to go on this river cruise and we talked about taking a French class together? Whatever happened to that idea?"

"We were still in the honeymoon stage of trip-planning back then," Tess said. "That's long gone. We've just passed through the oh-shit-I-don't-really-want-to-go stage and now we've arrived at the there's-an-app-for-that stage."

"That'll work," I said. "I'll see if I can find an English-to-French app to download as soon as I finish my school stuff today."

"Too late," Tess said. "I've already downloaded one. I'm now The Wildwater Walking Club's official translator."

"Great," Rosie said. "How do you say *OMG we are in serious trouble* in French?"

The health coach certificate students had been divided into triads to practice health coaching via Skype video call. Our assignment was to alternate the roles of coach, client and observer for three twenty-minute segments, with the observer taking notes and keeping track of time. At the end of each segment, we'd spend five minutes giving feedback that would consist of the make-believe client and the observer giving the person in the coach role three positive comments and one suggestion for improvement.

We'd continue to have health coaching videoconference practice throughout the twelve weeks of our training, and the triads would be reconfigured each time.

Our further instructions had been that prior to our first session we should each come up with a list of goals we had a real desire to be coached toward. A pre-prepared list would help the groups in terms of time management, and having meaningful goals would make the sessions realistic and theoretically even helpful.

Coming up with a list of goals turned out to be alarmingly easy for me. It was possible that I had enough issues to keep a health coach busy for her entire career.

Noreen's Goals for Practice and Life

- Walking daily without needing to be dragged out of bed by walking partners

- Grocery shopping while avoiding running into Ben & Jerry in the ice cream aisle
- Cooking occasionally
- Cooking healthy meals once I get the cooking occasionally part under control
- Remembering to stay mindful
- Being less stressed about not having a life
- Continuing to be less stressed once I get a life
- Figuring out how I'd like to earn a living and live my potential life before it's too late
- Working toward a healthy relationship with boyfriend
- If necessary, facing that it's not possible to have healthy relationship with said boyfriend
- Enjoying a once-in-lifetime trip to France without worrying about anything else on this list

I could have gone on and on, but just in case we had to share our lists, I didn't want to frighten my first triad partners away.

I'd already fake cleaned the part of my office right behind me that would show on camera during the Skype video call. After dusting off a slight layer of dust on them, I brought in a pair of bright red handheld weights from the fitness corner I'd made in my garage. I shoved some books over and then put the weights on the bookshelf behind me, added an old issue of *Shape* magazine and a fresh pair of Walk on By sneakers. I thought for a moment, then replaced the new sneakers with the most worn-out pair I could find so that it might possibly look like I was training for a marathon.

I did a quick camera check. On my screen it looked like I was in a cross between a gym and a library, which I could only hope would make me look both healthy and well read.

So the camera wouldn't make me look washed out, I put on some makeup for a change. Then I paired my favorite blue walking hoodie with a clean white T-shirt. I didn't see the sense in changing out of my drawstring pajama bottoms since the camera was only going to show me from the waist up. I tried putting my hair up in a cute messy bun like Tess's, but I only had enough hair for a distinctly uncute stubby ponytail, so I just ran my brush through it a few times and called it a hairdo.

My next stop was the kitchen, where I grabbed a water bottle from the fridge. I reconsidered and poured the contents of the water bottle into my BPA-free bottle with the built-in filter, hoped the filter would show on camera.

With two minutes to spare, I typed my password and signed in to Skype.

The other two women in my triad had already signed in. I joined the video call.

"I'll be the observer first," one of the women was saying as she waved her notebook.

"I call client," the other woman said.

No fair didn't seem like the best thing for a future health coach to say, so even though I would have preferred to watch someone else coach first, I smiled and said, "Okay, coach it is."

My pretend client, whose name was Liz, was wearing mascara and lipstick, too, I noticed. She jumped right in. "My goal is to give up yo-yo dieting forever by making permanent changes in the foods I eat to improve my overall health and well being." On a table behind Liz, I could see a half-eaten salad. I wondered if she'd really been eating it or if it was just a prop.

"So," I said as I launched into my best slow pendulum nod. "Your goal is to change your diet permanently to improve your overall health and well-being."

The observer, whose name was Sharon, was scribbling away in her notebook. I imagined her writing: *no more diet but change eating habits to improve overall health and well-being.* A tiny clothesline was stretched across the wall behind Observer Sharon. About a half dozen of those numbers they give you to pin on your shirt at road races were clipped to the clothesline with tiny clothespins. I wondered if Observer Sharon was really a runner or if she'd borrowed the numbers from a neighbor. I wondered if this was the kind of clothesline Tess would have when she bought her tiny house.

Belatedly I realized everybody was waiting for me to say something else.

I cleared my throat. "So. How confident are you that you're ready to make these changes?"

"Super duper confident," Client Liz said. "Probably like a 9 out of 10."

"Great," I said. I glanced down at the cheat sheet I'd made about SMART goals. "Your goal is specific and it sounds really relevant and also very achievable for you. What would that diet change look like? Can you visualize it for us?"

"Well," Client Liz said, "I'd stop eating processed foods entirely. And I'd stop eating grains and sugar of any kind, too. Every time I do those things I feel so much better, and the weight just melts off without even trying. And I'd drink lots of water and turn everything into a salad."

Client Liz looked over her shoulder to make sure her salad was still behind her. "Besides the greens," she said, "I'd eat plenty of cruciferous vegetables like broccoli and cauliflower and healthy fats like avocado and nuts and coconut oil."

"Wow," I said. "Impressive. I can barely get through a day lately without binging on a pint of Hazed and Confused."

My cohorts were both giving me saucer eyes on my computer screen.

"Oops," I said. "Scratch that." I got my pendulum action going while I took another peek at my cheat sheet. "Um, it sounds like you have a clear and measurable picture of the action-oriented specifics of your goal."

Client Liz nodded. Observer Sharon was writing like a maniac, no doubt detailing my Ben & Jerry's slip-up. Either that or writing down the name of the flavor for future reference.

I realized that nobody was saying anything. Apparently it was still my turn to talk.

"So do you have any thoughts on what might get in your way?" I said. "You know, besides getting stuck with a rookie coach like me?"

Nobody laughed.

"I mean, can you visualize any obstacles to your goal?" I said.

Client Liz let out a puff of air. "Yes, it's going to drive me absolutely insane when everybody at work is chowing down on all the things I can't have. I work in a pediatrician's office. Grateful patients are constantly dropping off cookies and candy and brownies and all sorts of junk. It's so not fair."

"Ohmigod, I hate that," I said. "It used to be like that when I worked at Balancing Act Shoes. Dunkin' Donuts in the snack room practically every day—chocolate munchkins were my downfall. I mean, we were an *athletic* shoe company. Couldn't they have sprung for carrot and celery sticks?"

Client Liz and Observer Sharon were giving me that wide-eyed judgy look again.

I cleared my throat. "So, what strategies might you try to overcome this baked-goods-in-the-office obstacle? Are there small steps you could take toward your goal?"

"You mean like cut back?" Client Liz said. "No way. If I have one cookie, it's all over. I have to keep sneaking back until I've finished the whole plate. It's like once I eat one I can even feel my blood sugar skyrocketing and then plummeting, and I simply need another cookie and then another cookie to try to level it out. I hate, hate people who can eat one cookie."

I tried to remember if I'd ever eaten just one cookie. "Hmm," I said. "Maybe I do that, too. I used to have a roommate who would buy a box of Mystic Mints and make them last for six months. She'd cut each one into about six pieces—actually saw them into sections with a steak knife—and eat one measly triangle each night. There was something really twisted about it. I mean, eat the Mystic Mints or don't eat them, you know?"

Those looks were back.

"Sorry," I said. "Can you visualize a strategy that *might* work?"

Client Liz shut her eyes, hopefully not just to block me out. "Well, I can picture how great I'd feel dropping this extra weight and seeing my blood pressure and blood sugar numbers go down. And having more energy. And rewarding myself with a new outfit, maybe some exercise clothes, too."

"Three minutes." A three-minute warning was part of Observer Sharon's job description.

I did another pendulum nod. "So, feeling great and dropping weight, seeing your numbers go down, having more energy. And maybe rewarding yourself with some new clothes. Can you visualize a reward that might include food, or would that be something that wouldn't work for you?"

"Let's see," Client Liz said. "On Saturday night I could have either a one-ounce square of 85% dark chocolate or a five-ounce glass of red wine. I'd portion them out, then I'd put whatever was left out of sight way in the back of the refrigerator, and then I'd brush my teeth immediately afterward."

Observer Sharon and I both nodded. She was probably writing: *Saturday night chocolate or wine.* Either that or *Coach Noreen is a total loser.*

"So," I said. I focused on nodding my head and not saying anything else.

"Oh, who am I kidding?" Client Liz said. "This totally sucks. It's completely unfair that everybody else at the office gets to have the cookies and I don't. One of the receptionists is so skinny and she tries every single thing that comes in, but she just takes a tiny pinch of a brownie and leaves the rest."

"Brownie pinchers are the worst," I said. "It's like those people who poke a finger in the bottom of every damn chocolate in the box to see what kind it is and end up ruining them for the rest of us. I mean, come on, take a chance, just pick a chocolate, life is short." I had to admit that this session was giving me a major urge to swing by the Ben & Jerry's aisle on the way home.

"Okay, what about this?" I said. "You could just throw everything in the trash as soon as it comes in. Or send a note to all the parents thanking them very much but telling them that from now on the office is a sweet-free zone. I mean, after all, a pediatrician's—"

"Time's up," Observer Sharon said.

Day 12

13, 013 steps

Rick and I were actually going to take turns making dinner for each other. That this seemed like a bold step forward in our relationship was yet more evidence of what slackers we'd been. Up until this point, we'd either eaten at a casual restaurant or nuked something we'd unearthed in one of our freezers. We'd also done at least quadruple our fair share of takeout. Anything more ambitious had simply seemed beyond us.

I was even going to be the first one to cook, another big leap. I'd decided to tweak a Gorgonzola chicken recipe I used to make a gazillion years ago. Back when I cooked, back when I cared.

I'd add avocado and nuts to make it aspiring health coach-worthy, as well as a touch of lavender in an attempt to turn it into something unique and even exotic. The lavender in my garden was just coming into bloom, but I still had some of the buds Rosie had helped me dry and store in hand-labeled tins at the end of last season. I'd use Munstead in the recipe because it was a nice sweet lavender. Mine had never been treated with chemicals, which made it culinary quality.

I'd found an old bottle of Cognac that had been lounging around in the back of one of my kitchen cabinets long enough that it was now aged well beyond the years on the label. In fact, it was so ancient that I couldn't even remember the story of how it had found its way into my house.

I felt a little bit guilty about the eating of chicken, as I always did now that I'd met The Supremes and Rod, but I was afraid if I substituted pork, somebody's pet pig would come barreling into my yard. In the end, I decided I'd deal with my meat-eating ambivalence once I finished working on some of my other issues.

When Rick called to check in around noon, I read my reinvented recipe to him over the phone.

"Sounds amazing," he said. "But are you sure health coaches are allowed to clog their dinner guest's arteries like that?"

"Actually," I said, "we just learned in class that there are two warring schools of thought in nutrition right now. One is the old low-fat, calorie-counting way. You know, cut back on your eating and keep it lean, then up your exercise and you'll be trim and healthy. The more cutting edge philosophy says that calories in do not equal calories out, and reducing caloric intake only makes you feel deprived, which is unsustainable and doesn't lead to long-term weight loss anyway. And processed foods, sugar and grains—not fats—are making us fat and sick, and if we ditch those and eat plenty of healthy fats and leafy greens and moderate amounts of protein, many of our health issues will disappear and the extra weight will come off as well."

I gulped down some air. "So this recipe is low carb, loaded with healthy fats, and uses spiralized zucchini, sometimes called zoodles, instead of pasta."

"Hey," he said. "You're really good at this stuff, aren't you?"

"Ha," I said. "You should have seen my first time playing coach via Skype video call. At the end of the session, the person I was coaching and the one observing me were supposed to give three positives about my coaching. I'll tell you, they really had to reach to come up with that third positive. Finally the observer said I had good enunciation."

Rick laughed. "I'm sure you did a great job."

I switched the phone to my other ear. "Thanks for the thought. I'm hanging on to the possibility that I might actually get better at it. The biggest challenge is letting the client come up with everything. I never realized how hard it is to resist telling people what to do."

"Remember that metal sculpting class I took right after we met?"

"Yeah," I said. "I wondered whatever happened with that."

"Well, I was working on my first big sculpture—it was supposed to be sort of a modern twist on a coat of arms. Anyway, I was really getting into it. And then when I came back the following week to work on it some more, somebody had taken the whole thing apart and put the pieces in the scrap pile. They thought it was junk."

"Ouch," I said.

"Yeah, that kind of cured me of metal sculpting. I never went back."

"Really?" I said. "Do you think you should have hung in there longer?"

"Nah, if there's one thing I know about myself, it's that I have a finite capacity for humiliation."

"Well, not to get all health coachy on you, but another thing we've been studying is the difference between having a fixed mindset and a growth mindset. In a fixed mindset, if you fail, you're a failure, end of story. In a growth mindset, our failures give us the information we need so we can continue to learn and grow and get better."

"Sort of like being in beta," Rick said.

"Huh?"

"You know, test phase. Beta is all about trying and failing, and then finding the bugs and tweaking from there. Not sure I buy it as far as people go, but it's an interesting thought. Anyway, I've been working on some other stuff on my own. No more metal—I've moved on to cement. I've been making these things out in my garage, kind of garden figures-slash-planters or whatever."

"I'd love to see them," I said. "Can you bring one when you come over tonight?"

"Yeah, sure. As long as you promise not to put it out with the trash."

"I wouldn't dream of it."

Silence came out of nowhere and stretched between us. We'd been so dialed in to each other that it took me completely by surprise. Normally I'd see something like this as not only a bad thing but as my fault, evidence of my own conversational incompetence. I'd scramble to find something to fill the silence with right away.

One Mississippi, two Mississippi, I counted to myself instead, just to see what would happen.

Rick didn't hang up. He didn't tell me I was boring. Instead he just waited another beat and then said, "Do you have everything you need, or do want me to swing by the grocery store on the way over?"

"Thanks, but I think I've got it under control." I had to admit it had actually been kind of fun to grocery shop with a list of ingredients and a purpose for a change instead of just wandering randomly up and down the aisles.

"I'll bring a bottle of wine then," Rick said. "And a healthy dessert—maybe edible flowers or something."

"Ha," I said. "Perfect. Just make sure you do your

research. If my cooking doesn't get us, it would be a shame if we both died of edible flower poisoning."

I stripped the sheets off my bed and loaded them in the washing machine. Even though I'd walked with Rosie and Tess this morning, I decided to do a second loop to the beach and back while my sheets were agitating. I wanted to make sure I hit my 10,000 steps early today so I didn't have to think about it later.

I had to admit I was also feeling kind of fluttery about tonight. In a crazy way, even though we'd been sleeping together for close to a year, it almost felt like tonight was Rick's and my first real date. So I figured a few extra endorphins couldn't hurt.

The tide was low, which gave me plenty of space to navigate past a clump of toddlers splashing in a tidal pool while their mothers kept an eye on them. Past a huge sand castle surrounded by a wide moat and dripped-sand turrets. Past a giggling group of teenage girls who'd moved their beach chairs into the water and were screaming like they were being shipwrecked with each peaceful wave that rolled in. Past the teenage boys shoving one another and pretending not to notice the screaming teenage girls.

I took off my sneakers and socks, rolled my exercise pants up over my knees. Then I walked farther and farther out into the frigid New England water. With true low tide magic, even though it felt like I'd been walking forever, the water was still shallow enough that everything above my shins stayed dry.

When I got home from my bonus walk, I sprayed my sheets with lavender water and threw them in the dryer. I only had one decent set of sheets, and there wasn't enough time to hang them out to line dry.

I jumped in the shower, washed my hair twice, let an extra

helping of conditioner do its work while I shaved my legs and armpits. After I dried off, I rubbed Rosie's lavender moisturizer on liberally.

I managed to locate a good bra and underpants, then slipped into a funky tie-dyed maxi dress with tiny lace insets at the hem. I was pretty sure it was casual enough that I wouldn't look like I was trying too hard, but I decided to go barefoot just to be on the safe side.

I spent a moment trying to visualize cooking without making a mess.

"How does that look?" I asked myself in my best health coach voice.

"Not happening," I answered. So I pulled a baggy T-shirt over my dress. I made a mental note to look for an apron someday if this cooking thing worked out. A crisp chef-like apron as opposed to something frilly inspired by *The Stepford Wives*.

My wardrobe complete, I pulled up my favorite classic rock station on my iPad. Etta James was singing "At Last," so I cranked up the volume, grabbed a zucchini to use as a makeshift microphone. I did a few spins around the kitchen as I sang along, my maxi dress fanning out around my ankles. I closed my eyes when I got to the line about my heart wrapped up in clover.

When Etta and I had finished our duet, I opened the vegetable spiralizer my mother had given me as a gift one Christmas. Last year? The year before? Once it was out of the box, I realized the spiralizer wasn't nearly as threatening as I'd imagined it to be. One of the assorted blades was even already in place. All it took was a few twists to attach the rotating handle to the thingamawhoosie that held the vegetable in place.

I washed my former microphone as well as the other zucchini I'd bought and gave it a go with one of them. As I cranked the handle of the spiralizer, ribbons of zucchini appeared miraculously, almost too beautiful to eat. They reminded me of the big box of ribbon candy my paternal grandparents would send us every Christmas when we were kids—ruffled works of art in an assortment of flavors from cinnamon to peppermint to clove.

How could I have let this spiralizer languish for so long? I wanted to spiralize everything I could get my hands on—cucumbers and apples and sweet potatoes and maybe even cabbage.

I did a quick time check and reminded myself to take this one meal at a time. I spiralized the second zucchini, and when I was finished, I had a towering pile of curlicues. Then I found my tiny spice mortar and pestle, another gift from my mom and her endless optimism, and ground the dried lavender buds. According to my research, using the mortar and pestle on the lavender would release the essential oils the way a spice grinder would, but it would also keep some of the buds intact, adding to the visual presentation. Given that my cooking repertoire consisted pretty much of things that were previously frozen, any kind of visual presentation at all would be a major triumph.

I cut the two boneless chicken breasts into cubes, put them back in the fridge. I paused for a long drink of water as I skimmed the recipe again. This cooking stuff was not for sissies. I minced the shallot and the garlic cloves. I chopped the pistachios, making sure I stopped at that crucial moment before they disintegrated into pistachio dust. I decided to hold off on chopping the avocado until right before it was time to put it into the sauce so that it didn't start to turn brown.

Prep work complete, I did another time check.

I cleaned up the mess I'd made so far while I helped Cat Stevens sing *Wild World* and Janis Joplin belt out *Summertime*. I peeled off my makeshift T-shirt apron, took a bathroom break, and while I was there I double-checked that I'd shaved both legs.

I remembered my sheets were still in the dryer when the dryer let out a series of retro musical chimes that always reminded me of the ice cream trucks of my childhood. I rescued the sheets and made my bed. I fluffed the pillows, evened out the comforter, said hello to the crack in my ceiling. I was actually glad Rick was running a little bit late so I didn't have to think about making the bed later either. Not that an unmade bed had ever stopped us before, but still.

I pictured Rick going back and forth between his cement garden creations, trying to decide which one to bring over to show off to me. I imagined him lingering over the selections as he chose the perfect bottle of wine to go with chicken and lavender and zoodles. I pictured him chatting with the florist at the grocery store, asking her if she was a hundred percent sure that daylilies weren't poisonous.

I decided to start sautéing the chicken in the butter and olive oil just to get a jumpstart. I took my time, and when the chicken was cooked through, I scooped it out of the skillet and onto a plate. I covered the plate with a piece of foil so it would stay warm, then I added the garlic and shallot and the lavender to the skillet, stirred it with the same wooden spoon I'd used for the chicken. The smell was amazing already— sweet and savory and almost musky, with a little bit of heaven thrown in.

My stomach growled in anticipation. I did another time check, took a lap around my house to add a few more steps to my daily count, listened to a couple more songs on my iPad. I added the cream and the broth and the Cognac to the skillet, stirred until it started to thicken, then turned the heat down low. I put the chicken back in the skillet and stirred some more until it was covered with creamy sauce.

I did another time check.

I turned the heat off under the skillet.

Then I turned the heat on again.

I turned the heat off again and covered the skillet with the same piece of foil I'd used to keep the chicken warm.

After that I checked my phone to see if I'd remembered to charge it. I walked to the front of the house and looked out the window to make sure Rick wasn't just pulling into my driveway.

Then I circled back to the kitchen and picked up the bottle of extra-aged Cognac.

How I would have loved to spend the night, the week, the rest of my life pretending Rick would be here any minute. But this wasn't my first rodeo. I'd learned more times than I cared to count that there is always that precise moment when the last shreds of denial slip away and your reality check bounces. The truth is right in front of you, and no matter how desperately you want to, you can't ignore it any longer.

Rick wasn't still trying to decide which of his creations to bring over to dazzle me with. He hadn't lost track of time in the wine aisle or in the florist section at the grocery store.

He was blowing me off. Intentionally or forgetfully, it didn't really matter. I'd worked my butt off, put myself out there, and he hadn't cared enough to show up.

So there it was.

I poured some Cognac into a vintage Flintstones glass. Growing up, Flintstones glasses were our favorite grocery store collectible. When you finished scraping out every last bit of the grape or strawberry jelly that came in them, you got to use them as glasses. My mother had parceled our collection out evenly, like they were the family jewels, to all four kids when we'd moved out. This one, Pebbles at the Beach, was the glass my mother used to fill with warm, flat ginger ale for me when I was in bed with the flu. I had to admit my stomach was doing that same kind of flip-flop thing right now.

I sat in the center of my couch as if I were company, rolled the amber liquid around in the clear glass with the Kelly green cartoon drawing. I sniffed it like I imagined a Cognac connoisseur would, then took a big swig. I started to choke, caught myself. I didn't realize how numb I'd been until I felt the Cognac burn as it went down.

I took another sip from my Flintstones glass. The Cognac was strong. It tasted like flowers and dried fruit and maybe citrus peel. I'd once read that all Cognacs are brandies but not all brandies are Cognacs, because they have to be grown and produced in the Cognac region of France. I'd forgotten that.

But if I lived to be a million, I'd never forget the night that Cognac became the taste of heartbreak and regret.

If it were possible to spiralize a man, or at least one of his outer extremities, I might be tempted. But then again, in order to spiralize someone, he has to show up first.

I took a smaller sip of Cognac. This one went down much easier. The next one even easier.

It would have been so much less embarrassing if we'd both died of edible flower poisoning. Tess would break into my house when I didn't show up to walk in the morning. She and Rosie would find Rick and me sprawled out on top of each other on my dining room floor like Juliet and Romeo. It would be sad, so sad. But in the end it would make a great story, one that might almost come across like the legacy of a life well lived. Ha.

I thought you were dead in a ditch, my mother had been known to yell when my brothers and sister and I were teens and one of us missed our curfew. Although messier than the Juliet and Romeo scenario, I could have lived with dead in a ditch, too. I wasn't sure what my role would be at the wake and funeral, since Rick and I weren't even engaged, let alone married, and he had adult kids as well as an ex who was their mother. But despite not quite fitting in, I'd be beautiful in black. I'd meet one of Rick's old friends at the cemetery. The spark would be undeniable, though we'd both be too classy and filled with anguish to act on it for at least a few months. We'd start out as friends, getting together to share memories of Rick over a glass of wine, and then one night when he drove me home—

Wait. What if Rick really *was* dead in a ditch? Or worse, not even all the way dead yet. There was still time to help him, and here I was fantasizing about hooking up with one of his old friends.

I grabbed my phone from the coffee table, found Rick's latest call, tapped his name on the screen.

Three rings and it went to voicemail. Was this the usual ring count? Or had he seen my name on his phone and pushed Reject instead of Accept?

"Rick, hi this is," Rick's voice said in his best Yoda imitation. "Message, leave at beep. No. Try not. Do or do not. There is no try."

If Rick was in the ditch but not dead, I was pretty sure he would have picked up, so I was off the hook on that. I had to admit it was a really good Yoda imitation. I wondered if he'd used some kind of Yoda-speak generator to create it. Who did things like that?

I took a sip of Cognac from my Flintstones glass. Pushed redial. Listened to Rick's Yoda voicemail message again.

I poured some more Cognac into the glass, took another small sip. It was like that TV drinking game where every time a politician tells a lie you have to do another shot. Maybe every time I pushed redial and listened to Rick's stupid Yoda voicemail greeting again, I had to take another drink. Maybe when I finally left a message for him, I had to chug the rest of the bottle.

I tried to keep the flashbacks away, but the warmth of the Cognac melted my resolve.

Michael, the guy who'd talked me into taking my buyout from Balancing Act, had stopped taking my calls and emails. Eventually I had to face the fact that his personal cellphone,

work voicemail and both email accounts weren't all coinciden-
tally down at the same time. When the emails I'd sent him
bounced back to me, they'd said *Returned Mail: Permanent Fatal
Errors*.

Just call me Noreen the Queen of the Permanent Fatal
Errors.

There was Steve of my early après college days. We'd been
dating for about a year and a half, and he'd pretty much
moved in to my crappy little apartment, when he asked me to
marry him. I said yes, and the next weekend we went shopping for wedding rings. We went back and forth between silver
and gold, trendy and classic, and in the end we decided to
think about it some more. When I got home from work the
next day, a wedding magazine clutched to my chest no less, all
his stuff was gone. Steve had officially ghosted me, back
before that was even an expression, and I never heard from
him again. In my most pathetic moments, I agonized over
whether or not it might have made a difference if I'd been
more decisive about my taste in jewelry. All these years later, it
occurred to me that it was possible that technically we were
still verbally engaged.

I called Rick's number again, listened to his stupid voicemail. My Flintstones glass seemed to have disappeared, so I
took a dainty sip from the Cognac bottle.

There was Wade, my very first boyfriend. We were going
steady, mostly by phone. Sixth grade? Seventh? He called to
break up with me, which I had to admit might have made him
my most mature boyfriend of them all. I must have been more
daring back then, because I asked him why. He said he wanted
to go steady with Penny, another girl in our class. So I asked
him why Penny. I really wanted to know what Penny had that
I didn't have. I mean, come on, not nickel or dime or half
dollar, but *Penny*? She's pretty and nice, he said. Pretty and
nice. Not brilliant or beautiful or multilingual or ambidex-

trous. I was pretty and nice, too. At least my friends said I was. What was wrong with *me*?

Without really planning it, somehow I found myself back in my kitchen. I cut the avocado with my sharpest knife, starting at the place where it had broken free of its stem and circling the blade around the swell of the circumference and back to where I'd begun. Then I separated the halves with a quick sideways twist of the knife. A flick of my wrist like I was throwing a dart, and I pierced the pit, wiggled the pit free from the tight flesh around it. Peeled the skin off the avocado and threw it away with the pit.

I chopped the flesh of the avocado ruthlessly, the sharp knife almost grazing my fingertips again and again. One slip and I'd have something worth getting upset about. If I bled to death, I wondered if it would make the local news. I wondered if Rick would be sorrier then than I was now.

After I added the avocado to the sauce, I turned the heat on under the saucepan to low. I crumbled the Gorgonzola and let it rain slowly down on the sauce. I added the unbearably beautiful ribbons of zucchini.

I mixed it all together, warmed everything through, turned off the heat. I found a big spoon, a single plate and fork. I served myself and then sprinkled pistachios on top.

It was amazing. A tour de force. A culinary work of art. Leaning back against the kitchen counter as if I didn't have a care in the world, I ate every damn bite, even if I couldn't quite taste it. The zucchini spirals didn't absorb the sauce the way pasta would, but at least I wasn't going to die a slow, white-flour death from them. And I was almost sure that this excruciating night wasn't going to kill me either.

When I finished, I relocated the leftovers to one of my mother's hand-me-down Tupperware containers and put them in the fridge. I rinsed my plate and silverware and loaded them in the dishwasher.

I was a little bit wobbly when I picked up the Cognac

bottle and my phone on the way to my bedroom, but it wasn't too bad. I stripped off my funky tie-dyed maxi dress with its little lace panels at the hem, my good bra and underpants.

Sitting naked on my bed, I called Rick's phone one more time. As an aspiring health coach, I knew I wasn't supposed to tell other people what to do. But I did it anyway.

"Cluck off," I said once his stupid message ended. "Permanently."

Then I chugged the rest of the Cognac.

Noreen's Luscious Lavender Chicken with Spiralized Zucchini

2 medium zucchini, made into zoodles with spiralizer or vegetable peeler
2 tablespoons butter
1 tablespoon extra virgin olive oil
2 boneless chicken breasts, cut into bite-size chunks
1 teaspoon sea salt
$^1/_2$ teaspoon pepper
1 minced shallot
2 cloves minced garlic
1 tablespoon dried culinary lavender buds, ground with spice grinder or mortar and pestle (or substitute Herbes de Provence)
1 cup heavy cream
1/3 cup chicken broth
2 tablespoon Cognac
1 ripe avocado, diced
1 cup Gorgonzola cheese, crumbled
$^1/_2$ cup pistachios, coarsely chopped

Sprinkle chicken with salt and pepper. Melt butter and olive oil in large skillet over medium heat. Add chicken and cook for 4 to 5 minutes or until cooked through, then remove chicken and set aside. Add shallots, garlic, and lavender to skillet and stir for 2-3 minutes. Add cream, broth, and Cognac and stir for 5 minutes or until thickened.

Reduce heat and stir in chicken and Gorgonzola and avocado. Add zoodles. Stir and heat through until zoodles are covered with sauce and just barely cooked. Transfer to plates and sprinkle with pistachios. Eat with company or all by yourself.

Day 13

18, 013 steps

The old Noreen would have stayed in bed. She might have found a new hiding place for her key so Tess and Rosie wouldn't be able to break in and find her. Or left a note for them on the front door saying she'd gone away unexpectedly and really looked forward to catching up when she got back. The old Noreen would have cried and moped and wallowed, possibly for the rest of her life. She might have eventually sent out for ice cream.

But I was the new Noreen.

"We are each entirely responsible for our own happiness," I said to the crack in my ceiling as soon as I opened one eye. "I have so much to be grateful for—this beautiful day, more than five months of salary and benefits left, the fact that the Cognac bottle wasn't full."

Somehow I'd never quite managed to get under the covers last night, but that only meant my sheets would be fresh tonight. I rolled out of bed, grabbed a robe. I swung by the bathroom. I found my disappeared Pebbles at the Beach Flintstones glass nestled in with the extra toilet paper rolls I kept in a wicker basket on a shelf.

"I have absolutely no idea how you got in there, Pebbles," I said as I scooped up the glass, "but if I had anything to do with it, I sincerely apologize for my part in your misadventure."

I walked cautiously into the kitchen and drank about eighteen gallons of water.

"Hydration," I said in my best coaching voice, "is crucial for health and well-being."

The cranial throbbing I was just holding at bay came crashing down and landed on the runway above my eyes. Since two glasses of wine was a wild night for me, I thought an immediate and generous dose of Advil might be prudent. I chased the Advil with more water and then microwaved a small plate of last night's leftovers to settle my stomach while the coffee was brewing.

When I opened my front door it was still twilight. I walked along sidewalks illuminated by streetlights and edged with long strips of dew-sprinkled lawn. The air was cool and fresh and damp, and it surrounded me like a cocoon. I could smell the salt air calling me from the beach. I thought I could smell the lavender from my garden, too, but maybe I was only imagining it. From the other side of the street, I picked out the sweet vanilla and honeycomb scent of honeysuckle climbing up an arbor.

I made it through the break in the seawall just as the sun was rising in pink and orange stripes, the reflection spilling over and waking up the gray blue sea. I stood there until the show was over, out of respect and awe and gratitude. I wondered why I'd missed so many sunrises in my life when they'd never once let me down.

A long time ago, John Lennon sang that you don't need a watch to waste your time. Oh, the time I had wasted in my life. No more. Rick and I were finished—an underrated f-word, the one that meant dead as a doornail. Obsolete. Over and out. Kaput. History. Past tense. Nonoperational. Defunct. Washed up.

Big deal. Everybody wasn't good at something. Tennis. Karaoke. Macramé. Okay, so I was really, really bad at love. It happens. All I had to do was zip up my heart and keep it zipped. And then go about living the rest of my life.

I took off down the beach, swinging my arms and stretching out my legs and waiting for the endorphins to kick in. Because no matter how many times in your life you've been done wrong, no matter how crappy you feel when you wake up in the morning, walking always helps.

"Step away from the key," I yelled. Too late, I realized that loud noises anywhere in the vicinity of my head were not a good thing.

Tess jumped at the sound of my voice. She dropped a large roll of paper that had been tucked under one arm. It tumbled down my front steps. Rosie ran after it and scooped it up.

Tess slid my key back under the mat. "Where have you been? And what's up with those fugly dark circles under your eyes?"

"Fugly?" Rosie said.

Tess shrugged. "It's the classy way of saying *f*-ing ugly. How can you not know that?"

Rosie bent over to retie one of her sneakers. "Um, because there *is* no classy way to say *f*-ing ugly?"

Since they seemed to have forgotten about me, I used the time to slide my sunglasses down from the top of my head and back over my eyes where they belonged.

Tess pivoted her head in my direction. "Okay, what's going on?"

"Late night studying," I said. "And I've got a ton of work to do today, so I walked early."

Tess put her hands on her hips. "Show us the mileage."

I sighed, held out my wrist and my Fitbit, hoped the smell of Cognac evaporating from every pore in my body wasn't all that noticeable.

"Wow," Rosie said. "Impressive."

"Thanks," I said. "The sunrise was inspiring."

I took a step in the direction of my house and another dose of Advil. "Okay, well, have a good walk. I'll see you tomorrow at the regular time."

"Hold your horses." Tess swung one arm around my shoulders and held up a roll of duct tape with her other hand.

"Get away from me." I slid out from under her arm. "The last time you showed up at my house with duct tape, you almost got me arrested."

Just before we'd left on our trip to the Sequim Lavender Festival last year, Tess had dragged me out of the house under the cover of darkness to protest Marshbury's official town clothesline ban. We covered poster boards with clothesline activism slogans like CLOTHESLINES ARE THE NEW COOL and HANG IT UP, BAN THE BAN and THERE'S NOTHING LIKE THE SMELL OF YOUR SHEETS FRESH OFF THE LINE. Then we'd duct taped our signs to a clothesline stretched across the Marshbury town common. Our final act of defiance had been to add bubbles to the elephant fountain. Perhaps a few too many bubbles, since overnight they'd multiplied and taken on a life of their own, overflowing the fountain and surging over the manicured grass.

When Tess, Rosie and I passed the common at the crack of dawn the next morning on the way to Logan Airport, the bubbles looked like a cross between a seriously late snowstorm and an effervescent tidal wave. And by the time we got to Sequim, a video of a hazy but identifiable me taking off my black ski mask and following a black ski-masked and unidentifiable Tess and her laundry detergent over to the fountain had found its way to Marshburytownonline.org.

"It was your own damn fault," Tess said. "I told you to keep your ski mask on."

"I mean it. I want absolutely nothing to do with you or your duct tape."

"Relax," Tess said. "We're just going to use it to hang up the map in your garage."

The little gym I'd created for us in the unused half of my garage hadn't been seeing a lot of action lately. Rosie and I held the world map over the United States map we'd used to track our miles for our Sequim trip while Tess taped the corners to the wall with duct tape.

The three of us stood back to admire our handiwork.

"Zaire?" Rosie said. "Didn't it change its name like two decades ago?"

"Fine," Tess said. She uncapped the marker she'd brought and crossed out Zaire and wrote Democratic Republic of Congo in her perfect teacher's block printing.

"Ceylon?" Rosie said. "Correct me if I'm wrong, but I'm pretty sure it's been Sri Lanka since right around the time Elton John's 'Rocket Man' came out."

Rosie grabbed the marker from Tess, crossed out Ceylon and wrote Sri Lanka. She tapped the marker against her chin a few times, then crossed out Burma and wrote Myanmar.

"You two are giving me a world geography complex," I said.

"Connor did a report for school on countries that have changed their names." Rosie held out the marker to me. "Here, you can cross out Saigon and write Ho Chi Minh City."

"Thanks," I said. "I feel so much smarter now."

"Okay, so I got a good deal on the map," Tess said. "It's not like we're walking over any of those countries anyway.

Let's see, the distance from Marshbury, Massachusetts to Paris, France is approximately 3,465 miles. There are three of us, so 3,465 divided by 3 equals . . ."

Rosie and I just looked at her.

Tess shook her head. "Come on, ladies. Math phobia is all in your head. The answer is 1155."

"Of course it is," I said.

"So," Tess said. "The three of us each have to walk 1155 miles over the next five days. Which means we have to walk . . ."

Rosie and I just looked at her some more.

Tess shook her head. "I'm appalled—you're not even trying. We each have to walk 231 miles a day, which I have to admit might be a tad optimistic. So rather than scale it up so that one step equals a quarter of a mile or something like that, which even I think feels a little bit like cheating, I think we're going to have to count our previous mileage to make this work."

I took what I hoped was an unnoticeable step in the direction of my next dose of Advil.

Tess kept talking. "Which means we're all going to have to go online and see how far back we can trace our mileage on our fitness tracker sites. We need all the mileage we can get if we're going to earn this trip."

I took another step toward the Advil and then stopped. "Wait. Did you just say we're leaving for France in five days?"

Day 14

10, OO2 steps

Walk. Study. Spiralize cucumber.

Day 15

10,026 steps

Walk. Study. Make spiralized cucumber-infused water.

Noreen's Health Coach-Worthy Infused Water

1 large organic cucumber, spiralized with spiralizer or
vegetable peeler
Cold filtered water
1 teaspoon culinary lavender buds
5 sprigs fresh mint

*Add cucumber spirals, lavender buds, and mint to clean glass pitcher. Fill
to top with filtered water. Cover and refrigerate. Attempt to drink your
troubles away.*

Day 16

10,001 steps

Walk. Study. Google Rick to make sure he's not dead in a ditch after all.

Day 17

10,002 steps

"Are you okay, Noreen?" Rosie asked as we cut across the beach parking lot.

I swallowed a sigh. "I'm fine. I was just thinking about everything I still have to do before we hit the road. I'm trying to get ahead on—"

"You'd better not let that health stuff get in our way," Tess said. "I have every intention of eating and drinking my way through Provence. And Lyon. And all the stops in between."

"Don't worry," I said, "I wouldn't dream of interrupting your binge. I think I'll have to do a practice coaching session from the ship, and maybe some reading, but other than that—"

"Did you and that hot boyfriend of yours break up or something?" Tess said.

"Do you ever let the other person finish a sentence before you interrupt?" I let out a puff of air. "You're really driving me up the walk. I mean, wall." I stepped around to the other side of Rosie.

"Driving me up the walk is actually pretty good," Rosie said. "We'll have to remember it."

Tess stepped around, too, then cut back in between Rosie and me. "Ohmigod, you *did* break up."

"Not so you'd notice." I picked a piece of lint off the shoulder of my T-shirt. "We had plans, he didn't show up, I haven't heard from him since, end of story."

"You haven't heard from him since?" Rosie said. "Oh, honey."

We walked single file through the opening in the seawall, spread out again across the sand. I tried to stay in the moment —blue skies overhead, morning sun gently warming my shoulders, ocean air coming in through my nose and going out through my mouth, calf muscles working as my heels sunk into the soft sand.

"I'll miss seeing him around," Tess said. "He had a tremendous ass."

Even though it wasn't really that funny, we all cracked up. We laughed and laughed, that crazy kind of out-of-control laughter, the gulls swooping and squawking above us as if they wanted in on the action.

Rosie wiped her eyes with the back of her hands. "Holy sunscreen in my eyes—I hate that. Okay, I know it probably doesn't feel this way now, but superior posterior or not, if that's the way he treats you, you're better off without him."

Tess gave me a series of awkward pats on the back like she was burping me. "Don't you worry, sweetie pie." She pulled up an app on her phone as we walked, typed something in. "We'll fix you up with *un homme séduisant* as soon as we get to France."

"I have no idea what you said after 'fix you up'," I said. "But whatever it was, don't even think about it."

Rosie leaned over so she could get a look at Tess's screen. "Ooh, an attractive man. Yes, please, I'll have one, too. Oh, wait, I forgot, I'm married. Although if my dad doesn't show up to help keep an eye on the boys like he promised, I might well be without a husband by the time we leave."

I stepped over a piece of driftwood, tried to look past Tess to make eye contact with Rosie. "Have you talked to your dad at all?"

Rosie took a little skip so she could see me. "Nope. I've left him three messages. How about your mom? Have you heard from her yet?"

I shook my head. "Not a word. Do you want me to leave a message on her voicemail asking her to tell your dad to call?"

"Good idea," Rosie said. "Maybe tag teaming them will do the trick."

"Hello," Tess said. "I'm right here."

"How could we ever forget?" I said.

My pushpin was blue, Rosie's was yellow, and Tess's was red, and they all had little matching flags attached to them. We'd already signed in to our fitness tracker accounts and traced our daily step counts back as far as we could. We'd totaled the mileage and now Tess was using a ruler to help us plot our way across the ocean from Massachusetts to France.

"Well done, ladies," Tess said. "Now give Iceland a big wave."

"If we can wave to Iceland," Rosie said, "I think we're in serious trouble."

"From a distance," Tess said. "We're waving from a distance. And if we keep this up, our step count should have us waving to the UK and walking into Paris just as our plane lands at Roissy Charles de Gaulle in real time."

"I'm confused," Rosie said. "If it's the Charles de Gaulle Airport, where does the Roissy come from?"

"Roissy is the name of a town near the airport," Tess said. "If we want to pass for locals, we should just call the airport Roissy."

"Yeah," I said. "I'm sure we'll totally pass for locals if we do that. We'll be lucky if we can manage to order coffee and a croissant and find the gate in time to make our flight to Marseille."

"Don't be ridiculous," Tess said. "We have almost four hours between flights. And let's not forget that you'll have the official Wildwater Walking Club translator traveling with you."

"Ha," I said.

Rosie gave her pushpin a little wiggle to make sure it wouldn't fall off the map and mess up our mileage. Tess and I did the same thing with our pushpins. Someday when I had more ambition, maybe I could cover this wall in cork tiles to make it work better.

"As silly as it is," I said, "plotting our mileage like this to earn our trip is a really good strategy. And having that specific, measurable, relevant daily step count goal that a fitness tracker or a step counter like a pedometer provides helps so much. It'll keep us on track with our walking while we're on the river cruise, too."

"It definitely helps," Rosie said, "but it just amazes me that even though I know how important walking 10,000 steps a day is, and I also know how much better I feel when I do it, I still have to fight with that self-destructive part of myself. I was really close to tying my Fitbit to the paddle fan last night to get my last two hundred steps in."

"Don't even think about it," Tess said. "If I'm resisting the air fluff cycle, your paddle fan is completely off limits."

"Maintaining change is the hardest part," I said. "We've been studying this in class, and it's incredible how often you change a behavior, it improves your life, and then you stop doing the thing that improved it. Kind of like once you feel better, you stop taking the medicine."

"I can see that," Tess said. "Like you're walking every day and eating well and then finally you look eat-your-heart-out-everybody fabulous. So you figure now you're done and you can stop. And then three months later you end up looking worse than if you'd never even started."

"So what's the answer?" Rosie said.

"Yeah," Tess said. "Let's hear it from the health coach."

I shrugged. "Well, first you're supposed to accept the fact that setbacks will happen. And you attempt to figure out what you can learn from each one. And then you try to use that information to figure out a better strategy for the next time you're in the same situation."

"Got it," Tess said. "So if I was trying not to eat a large buttered popcorn every time I go to the movies, it's okay if I end up doing it anyway, as long as I order a medium the next time."

"Good try," I said. "I think it's also that instead of thinking quick fixes, or what we can get away with, we need to be thinking about changes that are meaningful to us in terms of health and wellness. Things that will help us reach the life we want to live."

"Fine," Tess said. "Next time I'll order a small popcorn."

I ignored her and turned to Rosie. "So you could try to come up with a strategy to help. Instead of thinking about all the ways to get out of those last 200 steps, or cranking them out through sheer willpower, maybe you could try to visualize yourself doing a nice peaceful loop around the neighborhood after dinner as if it's an end-of-the-day treat. The Italians even have a name for that kind of walk—*passeggiata*. They catch the last bit of sunlight, chat with their neighbors while they digest their evening meal, get relaxed and ready for a good night's sleep."

"*Passeggiata*," Tess said. "Maybe we'll have to go to Italy for our next trip."

"I love the sound of that," Rosie said. "Both the *passeggiata* and the trip to Italy."

My head had launched into a slow pendulum nod on its own. "Or you could think about how good you'll feel when you hit that 10,000^th step. Or you could leave your sneakers on until you've reached your step quota for the day so it doesn't feel like too much work to put them back on again."

Rosie was nodding along with me now, so I kept going. "Everybody's different, so you have to picture what strategies might work for you. Basically you think about where you want to be and then you figure out how you're going to get there by setting a series of small goals, each with a high probability of success. You know, one step at a time."

"You're really getting good at this coaching thing," Rosie said.

"Thanks," I said. "Now if only I could figure out how to apply it to my own life."

Tess had just gone next door to her house. Rosie was cutting through my backyard to the path that led to her house.

I was standing in my front yard, at loose ends, trying to decide whether to run to the grocery store, or do some health coach reading, or finally jump in to the completely daunting task of trying to decide what to pack for France.

I noticed something on my front steps.

I walked over to it slowly, almost afraid it might jump out at me like a Jack-in-the-box. Or blow up or something.

I'd never seen anything like it. It was shaped like a woman's head and neck, with the shoulders and collarbones acting as a pedestal. It was made out of rough gray cement with the tiniest bits of multicolored sea glass sparkling in it.

The top of the head had been scooped out and filled with soil. Long rosary bead-like strands of some kind of green plant were mixed with a leafier green plant that had tiny white flowers. The plants cascaded out of the soil like an explosion of hair. A pair of reading glasses I must have left at Rick's house at some point perched on a cement nose shaped a lot like mine. A big red flower was tucked behind one ear. A strand of heart-shaped ivy grew out of the soil and wrapped around the neck twice to make a necklace. A little cement heart with an $\mathcal{N}$ carved on it hung from a tiny metal loop in the center of the ivy necklace.

It was bizarre. It was magnificent. Was it a note-less apology? Or some kind of voodoo planter filled with nonedible plants? A peace offering? Or an excuse—here's the head pot I was so busy making that I missed dinner? Just because it was spectacular didn't mean Rick and I weren't history.

I ran through the path between my yard and Rosie's.

She turned when she heard me, one hand on the doorknob of her back door. "Hey, what's up?"

"Can I borrow your tussie-mussie book again?" I said.

While I really should have been studying, while I definitely should have been packing, I flipped through Rosie's book. Tussie-mussies were Victorian speaking bouquets. The Victorians used to exchange symbolic flower arrangements instead of letters, little lace doily-wrapped nosegays that were their unique way of cryptically yet gracefully expressing their repressed feelings.

It was a shame tussie-mussies had never caught on in any lasting way. The world would be a kinder and gentler place if we all exchanged tussie-mussies instead of badmouthing people behind their backs or unfriending them on Facebook. I'd designed a tussie-mussie for Michael after he'd dumped me, and I had to admit it had been pretty cathartic.

Rick's tussie-mussie would have poppies to remind him of the deadly poppy fields in the *Wizard of Oz* that I'd learned way back in high school symbolized the dangers of complacency.

I'd add ornamental grass to Rick's tussie-mussie, too. One of the few bits of dialog I remembered from *Star Wars* was when Princess Leia said, "The grass doesn't mind being walked on, but it does feel it." I'd tiptoed over grass for years after hearing her say that. The grass in Rick's tussie-mussie would be my way of saying that when it comes right down to it, we all mind being walked on.

My next thought was that I'd take the plants out of the top of Rick's planter and replace them with his tussie-mussie. Then I'd drive the planter over to his house under the cover of darkness and leave it on his front steps. Let him see what it felt like to find it. No note. No explanation.

But then I worried he'd think I didn't like his cement sculpture, and he'd stop working in cement just like he'd quit metal sculpture.

In the end, I decided that I didn't need the drama. Making a tussie-mussie only in my head was a lot like writing a letter telling someone off and then not sending it. The closure is for you, not the other person.

TUSSIE-MUSSIE FUCKIE-YOUIE BOUQUET 2.0

Poppies = you were asleep at the wheel
Ornamental grass = we all feel it and we mind
Bittersweet = truth
Dead leaves = sadness
Yarrow = cure for heartache
Black rose = you are from Mars
Green rose = I am from Venus
Love in a mist = you puzzle me
Buttercup = childishness
Cactus = endurance

Carnation = alas, my poor heart
Cyclamen = resignation and goodbye
Wormwood = absence
Verbena = let it go
Bells of Ireland = good luck

Day 18

10,500 steps

"Where did you get that fantastic planter?" Rosie bent down to get a closer look. "She actually kind of looks like you."

"Thanks," I said. "I, um, it just sort of showed up."

Tess made a kissing sound. I glared at her.

Rosie gave Tess a look. "Well," Rosie said, "whoever made it is really talented."

We'd finished walking and recording our mileage. Rosie and Tess followed me into my house and we sat around my kitchen table. I passed out pens and sheets of computer paper and generic supermarket water bottles all around.

Tess clapped her hands to get our attention as if we were her third-grade students. "Okay, we're probably a couple weeks late on this, but we need to agree on exactly what kind of clothes and how many of them we're going to bring."

"Yikes," I said. "I can't believe I've barely started to pack. At least since we're going to France the good news is that we don't have to pay extra to check the first bag. Between one suitcase and a carry-on, we should have plenty of space."

Rosie looked up at my kitchen clock. "I'm a lot more

worried about the fact that my dad hasn't shown up yet than I am about what to pack—I'm used to packing for four people. By the time I get around to my stuff, I just start grabbing things by the handful and throwing them in."

"I left my mother three more messages," I said. "I'd say it's not like her to not call me back, but the truth is I have no idea who she is anymore."

Rosie just shook her head.

"The important thing," Tess said, "is that we don't bring too much stuff. I always over-pack and spend half the trip trying to decide what to wear, and then I end up wearing the same three things over and over again."

"I do that, too," Rosie said. "It's ridiculous."

"Yeah, me too," I said.

"So," Tess said. "What we're going to do is come up with a mandatory Wildwater Walking Club wardrobe, a uniform of sorts, and after we agree to it, there will be no deviation."

"You are seriously unhinged," I said.

"Not that I disagree that Tess is unhinged," Rosie said, "but I actually think it's a good idea, and I'm all for anything that will take the packing pressure off. So what, like one pair of jeans?"

"One pair of jeans," Tess said. "Plus two pairs of black or navy pants, any length from ankle to capri to walking shorts. White won't work because there's a universal law that the minute you put white pants on, you spill red wine on them."

"Dark pants hide a multitude of spills," I said as if I was still a Senior Manager of Brand Identity and this was a pitch brainstorming session.

"One beachy dress," Rosie said. "Plus a summer weight sweater and a jean jacket."

"One pair of sneakers," I said, since my former career in the athletic shoe industry made me the resident footwear expert. "Plus walking shoes, flip-flops, and dressier sandals or ballet flats."

"And one sun hat, so we'll blend in," Tess said.

"Once again," I said, "why do I think the three of us blending in is not going to happen?"

"Two pairs of sunglasses and two pairs of reading glasses," Tess said, "because if you lose one pair, it's probably crazy expensive to replace them in France."

We all scribbled away on our sheets of paper.

"Two pairs of yoga pants," I said. "Or exercise tights, any length."

We scribbled some more. Tess wrote in neat block letters. Rosie made quick little sketches next to some of the items on her list. My own list looked as confused as I was—half cursive, half printing, the words mostly slanting uphill with an occasional steep downward dip.

"Five shirts of your choice," Rosie said. "T-shirt, button-down, camisole, whatever. And something to sleep in. And underwear. Plus seven pairs of sneaker socks. We can always wash them by hand if we run out of clean ones. I'll bring some liquid detergent. And some of those little suction cups with hooks. We can attach them to the glass shower enclosure and hang things to dry on them."

"Do you think I should bring one of my retractable clotheslines?" I said. I'd decorated some retractable clotheslines, and we'd put them up for sale at Rosie's lavender farm shop and on the website.

"Nah," Rosie said. "Then you'd need to bring power tools to install it, which probably wouldn't go over too well with whoever's in charge of the ship."

"Good point," I said. "I wish I'd thought of it earlier. I could have come up with a travel version—a tiny clothesline that attaches to two suction cups and some mini clothespins."

"Even I think we can survive without a clothesline for eight days," Tess said. "Okay, no serious makeup. Tinted sunscreen, concealer, mascara, lip balm or gloss, blush if you absolutely have to. Oh, and travel magnifying mirrors with suction cups to stick on the bathroom mirror are allowed—even if we're going light on the makeup, it's helpful to be able to see to put it on."

"I hate it when my mascara ends up on my nose," Rosie said.

"Don't be a smartass," Tess said.

"Make sure you don't forget your chargers," I said. "And I've got some extra power strips—I can bring one for each room so we're not fighting over plugs."

"The bathroom on that video they sent us was ultra sleek and modern," Tess said, "but there's not much counter space. So we'll need one of those over-the-door storage organizers for each room—you know, the clear plastic kind with all those pockets."

Rosie reached for her water. "There's no way I have time to go shopping before we leave."

"I've got two," Tess said. "I bought them for Hannah before she went off to college—one for her and one for her roommate. My darling daughter told me they were lame." Tess rolled her eyes. "I never got around to returning them."

"I'll bring bug spray," Rosie said.

"We won't need it," Tess said. "France doesn't have mosquitoes."

"How could they not have mosquitoes?" Rosie said.

"I have no idea," Tess said. "Maybe they passed an ordinance."

"I read about this," I said. "It's a myth that France doesn't have mosquitoes. It comes from an old joke: 'Why are there no mosquitoes in France? Because there are so many frogs.'"

"I don't get it," Tess said. "And as a third-grade teacher I'm pretty good at getting bad jokes."

"You know, frog is a nickname for French people." I closed my eyes while I tried to remember the whole story. "Apparently the British started making fun of the French for eating frogs' legs way back in the 16th century. They called them frog-eaters. It stuck and eventually it was shortened to frogs."

"It's still not much of a joke," Tess said. "And it could easily be interpreted as xenophobic. I don't mind Yankee, but I'm not sure how the British feel about Limey or the Irish about Mick."

"Ooh," Rosie said. "But if your kids were half Irish and half French, you could call them McFrogs."

"Good one," I said. "Okay, I've got a big bottle of sunscreen. And I'll bring a stain stick to share."

We scribbled some more, reached for our water bottles.

"I'll bring the duct tape," Tess said.

"Funny," I said.

"I'm not kidding." Tess wrote DUCT TAPE on her list in big block letters. "I never travel without it. It works better than those lint rollers, you can use it to tape the curtains in your room together if the sun peeks through, and we could even use it for a clothesline in a pinch. Plus it fixes all sorts of wardrobe malfunctions from gaping shirts to broken bra straps to unraveling hems to separated sandal soles. There's actually a saying that duct tape fixes everything but a broken heart."

"Thanks," I said. "I needed that."

"Final thing," Tess pushed herself up from the chair. "Wait right here."

"Come on, Tess," Rosie said. "I've got a million things to do."

By the time Rosie and I had finished leaving our parents another message on their cellphones, Tess was back. She handed Rosie and me each a little polka dot gift bag. One thing I'd noticed about elementary school teachers is that they always have plenty of gift bags.

Rosie and I each pulled an identical long loop of shiny silver from our bag.

"It's a twisty necklace," Tess said. "Look." Tess pulled a triplet to the necklaces she'd given us over her head. When she twisted one end into a figure 8, it held its shape. Then she made it into a knot and it held its shape again. She pulled the necklace straight, twisted it around a few times and threaded her reading glasses through a loop at the bottom. Her reading glasses held perfectly.

"Wicked cool," I said. Wicked cool was one of those childhood expressions reserved for truly awesome things. I twisted my twisty necklace into the shape of a bowtie. "Thanks so much for this."

"I love it," Rosie said. Rosie pulled hers up over her red curls and twisted it into a series of loops on top of her head. It looked like a cross between a tiara and a headband. "Thank you, Tess."

"And now," Tess said, "the other shoe drops. The official Wildwater Walking Club challenge is that this is the only piece of jewelry we're allowed to bring on our trip."

"I don't get it," I said.

Rosie just kept playing with her twisty headband.

Tess unhooked her reading glasses and gave the necklace another twist. "It's always such a hassle trying to remember to put your jewelry in the safe deposit box. It's just one more thing to think about. Plus I have to admit I'm kind of over having to take care of anything, including jewelry."

"I'm all for simplifying," Rosie said. "And we can have contests to see who comes up with the most creative ways to wear our twisty necklaces."

"And if we run into any turbulence on the flight," I said, "they can double as prayer beads."

Rosie stopped twisting her necklace. Her freckles popped against her suddenly pale skin.

"Sorry," I said. "I forgot."

Rosie was terrified of flying. On our last trip, Tess had given Rosie one of her vitamins and pretended it was Valium. While Rosie snoozed away, Tess had informed me as well as everyone on the plane within earshot that she'd once given her husband one of her kids' old vitamins—Smurf blue and probably ten years old—and told him it was Viagra. She said it had worked like a charm.

Rosie had not been pleased when she found out that Tess had tricked her.

Silence filled my kitchen as we all had the same flashback. And then it passed, the way things do when you put them behind you because you know that even though friendships aren't perfect, having a group of women who are up for walking every day as well as taking an occasional trip together is a rare and beautiful thing.

"I'm in," Rosie said. "One twisty necklace only in the jewelry department of the official Wildwater Walking Club packing list."

"I'm in, too," I said. "Wait. You bought a necklace for Joy, too, right?"

"Oops," Tess said. She opened her pale blue eyes wide.

"Tess," Rosie said.

I shook my head.

Tess burst out laughing. "Of course I got a twisty necklace for Joy. And she's going to meet us at Roissy aka CDG. Her flight comes in just before ours. From San Antonio or Santa Barbara or San wherever it is she's coming from. And we're all booked on the same flight to Marseille."

"I can't wait to meet her," Rosie said.

"Yeah, me, too," I said. "I'm really looking forward to expressing my deepest sympathy to her on her roommate situation."

I broke down and gave Rick's planter a quick watering. On the one hand I didn't think this was necessarily my responsibility just because the planter looked a little bit like me. But on the other hand all that green plant hair was so beautiful it would be a shame to see it die of thirst.

I carried the watering can around to my backyard to say a quick goodbye to my lavender before I finally dug in to my packing. The dark purple flowers of my Hidcote had started to bloom. I'd noticed that the Hidcote seemed to thrive in the still relatively cool earlier summer weather, while my Munstead tolerated the later summer heat better.

"Sorry," I whispered as I pinched off some flowering stems from the Hidcote. This was almost painful, for me if not for the plant, when the blooms were this pretty. But I knew the best time to pick a lavender flower is when it's just opened and before it begins to turn brown, because waiting affects the taste. Rosie had also taught me that in terms of flavor it's also better to pull the flowers away from the little green cap that holds them and eat only the flower petals.

In this case I wasn't going to actually eat the lavender. I'd add a few lavender cuttings, stems and all, to a pitcher of Earl Grey iced tea I'd brewed to fortify me while I packed.

I heard a shrill scream from Rosie's yard, followed by a cock-a-doodle-doo that could only be Rod Stewart. The Supremes began clucking nonstop. Another ear-piercing scream followed.

I ran through the wooded path between Rosie's and my yards, still carrying the lavender and the watering can.

In the clearing next to the lavender shed, The Supremes were clucking away as they circled a picnic table in well-choreographed formation, while Rod stood by in case they ran into any trouble. My mother was standing on top of the picnic table, screaming her head off. Rosie's dad had one hand over his eyes like a mountain climber trying to assess the best way up.

Rosie headed me off at the path.

"Avert your eyes," Rosie whispered. "I'm pretty sure it's foreplay."

"Oh, gross," I said.

I made an about face and got back to my house just as a massive truck finished depositing a red and white storage pod in my driveway. The truck driver climbed back in the truck and started pulling away.

"Wait," I yelled.

He beeped and waved and kept driving.

I looked at the storage pod, which was roughly the size of a large bedroom or possibly even two. With high ceilings. I tried to imagine backing my car out of the garage without tearing off a bumper.

The good news was as least I didn't have to drive anywhere for the next eight days or so.

The picnic table lovebirds had apparently managed to drag themselves away from each other, since my mom was now sprawled across my bed while I packed. She took a sip from the tall glass of iced tea I'd graciously provided. "Just lovely, sweetie. The lavender complements the oil of bergamot in the Earl Grey beautifully."

"Thanks," I said. "You want to explain that red and white monstrosity in my driveway?"

"Oh, that." She gave the hand not holding her iced tea an airy wave. "You won't even know it's there, honey."

"I'll totally know it's there." I folded the closest thing I had to a France-worthy pair of jeans and put them in my suitcase. "The question is how long will it be taking up most of my driveway?"

My mother smiled. Her eyes sparkled.

I shook my head. "And talk about under the wire. Rosie and I were really worried when you two didn't return our calls. I mean, we had no idea *where* you were."

"Payback's a bitch." My mother threw back her head and laughed.

"Did you really just say that?" I grabbed a pair of navy pants from my closet.

My mother put her glass down on one of my bedside tables. She leaned back against my headboard and crossed one ankle over the other like a movie star. "Which part? Payback or bitch?"

"Hmm," I said, "I'd have to say that the language was probably slightly more shocking than the sentiment."

My old mother would have taken over my packing by now. I'd hand her my clothes and she'd find the most strategic way to arrange them in the suitcase. Eventually, I might have been able to gracefully slip away, under the guise of doing my homework, while she finished up.

My new mother said, "Studies show that people who swear are not only more intelligent but actually have more fun and live longer."

I looked up from counting sneaker socks. "Where were those studies when I was growing up? I mean, come on, we even had a *swear jar* on the mantel."

My mother's new spiky black Joan Jett hair looked like it had been recently shoe-polished. She was wearing dangly fish earrings, maybe rainbow trout, and an ear clip on one ear made out of a multitude of puka shells. Turquoise capris and a low cut hot pink top and strappy hot pink exercise shoes completed her ensemble. She looked great. I also had to admit it was a little bit disorienting that she seemed to be acting younger than I felt.

My mother laughed again. Basically, she hadn't stopped laughing since she'd shown up. "Funny you should bring that up. Kent and I just decided we're going to start a swear jar. A five dollar bill for each curse word, and when the jar's full, we'll take a trip to an exotic country where we can learn to swear in a new language." My mother giggled.

"Kent loves it when I swear like a sailor. It really turns him on."

Parents should never, ever talk like that in front of their kids, no matter how old they are. I scrunched my eyes shut to block out the image, even though it was probably already seared into my brain forever.

My mother was still laughing. Belatedly, I wished I'd thought to count her peals of laughter—maybe there was a Guinness Record she could break. Then I could be her manager and not have to worry about what my next career move would be.

I opened my eyes and reached for a T-shirt, tried to remember whether I'd already packed two or three.

"Wait," I said. "Where exactly would this swear jar reside?"

My mother made that same airy gesture, this time with both hands. "Oh, we'll probably just flit back and forth since there's plenty of space at both places."

"I don't get it," I said. The pod in my driveway appeared like a vision. I tried to block it out. "I mean, Florida is not exactly flitting distance from Massachusetts."

"Did I forget to tell you? I sold my condo. In three days and well over asking price, I might add." My mother let out another peal of laughter. "Kent likes to think it was his strutting back and forth on the front porch looking like he came with the property that caused the bidding war."

"So," I said. I was having a really hard time doing the math here. "That new swear jar will be dividing its time while you flit back and forth between Rosie's place and . . . the pod?"

"Oh, you," my mother said. "You get that sense of humor from your father, you know."

It was like I'd fallen into a bad game of twenty questions. "Here?" I said as calmly as I could.

My mother's laughter was a bottomless pit. "Of course,

here, honey. Rosie and her husband and their brood have taken over most of Kent's house and banished him to the basement—"

I reached for another T-shirt. "They didn't banish him to the basement. They built him a beautiful lower level apartment."

"It's lovely. If you like grab-bars in the bathroom and wheelchair-width doorways. And spending the rest of your life partially buried underground."

I opened my mouth to say something, closed it again because it was true.

My mother shrugged and laughed at the same time. "We might have some fun pretending we're old geezers over there sometimes, but there's a lot going on in that house. So we think the relative calm over here will be a nice balance for us. And of course we'll shake things up sometimes, and he can stay there while I'm here and then he'll come a calling."

My mother actually wiggled her eyebrows. "It leaves room for all sorts of adventures. You know, everything from escaped convict and the prison warden's wife to—"

"Eww," I said. "Please stop."

My mother giggled. "Why don't you finish packing and invite Rick over. Kent promised to sneak over here a little later so the four of us can get a few strings of Wii bowling in before you leave on your trip."

"Wii bowling?" I said.

My mother touched her fish earrings, maybe to make sure they hadn't swum away since she'd last checked. "Yes, Kent and I want Rick to show us a few more tricks—he really helped us out last time. When you get back from France, we'll turn you on to pickleball, which is the new big thing. I have to warn you, Kent and I have our own regulation portable net and we're really getting good. But playing up is how you learn, so just keep that in mind while we're kicking your butts."

My mother laughed some more. It was like she had this

endless well of laughter that just kept bubbling up. Maybe she and Rosie's dad had discovered the fountain of youth while they were missing in action. Instead of bubbles coming out of the elephant fountain, an avalanche of laughter bubbled out of the fountain of youth. And when you drank from it, laughter bubbled out of you, too. The upside was that the fountain of youth kept your neurons firing and your joints lubricated. The downside was that it was like having chronic hiccups—you couldn't stop laughing.

I thought for a moment, trying to decide whether to tell my mother that Rick was out of town or down with the flu or even dead in a ditch. How many times had I been here? My mother would call and ask me about some guy I'd been seeing and he'd be long gone. Sometimes I'd lie and say he was just fine and hope she'd have forgotten about him by the next time I heard from her.

I sighed. "Rick and I aren't seeing each other any more."

When I reached for my funky tie-dyed maxi dress with the little insets of lace at the hem, my eyes surprised me by tearing up. I started to reach for another beachy dress instead, decided I wasn't going to let Rick ruin this dress for me. I folded the dress firmly and placed it on top of my yoga pants.

My mother tilted her head. She re-crossed her movie star ankles so that the other one was on top. "What happened?"

I shrugged. "We had plans, he didn't show up, I haven't heard from him since, the end."

My mother shook her head. "That's not an end. That's an adult conversation that needs to happen."

"Mom, you weren't there. I cooked an elaborate meal for him. I *spiralized* zucchini." I searched for more ammunition. "With the spiralizer you gave me, I might add."

"If you both choose to take the exit door, that's one thing, but you have to earn your way to it by talking it through. If Rick hasn't called you, you need to call him."

"I did call him. That night. Repeatedly. He didn't answer."

"Did you leave a message?"

"I most certainly did leave a message," I said. "I told him to cluck off. Permanently."

"Noreen," my mother said. "If you're going to swear, do it like a grownup."

"I'm close," I said. "But you gave birth to me so I'm restraining myself."

My mother burst out laughing.

"Would you knock it off with the laughter thing," I said. "It's really annoying."

My mother hooked a lacy black bra strap that had slipped down over her shoulder with one finger and pulled it back into place. "Lighten up, honey. And listen up, too. Nobody avoids pain. You need to stop running away from it. Either that or you're going to end up living a long dreary life. You can't just cut and run in a relationship. You have to try to work things out first. You take a deep breath, maybe throw a few high drama zucchini spirals—"

"Cute," I said.

"I love you, honey, but I hope you know that you're your own worst enemy."

"Thanks," I said. "I appreciate that."

"So that was it?" my mother said. "And you haven't heard a word from him since?"

"Nope. Well, he left a planter he made on my front steps."

My mother's eyes lit up. "That adorable planter? The one that looks just like you, with the N on the necklace and those gorgeous plants tumbling out like a mane of hair? I was actually waiting for the right moment to drop a hint that I'd love one for Christmas. Maybe Rosie could get one for Kent, too."

"Mom," I said. "Newsflash: This isn't about you."

My mother and I locked eyes.

"Rick made that for you?" she said.

I nodded.

"Before or after you told him to cluck off?"

"After."

She crossed her arms over her chest. "I rest my case."

Lavender Earl Grey Iced Tea for a Summer Day

3 Earl Grey teabags
3-4 sprigs of lavender, flowers and leaves, rinsed
Sugar or honey, if desired

Bring kettle of water to boil. Put teabags in glass pitcher and pour water in. Steep for 5-6 minutes. Remove teabags. If using sweetener, add and stir until dissolved. Add lavender.

Refrigerate until cold. Serve over ice in tall glass.

Day 19

10,144 steps

My mother and Kent were sitting at my table drinking coffee when I shuffled barefoot into my kitchen. They were wearing matching white terrycloth robes, which I could have happily missed seeing, but at least the two of them were mostly covered up.

Kent stood when he saw me, crossed the kitchen to give me a kiss on the cheek. "Hope you don't mind me bunking in, Noreen."

I gave my sleep T-shirt a subtle yank so it covered more of my legs. "Of course not. It's nice to see you again, Mr. Stockton."

They both burst out laughing. Apparently my fountain of youth theory had been spot on.

"Kent, honey," Rosie's father said. "Call me Kent."

"We're all family now," my mother said.

I seriously needed caffeine for this. I opened a cabinet, reached for a coffee mug, waited for my mother to get up and take over. She didn't.

My mother held out her mug for me to get her a refill.

"The plan is that while you and your friends are gone, Kent and I will spend the day with the boys while their dad's at work, then sneak over here at night for a little peace and quiet."

Rosie's dad wiggled his eyebrows. "And a little romance. Right, Lo?"

"Oh, you," my mother said. And then my mom and Rosie's dad dissolved into what could only be described as orgasmic peals of simultaneous laughter.

I handed my mother her coffee, splashed cream in mine, grabbed a handful of almonds.

"Walk," I said. "Must walk."

The first person I saw when I rolled my suitcases out to my storage pod-filled driveway was Tess's daughter. Her long blond hair hung in beachy waves down her back, and her legs were a mile long in her short white shorts. She still had that effortless teenage beauty that she'd look back on one day and wonder why she hadn't taken the time to appreciate it.

"Hannah!" I yelled.

I parked my suitcases and went over to give her a hug. "You look terrific," I said.

"Thanks." She looked at me doubtfully. "You, too."

I smiled. "What are you doing here?"

"A friend had to drive home to get something, so I just came for the weekend to keep her company."

Tess sashayed across the driveway in sunglasses and a wide-brimmed hat. "And it's been lovely to see you for all of five minutes. Your timing is impeccable."

"Mo-om," Hannah said. "I told you I didn't remember when you were going on your trip. I do have a life of my own, you know."

"I realize that," Tess said. "In fact, I pay for it."

When Hannah put her hands on her hips, she looked exactly like Tess. "You do not. I have a paid internship. Okay, so it doesn't exactly cover all my—"

Tess's husband jumped in between them and put his arms around their shoulders. "Come on, let's have a nice goodbye and then you can start the next round when we have more time."

"Group hug," Hannah said. She looped her free arm around Tess.

It reminded me of everything I didn't have in my own life, so I looked away.

When their hug broke up, Hannah reached over and twirled Tess's twisty necklace into a new shape. "Have a great time, Mom. And whatever you do, don't buy me one of these necklaces. Ever. But if you see any really French-looking silk scarves while you're there, just so you know, I've always wanted one."

"Since when?" Tess said.

Hannah shrugged. "Since I Googled France? Anyway, don't just pick one out. Send me a picture first to make sure I like it."

Tess put her hands on Hannah's shoulders and gave her a kiss on her forehead. "I love you, honey. And some day I know I'll even like you again."

"Is that a yes?" Hannah said.

The two of them cracked up. Tess's husband shook his head.

Rosie was chatting quietly with her husband while Connor and Nick kicked a soccer ball around with their grandfather and my mother. Somehow since the last time I'd seen her, my mother had even ramped up her soccer skills. The woman had *moves*.

"Go, Lo," Connor, or maybe it was Nick, yelled as my mother scooped the ball away from Kent with one well-angled foot and started dribbling it in the opposite direction.

I stood there, once again the cheese that stands alone at the end of "The Farmer in the Dell," watching this assortment of people of all ages and shapes and sizes. The one thing they all seemed to have in common was that they were so much better at life than I was.

Rosie walked over. "Nice pod," she said as she leaned back against it.

I leaned back beside her. "Thanks. But I think it might look even nicer in your driveway."

Connor and Nick let out a roar from the makeshift soccer field.

"Not a chance," Rosie said. "But hey, look on the bright side. Maybe we can just stay in France and then we won't have to worry about the pod or anything else."

The car we'd arranged to drive us to Logan Airport pulled into my driveway. We'd hired the same airport shuttle service last year for our Sequim trip. If you factored in the crazy cost of airport parking, plus the fact that we could split the cost three ways, it was definitely the way to go.

"At least the pickup time is lot more civilized for this flight than our last one," Tess said. "2:30 P.M. vs. 3:30 A.M., as I remember."

The driver popped the trunk and managed to cram our luggage in.

Rosie and Tess and I gave our twisty necklaces a final adjustment. Tess made Rosie and me put on our hats, too, so we'd all blend in when we got to France. We climbed into the backseat so we could sit together, Rosie squished into the middle since she had the shortest legs.

Tess and I lowered our windows.

"Bon Voyage," the three of us yelled as we wiggled our wrists back and forth in queen-like waves.

"Bon Voyage," everybody yelled back.

I wondered which would be worse when I got home again:

to see the storage pod still in my driveway or to find out the pod was gone but its contents had taken over my house.

"Déjà vu all over again," Tess said as we drove past the Marshbury town common a few minutes later. "I'm seeing those bubbles we poured in that fountain last year like it was yesterday."

The driver looked at us in the rearview mirror. "That was *you?*"

"We're going to plead the fifth on that," Tess said.

I didn't say anything. I was too busy looking out my window and imagining Rick splashing through the elephant fountain, looking like a really nice guy who'd gotten a little bit lost.

Day 20

11,322 steps

Our nonstop overnight flight was scheduled to leave Boston at 6:45 P.M. and arrive in Paris at 7:40 A.M. the next morning. The time in Paris is six hours ahead of the time in Boston. Rather than risk a math headache by trying to figure out how long the flight was, I'd cheated and looked it up: 6 hours and 55 minutes. We'd scheduled our ride to the airport an hour earlier than the crazy early time we needed to arrive for an international flight so we could get the rest of our daily steps in before we boarded.

Our driver let us out at Logan's international terminal, Terminal E, and we managed to find the right line to check our baggage. We'd already attached the red leather tags that the cruise company had mailed us, along with our cruise documents, in chic zip-up toiletry bags. For back up, we'd filled out index cards with our snail mail and email addresses, as well as our cell number and the ship's number, and put the cards inside our suitcases. We'd also taken photos of our checked bags with our cell phones in case we needed them for identification purposes. We agreed that, in a reverse Murphy's

Law kind of way, going to all this trouble would seriously minimize the chances of the airlines losing our luggage.

Once we'd made it through the security check, we walked our carry-ons up and down the terminal until we all hit 10,000 steps. To celebrate, we stopped at the water bottle filling station and refilled the big water bottles we'd emptied so we could bring them through security.

We tapped water bottles all around. "*Santé*," I said. "That's the short version of *a votre santé*, a French toast that means 'to your health.' It seemed like something a potential health coach going to France should know."

"We'll have no upstaging the official Wildwater Walking Club translator," Tess said. She looked at her wrist. "Okay, we still have time to hit Durgin-Park. I haven't been insulted by a server in ages."

"I think you might have to go to their Faneuil Hall restaurant for that," Rosie said. "I bet they tone down the insults here so they don't frighten visitors just coming into the country. But I used to love going to Durgin-Park with my parents when we were kids. The tin ceilings, the uneven wood floors, the long shared tables with the red and white checked tablecloths. We always requested Gina as our waitress because she was tough as nails and never failed to tell us we'd be lucky if our Yankee pot roast came on a plate."

Tess, who was leading the way, turned her head so we could hear her. "I remember asking my mom if the waitresses were nurses because they all wore those fugly white uniforms."

"What I remember most," I said, "besides the New England clam chowder, is that I could never understand a word anybody said. If you want to hear a real Boston accent, that's the place to go. And I loved the sign out front—"

"Look," Rosie said. The Terminal E airport Durgin-Park had the same sign: Established Before You Were Born.

We stood in line and ordered clam chowder all around. Nobody insulted us, which was a little bit disappointing.

Tess took a break from inhaling her chowder to point to a couple walking by. "What do you think their story is?"

"Easy," I said. "They met for the first time at Starbucks a few minutes ago. His name is Alphonse and he has a wife back home and he's here for a conference. Her name is Fiona, and she got dumped by her boyfriend right before she left to catch her plane for the same conference."

"Even though," Rosie said, "Fiona just this minute noticed the tan line from the wedding ring Alphonse took off before he boarded his flight, they'll hook up for the night."

"And then tomorrow," I said, "Fiona will eat peanut M&Ms and drink a tiny screw-top bottle of Chardonnay from the minibar for dinner, while she toys with mildly suicidal impulses."

"She'll feel guilty," Tess said, "about cheating on the boyfriend who dumped her and less guilty that, while he was in the bathroom, she stole Alphonse's wedding ring from his wallet to keep as a souvenir."

"Ooh," Rosie said. "I like it. Okay, after a four-course meal in the hotel dining room, Alphonse will smoke a cigar on the balcony of his room while he calls his wife and tells her how much he misses her."

I nodded. "And when Alphonse goes to put his wedding ring back on before he gets on his return flight, Fiona will feel the exact moment he realizes it's missing. And she'll smile."

"The end," I added. I went back to fishing for pieces of clam with my plastic soupspoon.

"I have to admit," Tess said. "I kind of feel like we should go after Fiona and save her from having to go through all that. Maybe we could bring her to France with us."

Rosie sighed. "Here we go again. I knew it was just a matter of time before your do-gooder impulses kicked in again. Let me just point out that Fiona doesn't exist, so we don't need to save her from anything. And I never get any time to myself, so all I want to do on this trip is have some fun."

I started to sing Sheryl Crow's "All I Want to Do" into my soupspoon.

At the exact same time, Tess began singing Cyndi Lauper's "Girls Just Wanna Have Fun," into her spoon. The songs actually sounded pretty good together. Maybe I could write a letter to Cyndi and Sheryl suggesting they record them together, one overlapping the other. It would be a colossal hit and they'd fight over which one got to hire me as her Senior Manager of Brand Identity, with a special emphasis on counterpoint collaborations. Or something.

"Hey," Rosie said. "Why is everybody staring at us?"

Tess and I looked around. People were definitely staring at us.

"The singing?" Tess said.

"Or you think it might be the hats?" I said.

We all reached up to touch our hats at the same time. Mine was a wide-brimmed overly floppy straw hat I'd bought years ago to wear to a wedding and then chickened out. Tess's hat had a brim like a skating rink and a monster taupe silk peony on one side. Rosie's was made out of bright purple canvas with a pleated neck cape to protect her from the sun. All three hats had chinstraps of varying widths, which I could only imagine made us look like fashionista-wannabe cowgirls.

"If we'd remembered our little white gloves, we could have passed them off as our Easter bonnets," I said. "Perhaps it would have been a good idea for us to try hat shopping again in this millennium."

"I knew I should have gone with my Red Sox baseball hat," Rosie said as two women walking by turned around to stare at us.

"Trust me. We'll fit right in once we get to France." Tess patted her mouth with her napkin. "That was actually pretty good for airport food."

"Nostalgia," I said, "makes everything taste better."

Rosie crumpled her napkin and stuffed it into her still half-full chowder takeout container. Her freckles were starting to jump out against her pale skin already.

We'd let the river cruise company book our flights, and they'd managed to get us seats next to one another, as well as a lot closer to the front of the coach section than we would have been able to get on our own.

We put our hats in a pile when we hit a logjam on the jetway to the plane. Tess put the pile on top of her head. "*Caps for Sale*," she sang in her best elementary teacher's voice.

"Good luck with that," Rosie said. "I'm not sure you could give them away."

"I loved *Caps for Sale*," I said. "I remember making my father read it to me every night for the longest time. Until I moved on to *Harold and the Purple Crayon*. I definitely had a thing for Harold."

"Harold had a nice ass, too," Tess said. "In case you're looking for a unifying theme in your taste in men."

"Shut up," I said. Tess smiled. A woman up ahead turned to get a look at us.

Eventually we made it inside the plane and crept our way down one of the aisles to our row. Rosie stood on tiptoe to put her carry-on overhead and climbed across to the window seat. Tess put her carry-on next to Rosie's and tucked the pile of hats in between.

Tess hesitated, torn between her extreme need to be in the center of things and getting an aisle seat.

I checked my boarding pass. "Technically I've got the middle seat, but I guess I could let you have it so you don't feel left out."

"No way am I falling for that one." Tess stepped back to

let me go first. "The aisle seat is much more valuable real estate."

I managed to get my carry-on stowed away overhead and a smaller bag crammed under the seat in front of me.

Tess passed out wipes as soon as we were seated. We all disinfected our trays and armrests and the screens in front of us. A man up ahead and across the aisle pulled out an enormous paper seat cover and draped it over his entire seat.

"He probably travels with his own package of disposable toilet seat covers," Tess said.

"Did you know," Rosie said, "that you can use pieces of disposable toilet seat covers to blot your face when it gets oily? They're made out of the exact same material they use for those facial-blotting sheets. And at a much better price per square inch, I might add."

"Who knew," I said.

"Okay, you two," Tess said. "Put your phones and iPads or whatever you brought in airplane mode. And don't forget we have to leave them in airplane mode until we're back in the U.S. so we don't rack up insane roaming fees. We can turn on Wi-Fi once we get to the ship. Unless either of you plans to buy a SIM card in France so you can have phone service?"

"Nope," I said. "I only need Wi-Fi for my school stuff."

Rosie didn't say anything. She just pulled a big purple pashmina out of her bag and draped it over her head like a tent.

"Okay," I said. "Even though our water bottles are full, we still need to take a bottle of water every time the flight attendants offer them so we'll stay hydrated, because a long flight like this is the equivalent of spending the same amount of time trudging across a desert."

"Good idea," Tess said. "It'll help balance out the free wine we get since it's an international flight."

I clicked in to health coach mode. "Up to you, of course, but the cabin air has far less oxygen than the air we usually breathe, which can make the effect of alcohol stronger, and there's also the dehydration issue, and we have a long night ahead of us as well as another plane to catch in the morning. Plus, they'll have plenty of free wine on the river cruise. So my vote—"

"Buzz kill," Tess said. "Fine."

Rosie brought her knees up under her purple pashmina.

I reached over and gave one of Rosie's knees a little pat.

"Moving on," I said. "I've set the timer on my phone— which by the way still works when it's in airplane mode in case you were wondering—to go off every hour to remind us to get up and walk around the plane."

The man in the seat in front of me let out a soft groan. I ignored him. "We can also point and flex our toes while we're sitting, and lift our feet off the floor and do clockwise and counterclockwise ankle circles. And I also downloaded a series of upper body plane exercises, so I can pull them up on my iPad later if we need them."

The man in front of us groaned again. I resisted a powerful urge to kick the back of his seat.

"I have to tell you," Tess said, "you're getting a little bit bossy."

"Takes one to know one," I said.

"Exercise all you want," Tess said. "But come health or high water, my plan is to watch three full movies before we land."

I took a long sip of water while Tess pulled up her first movie on her tablet. "*Paris, T'Aime,*" she read along with the credits.

She paused the movie and pulled up her translation app on her phone. "That means *Paris, I Love You,*" she said.

I took another sip of water. "Good to know."

Tess put her phone away. "Do you want to watch it with me?" She held out one of her ear buds in my direction. "It's a collection of vignettes and short films about romance set all around Paris. Great ensemble cast."

"Thanks," I said. "But I think I'll just catch up on my health coach reading."

As soon as Tess was plugged into her movie, the captain told the crew to prepare for takeoff. I heard a little gasp beside me.

"You okay?" I whispered to Rosie.

The top of her pashmina was going up and down, up and down.

I leaned a little closer. "*What* are you doing under there?"

Rosie lifted up a corner of her big purple scarf. "It's called tapping. It's kind of like acupressure. You tap your body's meridian points with your fingertips. It's supposed to help with—"

The plane's wheels made a grinding sound as they retracted into the wheel wells.

"Noooo," Rosie said.

"Hey," I said. I grabbed the end of Rosie's pashmina closest to me and ducked my head under. "So you know all the reasons you shouldn't be afraid of flying, right?"

Rosie pressed her head against my shoulder. "That I have a better chance of being killed on the highway? That the whole plane won't actually tilt if I move?"

I launched into my pendulum nod. "Tell me about this tapping thing and what you hope it will accomplish."

Rosie took a couple of shallow breaths. "It's supposed to help you feel less anxious."

I nodded my head some more, even though Rosie couldn't see me because the pashmina had created a little tent of darkness. "So, you're hoping the tapping will make you feel less anxious about flying. On a scale of one to ten, how anxious do you feel right now?"

"Um, a billion and nine. Okay, I'm supposed to rub the lymph area on either side of my chest about two inches or so below the collarbone. They're called the sore spots—you'll know when you hit them because you'll feel the sensitivity."

I found my own sore spots. "Cool."

"And now I'm supposed to rub them and tell myself a few times that even though I'm deeply afraid of flying, I completely accept myself."

I tried to come up with a version that would work for me. *Even though I'm deeply afraid of living my life*, I thought as I rubbed my sore spots, *I completely accept myself*. The completely accepting myself part was a bit of a stretch, but I had to admit I liked the concept.

"Okay, now what?" I said.

"So now you take your index and middle fingers and tap each of your meridian points seven times as you think *fear of flying*."

"I loved *Fear of Flying*," Tess said from the other side of Rosie's pashmina. "It was the first racy book I ever read. I found it in my sister's room when she went off to college and hid it under my—"

"Not now," I said.

Rosie started tapping. "The top of your head . . ."

Fear of life, I thought. Even though it seemed a little bit over-dramatic, it also had the distinct ring of truth, so I just kept thinking it as I tapped the top of my head seven times.

"The inside of your eyebrows . . ."

Fear of life, I thought again as I tapped the inside of my eyebrows seven times.

"The bones on the outside corner of your eyes . . ."

Tap-tap-tap-tap-tap-tap-tap.

"Under the eyes about an inch under the pupil . . ."

Tap-tap-tap-tap-tap-tap-tap.

"Between your nose and upper lip . . .between your bottom lip and your chin . . . on your sore spots again . . . about four inches below your armpit . . . on the web between your thumb and first finger . . . on the outside part of the hand between the top of your wrist and the bottom of your pinkie."

We tapped away.

"How do you feel now?" I whispered. "On a scale of one to ten?"

"A little bit better," Rosie whispered. "At least I think I do. Maybe like a billion and three. Okay, now we're supposed to tap the gamut point, which is on the back of the hand between the pinkie and the ring finger and about half an inch back toward the wrist. Just keep tapping there for a while. And then if we need to, we can go back to the beginning and start the whole thing over again."

"What an awesome thing to add to my bag of tricks," I said once we'd stopped tapping. "Thank you."

I slid out from under the purple pashmina and patted my hair back into place. Rosie slid out, too. The guy in front of me turned around and tried to peek between the seats to get a look at us.

Tess paused her movie and pointed. "He thinks you're lesbians. Not that there's anything wrong with that."

I gave his seat a little kick as I reached for my water bottle.

"Thank you, honey," Rosie said in a swoony voice. "I hope that was as good for you as it was for me."

"Ohmigod," Tess said. "That just reminded me. Did you hear about the woman who got arrested for stealing a vibrator from Marshbury Provisions?"

Water spurted from my mouth and all over the back of the seat in front of me. The man in front of me blew out a disgusted puff of air. A few people across the aisle turned to look at us.

Rosie handed me a napkin.

I elbowed Tess. "Why do you always do that?"

Tess elbowed me back. "What?"

"Ouch," I said. "You always wait until we're in a crowded

place surrounded by strangers to say something like that. You did it on the plane to Sequim last year, too."

"I have no idea what you're talking about," Tess said.

"I'm still waiting to hear the vibrator story," Rosie whispered.

"Me, too," the woman seated across the aisle from Tess said.

"Well," Tess said, "Apparently the perpetrator—"

"Perpetrator?" I said.

"What would you prefer?" Tess said. "Masturbator-to-be? Anyway, she took the vibrator out of its packaging and left the store without paying for it. The manager saw her do it and called the police, who came immediately—"

"No pun intended," Rosie said.

"Good one," Tess said. She reached past me and knuckle-bumped Rosie. "So the police watched the whole thing on the store's surveillance."

"Oh, the poor woman," I said. "She probably went to high school with the person at the register and didn't think saying she was buying the vibrator for a friend would fly."

"Maybe she left the money in the empty package," Rosie said. "I hope the police at least checked."

"Anyway," Tess said. "After watching the surveillance video, one of the policemen was able to identify the woman."

"From a long string of previous vibrator thefts?" Rosie said.

Our little corner of the plane cracked up.

"No," Tess said. "Apparently she was in a book club with the cop's wife. And no, he didn't know what book they were reading that month."

"Yikes," I said. "Welcome to small town America. So what happened?"

Tess shrugged. "They tracked her down at her house, charged her with shoplifting, and recovered the item."

"Eww," Rosie said. "I hope they at least washed it before they put it back on the shelf."

A flight attendant stopped his cart next to us to deliver our dinners. "Let that be a lesson to you ladies," he said. "This is why God invented online shopping."

Day 21

12, 199 steps

By the time we landed, I'd come to the undeniable realization that I no longer possessed the ability to handle an all-nighter the way I'd been able to back in my college days.

The night had stretched on endlessly. We'd each brought a pashmina to use as a blanket, so we didn't have to take a chance on whether or not the airline blankets had been cleaned lately or just fluffed up and refolded. The sleep masks the flight attendants passed out had been safely sealed in plastic. The foam earplugs they'd handed out had been sealed in plastic, too, and had really come in handy, especially since Rosie still had the same aggravating little snore I remembered from our last trip.

Sometime in the middle of the night, I'd peeled off my sleep mask to see Tess leaning over me with an entire disposable toilet seat cover stuck to her face.

We'd giggled like teenagers. Rosie had woken up and we'd all giggled some more.

I'd watched *Chocolat* with Tess. And then parts of *Le Divorce* as I drifted in and out of sleep.

The interior lights came back on and the flight attendants served us a continental breakfast. The plane landed. Eventually we taxied to a gate.

We put our hats back on to camouflage our plane hair as we inched our way toward freedom with the crowd of sleepy passengers.

"Moisturizer," I croaked. "And then more caffeine. Or maybe caffeine and then a toothbrush and then moisturizer."

"I actually slept like a baby for half an hour or so," Tess said. "As soon as you unscheduled that obnoxious exercise alarm of yours."

"It wasn't obnoxious," I said. "It was a gentle meditation chime. But I definitely learned that having to unbuckle and climb out to the aisle on a plane is a bigger obstacle to exercising every hour than I thought it would be. I didn't get much reading done either."

Rosie let out a huge yawn.

"Hey," I said. "You did pretty well, didn't you?"

Rosie rubbed her eyes with her free hand. "I only had to tap at takeoff and at landing. I still absolutely hate flying, but I think the tapping made it a little bit more manageable."

As soon as we got off the plane, we were herded through the non-EU passport control line.

"Look, it says ROISSY-CDG." I said as I checked out the new stamp on my passport. "This trip is starting to feel real now."

"All these blank pages in my new passport are embarrassing," Tess said. "I'm going to have to do some serious traveling. I hope they let you drive a tiny house across international borders."

Next we were herded through a carry-on security check. Security people zipped open our carry-ons. I cringed as a woman held up one of my bras with a latex-gloved hand as she rifled through the rest of my stuff with her other hand. She seemed to be giving the entire contents of my carry-on a disdainful look, as if her job was to check not for contraband items, but for wardrobe worthiness before being allowed to enter France. Clearly I was flunking the test with flying colors.

"That wasn't so bad," Rosie said as we entered the secure part of Terminal 2E. "Should we find our gate first?"

Tess was already pulling out a map from the front pocket of her carry-on. "Okay, so we're in 2E and we have to go to 2F. Piece of *gâteau*. That's cake in French."

My stomach growled. "Hurry. I want to make sure we have time to get coffee and eat something besides airplane food."

"Relax," Tess said. "We have almost three-and-a-half hours before the next flight."

One bus, at least two elevators, another passport control line, another security checkpoint, plus lots and lots of walking past construction, and we finally found our gate.

Tess looked at her wrist. "The good news is we have almost six thousand steps in already today."

"That was crazy," Rosie said. "And to think 2E and 2F sounded so close."

I looked up at the high domed glass ceiling over our heads. "You have to admit it's pretty cool here though. I read that the music video for the U2 song "Beautiful Day" was filmed right here in Terminal 2F. The cover picture of the album the song is on was taken here, too."

"Fascinating," Tess said. "But I really need to pee."

We followed stick figure signs and an arrow pointing downstairs. We rolled our carry-ons into the women's restroom.

"Wow," Rosie said. "What an amazing place—I think it might be the most modern restroom I've ever seen."

I blinked my jet-lagged eyes and tried to take it in. Shiny orange and fuchsia doors, mirrors suspended over an enormous slab sink in the center of the room with individual chrome faucets that appeared to sprout out of nowhere.

We managed to find our way out of the glamorous bathroom without getting locked in a stall or breaking anything.
We dragged our tired butts down a dark hallway and stood
outside a small café.

"This place looks a little sad," Rosie whispered.

"As long as it has coffee," Tess said. "Okay, the French
custom is to acknowledge people before you get down to business, so just make sure you say *'Bonjour, Madame'* before we
order so we don't insult anybody."

"Even if it's a guy?" Rosie said.

"Cute," Tess said.

Tess took a step toward the counter. *"Bonjour, Monsieur."*

"Bonjour, Monsieur," Rosie and I parroted.

"Bonjour, Madames," the guy behind the counter said. *"Trois
cafés américains?"*

"What was your first clue?" I said.

All four of us burst out laughing.

"Say cheese," a women's voice said behind us.

We turned around. A flash went off in our tired puffy
eyes.

"Aloha," the woman holding the camera said. "I'm Joy."

Tess introduced us all around. Joy gave us each a quick air kiss
then flitted past us and up to the counter. Tess, Rosie and I
stood in the dark hallway outside the little café checking
her out.

Joy looked remarkably fresh for someone who'd been up
all night traveling. In contrast to our yoga pants that by this
point had some serious bagging going on at the knees, her
jeans were still tight. I took a moment to wonder what kind of
midlife woman wears skintight jeans on an overnight flight to
France.

Rosie adjusted her purple garden hat. "Do you believe

those heels? How the hell can she walk in them after flying all night? I'm practically falling off my flip-flops."

I pulled my hat down a little to camouflage my face. "Do you think she just put on fresh lipstick, or are her lips tattooed? And those eyelashes can't be hers, can they? I mean, who still has long thick lashes at our age?"

Tess didn't say anything.

"It's the jewelry that's getting me," Rosie said. "Can you imagine having to take off all that stuff every time you go through security?"

We watched Joy give her thick blond-highlighted hair a flip. It undulated gracefully and fell back into place just a little bit fluffier.

Tess took off her hat and gave her own scraggly blond-highlighted hair a flip.

"Ohmigod," I said. "You're jealous."

Tess's lips fluttered as she made a horse-like sound. "Don't be ridiculous. I'm not the least bit jealous. I just don't want to miss our flight to Marseille."

Joy leaned over the counter and whispered something to the guy standing behind it. He laughed. She took his picture.

"Come on," Tess said. "Let's go. We can meet her at the gate."

"We can't just take off without saying anything," I said.

"Fine," Tess said. She pulled up her translation app on her phone. She took a step toward the café. "We'll meet you at the gate," she yelled. "*Au revoir.*"

Joy kept talking.

"That means goodbye," Tess yelled to Joy.

We trudged up the stairs, lugging our carry-ons with one hand and holding our coffee in the other. We managed to find seats relatively near our gate. I dug out a plastic bag full of almonds and passed them around. Rosie found some dark chocolate and broke it into three pieces.

There were no zones on the flight from Paris to Marseille,

so everybody just started surging toward the plane when a flight attendant made the boarding announcement in French and then English.

"She's going to miss the flight," Rosie said.

"Not our problem," Tess said.

It was a small plane, so Rosie and I were seated next to each other and Tess was seated across the aisle from us. The river cruise company had sent us big round stickers printed with their logo to wear on our shirts, so their staff could find us at the baggage claim in Marseille to transfer us to the ship. We all put them on so we wouldn't have to remember to do it later.

Just before the plane door closed, Joy appeared. Her eyes grazed ours. She smiled a brilliant smile at one of the flight attendants, then sat in an empty seat toward the front of the plane.

"I can't believe she just did that," Tess said. Tess looked at the empty seat beside her. "I'm pretty sure this is her seat."

"Cut her some slack," Rosie said. "Her feet are probably tired from those heels and she didn't want to walk all the way back here."

"Yeah," I said. "I'm sure once we get to know her, we're all really going to like her."

"Fine," Tess said. "You can be her roommate then."

I drifted into a daze, half listening to the subdued rhythmic sound of French voices all around me. Joy's laughter broke through, loud and distinctly American, from the front of the plane.

We touched down at Marseille Provence Airport just before 11 A.M. French time. I counted on my fingers and managed to figure out that it was almost 6 A.M. Marshbury time and we'd been awake for most of the last 24 hours.

Once we finally shuffled our tired bodies off the plane, there was no sign of Joy.

"Whatever," Tess said.

As we approached baggage claim, a pretty woman with a scarf around her neck and a shirt with a logo that matched our stickers held up a sign with all four of our last names written on it in big bold letters.

"*Bonjour, Madame,*" we all yelled, oversmiling and waving like the Americans we were.

"Hello," she said in French-tinged English. "My name is Adèle. And no I don't sing."

"Too bad," Rosie said. "You could have been in our girl group."

She smiled. "*C'est dommage.*"

Tess pulled up her app. "Too bad. It's a pity."

"Thanks," I said. "I never would have guessed."

Adèle gave us directions in French-accented English to *les toilettes* around the corner. By the time we came back, she was identifying our suitcases by their red leather tags and grabbing them as they rolled by on the carousel. We watched spacily for a moment and then kicked into gear and began to help. Joy sidled up to us, still looking fresh as a daisy, her carry-on resting comfortably on top of her larger suitcase.

A big black SUV was waiting for us just outside the airport door. The driver jumped out to greet us.

Joy held up her camera, which was small but serious-looking. "*Bonjour! Je peux, Monsieur?*"

"*Attention, voilà les Paparazzi!*" the driver yelled. He put one hand on the car and struck a pose.

We all laughed and Joy snapped a photo. Adèle helped the driver put our luggage in the trunk.

Joy climbed in the front seat and the three of us climbed in the back. We said our goodbyes to Adèle.

"*Merci beaucoup!*" Tess yelled.

"*Merci beaucoup!*" Rosie and I parroted.

"That means thanks a lot," Tess said as we drove away.

"No shit," I said.

Tess typed something into her app. "No shit is *pas de la merde.*"

Joy turned around to look at us. "Just so you know, she was always like that."

Tess glared at her. "What's *that* supposed to mean?"

Joy met her eyes. "Just what I said."

They stared each other down for a long moment, then Joy smiled and turned around.

"*Salope,*" Joy said from the front seat. "That means bitch, just so you don't have to look it up."

An awkward beat of silence filled the SUV.

I made a sound that came out like a cross between a laugh and a croak. "Good to know." I elbowed Tess. "*Salope.*"

The driver kept his eyes on the road.

Tess didn't say anything.

Out on the highway, we passed signs for Paris and for Nice. I thought about all the places in France we weren't going to get to see on this trip. Then I switched into glass half full mode and thought about all the places we *were* going to see.

Rosie sighed. "Is this the way to travel or what? Being escorted through the airport to your awaiting car is such an incredible luxury."

I leaned my head back against the seat. "It's amazing. We'd still be back there looking for *les toilettes* if we were traveling on our own."

"I'm not going to think for the entire week," Rosie said. "I'm just going to let people herd me around the way I usually have to herd my family."

"So," I said when the silence seemed to have gone on for a little too long. "Where is it you live again, Joy?"

"Austin," she said.

I looked at Tess. She shrugged.

"Great city," I said.

Joy didn't acknowledge my comment.

I decided I had no aptitude for being the social director,

especially this exhausted, so I just shut up. The driver turned on the radio and we listened to something instrumental and unidentifiable.

About an hour later, we pulled off the highway and drove into Avignon.

"Ooh, look," Rosie said. "A patch of lavender growing on the bank of the Rhône River. I can't believe we're actually seeing that. I can die a happy woman."

"Pont Saint-Bénézet," our driver said a few minutes later. He pointed at a bridge—four stone arches jutted into the river and then ended in a stonewall with ruins artfully arranged off to the side.

"I've read about this," I said. "I think it's also called Pont d'Avignon. It used to have something like 22 stone arches, but they kept collapsing whenever the Rhône flooded. So now what's left of the bridge is a World Heritage Site."

Tess snapped a picture with her phone. *"Sur le pont d'Avignon,"* she sang. *"On y danse, on y danse, Sur le pont d'Avignon, On y danse, tous en rond."*

"Aww," Rosie said. "My mom used to sing that song to me when I was little."

"I'm on it," Tess said. "I'm going to teach the song to my kids on the first day of school. Maybe with a little London Bridge is falling down dance action thrown in, which I realize is a little bit of cultural fusion, but they'll never know. Then my students can go classroom to classroom and teach it to all the other kids in the school."

"Look," Rosie said. "There's old town Avignon—it looks like a set from *Game of Thrones*. The information packet they sent us said it's completely encircled by medieval fortification walls. Those towers are the entrances. And I think that's the Palais des Papes back behind the walls."

Tess looked up from her app. "That means Palace of Popes."

The driver put his blinker on and pulled over behind some other cars at the side of the road.

Our ship was docked right beside us, a red-carpeted gangway leading up to it. Two big welcome banners flanked the entrance and also matched the stickers we were still wearing, which in my professional opinion was excellent branding. Uniformed crewmembers awaited us on the lower deck, laughing and handing out bottled water to people as they boarded.

"Wow," Rosie said. "What a beautiful ship. Now I get why they call it a longboat—it goes on forever. And look at that huge sun deck up on top."

Our driver clicked the trunk open. Two smiling crewmembers made a beeline for our car to get our luggage.

"I call the first *douche*," Joy said. "That's shower in French."

Tess finished using Rosie's and my bathroom and joined us out on our little stateroom balcony. "Wouldn't you think she would have at least given me a chance to go to the bathroom first before she hogged our shower? And how about that douche comment? She was just daring me to make a crack about *her* being the first douche. Fortunately, I'm far too mature to make misogynistic comments."

I yawned. "Let it go. It's not worth it."

Rosie looked up from scanning the ship's daily newsletter and yawned, too. "Okay, so it says there's an embarkation buffet with salads, sandwiches and soup in the lounge that began at 11 and lasts until 3. Or maybe we should take a nap instead and wake up before the welcome briefing at 6:30. Or we could skip the welcome thing completely and wake up just before dinner starts at 7."

I checked my Fitbit. "I say we get the rest of our steps in

before we do anything. I have a feeling that if we don't put our sneakers on right now and start walking, it's not going to happen today. Plus, I think we'd be better off toughing it out instead of napping so we'll sleep well tonight. Also, from a health perspective, getting some sunlight is supposed to help your body adjust to a new time zone."

"I definitely can't wait till 7 to eat," Tess said. "How about this—we put our sneakers on, then do a quick loop through the buffet. We can each grab a sandwich or something and keep walking. Eat while we walk or store everything in your refrigerator until we get back. No way I'm going to put anything in my fridge—you-know-who will eat it on me the minute my back is turned."

I took a step toward the stateroom and my sneakers. "Fine. We'll meet in the hallway between our rooms in two minutes. Make sure you invite Joy to come with us."

"Don't either of you dare change your clothes and make me look bad," Tess said. "We can all shower and change after we finish our walk."

"Hats or no hats?" I said.

"I have to admit these hats are not the foreign fashion statements I'd hoped they'd be," Tess said. "But I don't think our hair should see the light of France until it gets a good shampoo and conditioning."

"Okay," Rosie said. "Hats it is."

By the time Rosie and I laced up our sneakers and made it out to the hallway, Tess was waiting.

"Is Joy coming with us?" I said.

"She's still in the freakin' shower," Tess said. "I mean, come on, water doesn't grow on boats."

"Did you leave her a note?" Rosie said.

Tess shrugged. "She'll figure it out."

I shook my head. "At least send her a quick email and tell her you'll catch up with her for dinner."

Tess rolled her eyes, but she pulled out her phone, connected to the ship's Wi-Fi, sent the email.

We walked along a short hallway to the atrium, past a little library and a computer nook, down a flight of stairs.

"This ship is so beautiful," Rosie said.

"Yeah," Tess said. "It's like Ikea and a sleek Scandinavian ship builder got together and had a baby."

We followed a travel-weary couple into the lounge. They stopped at a white tablecloth-covered table. We headed right for the buffet.

"Just grab a napkin and something portable and keep walking," Tess said. "We can divvy it all up later."

A guy in a white jacket and a tall white chef's hat stood behind a table at one end of the buffet. Another guy in a white jacket was grilling custom-ordered sandwiches. We bypassed them. Tess and Rosie each grabbed a pre-made sandwich from a platter. I headed for an assortment of French cheeses.

A server with brown hair and a pretty smile stepped up to us. "Hello, I'm Andi. How can I help you?"

We all froze and gave her a guilty look.

Rosie and I turned to Tess, since it was her big idea in the first place.

Tess shrugged. "We don't have time to sit because we're heading out for a long walk. But my friends insisted we grab a little snack to eat when we get back to tide us over until dinner."

"Nice," Rosie said. "Throw us under the boat."

Andi reached for a stack of plates. "Pile your plates high and put them in your refrigerator to reward yourselves after your exercise. I will get you three glasses of wine to complete your feast. Red or white?"

We managed to jam three plates overloaded with cheeses and olives and veggies and sandwiches into Rosie's and my little refrigerator. We lined up the three glasses of red wine on top of a long chest of drawers.

"Ohmigod," Rosie said. "That wine looks so good. Maybe we should have just a teensy weensy sip before we go."

"No way," I said. "You know the official Wildwater Walking Club rule: Walk first. Drink wine later."

We managed to walk away from the wine. We found our way past a smiling concierge and out an automatic door. We walked down the gangway.

Across the street from where our ship was docked, a huge Ferris wheel turned slowly. "I bet that would be a great way to watch the sunset later on," I said.

"Bite your tongue," Rosie said. "I just barely survived two flights. There's no way I'm going up in the air again until I have to."

"Sorry," I said. "Okay, let's make a loop through old town first."

"It's too bad Andi couldn't come with us for a walk," Tess said. "I bet she could use a little time off. Or even Adèle—she probably works hard, too."

"You're doing it again," Rosie said. "Pretending we know people that we don't."

"No I'm not," Tess said. "I'm just trying to take my mind off my roommate situation. I was actually thinking how great it would be if Joy could magically trade places with one of them. You know, like in *Freaky Friday*."

"No offense to Andi or Adèle," I said, "but if we're going to go the magic route, I'd much rather have Jamie Lee Curtis come hang out with us."

We crossed the street and headed for two tall towers that flanked an entrance to old town.

I swiveled my tired neck to look at Tess. "How exactly did the Joy thing come about anyway? You've never really said, except that it had something to do with Facebook."

"What was I *thinking*?" Tess said.

When she grabbed the brim on her hat against a burst of wind, its monster taupe flower fluttered in the warm breeze. "We'd been Facebook friends for a while—most of our high school class has friended one another by this point—and I think I posted something asking if anyone else had taken this particular river cruise and had any recommendations. Anyway, Joy sent me a private message saying she's always wanted to take a trip like that and to let her know if I needed a roommate."

Tess and I walked in place while Rosie stopped to tie a shoe. We picked up our pace again, then reconfigured into a single file to navigate past a clump of tourists.

"Anyway," Tess said. "There were three of us, so we obviously needed a fourth to keep the cost down. It seemed like such serendipity that one fell right in my lap. I mean, there were plenty of other people I could have asked. It's just such a hassle—people always talk about how they want to have more adventure in their lives, but when you try to get them to commit, they've got a million excuses."

"So you and Joy were friends in high school though, right?" Rosie said as we spread out again.

"Here's the weird thing," Tess said. "For a while there I thought we must have been friends, just because of the way she was acting. But then the more I thought about it, I realized I didn't have a single memory of her from high school. Not a shared class, not hanging out. Nothing. But by then it was too late. Maybe I just blocked out all my memories because she's such a *salope*."

Tess smiled. "That means bitch."

"I love you," Rosie said. "But if you don't ditch that translation app of yours, you're going overboard."

Tess typed something into her phone. "*Dûment noté*," she said. "That means duly noted."

"So," I said. "What's your goal for this trip as far as Joy is concerned?"

"Survival?" Tess said.

I went into my slow pendulum nod. "How would that look?"

"Let's see," Tess said. "I think we'd just have to be civil to each other. You know, maybe it was a mistake, but if we both behave ourselves, we can get through it."

I kept nodding. "And what do you think your first step might be?"

Tess shrugged. "I guess I could make an effort to be kind and inclusive and see what happens. Maybe we're making her feel left out."

"So," I said. "Your first step is to make an effort to be kind and inclusive."

"Exactly," Tess said. "And if that doesn't work, we're going to call housekeeping and get them to cram a cot for me between your two beds."

We walked and walked, our tired feet taking turns tripping over cobblestones. We mingled with tourists from all over the world, stepped out of the reach of the photos they were taking.

"Maybe we should photobomb them instead of trying to get out of the way," Tess said as we circled around a couple taking a picture with a selfie stick. "Then all these people would go home with photos of us, and in a couple years they'd scroll through them again and it would be like they know we're old friends but they can't quite remember our names."

"Whatever happened to photobombing anyway?" I said. "Do people still do it, or has it jumped the shark?"

"I think you can still do it," Tess said, "but you can't just invade somebody's photo randomly. Now that photobombing is past its infancy, it has to be really genius."

"I'm too tired to photobomb," Rosie said. "Whatever is beyond tired, that's what I am."

We cut through a huge courtyard in front of the immense Palace of Popes. The beige interconnected sections and pointy

Gothic spires made me think of a sandcastle on steroids. Living in New England, we were used to old. But Europe was a whole other level of old. We circled back out to the street, walked some more.

"Let's go to Les Halles market," Rosie said. "I want to see the green wall."

Tess pulled out a map, attempted to walk and read at the same time.

Rosie and I each grabbed an arm as Tess tripped on the edge of a cobblestone.

We held onto Tess and walked in place while she looked at the map.

"Avignon Les Halles is right next to Place Pie," Tess said.

"That means Pie Place," Rosie said.

"Don't be a smart ass." Tess pointed. "Okay, I think it's this way. If not, we'll just turn around and try the other way."

We walked for maybe another twenty minutes. Along our route, Rosie pointed out a row of trees with scaling bark that looked like camouflage. "They're plane trees. They look a lot like our sycamore trees at home. I think the plane trees here are actually a hybrid of Asian and American sycamores."

Rosie jumped on a small hard brown ball on the sidewalk. It burst like a dandelion head. "Those are the seeds."

Tess and I started stepping on seedpods as we walked.

"This is so addictive," I said. "It's like popping bubble wrap."

Place Pie turned out to be a public plaza with pedestrian-friendly streets. There were shops and restaurants with outside seating—people chatted at round tables and drank in the hot sun along with their cold drinks. A band played what sounded to my unskilled ears like New Orleans Jazz. Motorcycles shared racks with bicycles. Round topiaries grew in square planters.

"Look," Rosie said. "Avignon Les Halles." An entire

massive wall was covered, jungle-like, in green plants that seemed to sprout from the roofs of the old buildings below it.

"Wow," I said. "It's so dramatic."

"I know, right," Rosie said. "What a brilliant way to disguise a parking lot. And it's all hydroponic."

Tess jumped. "Ten thousand steps. Damn, that buzzer makes me think I'm being electrocuted every time. So this is a covered market, right?"

Rosie nodded. "Yes, it's supposed to be a foodie's paradise. You know, meats, seafood, pastry, cheeses, olives, tapenade, bread, herbs, produce, the whole nine yards."

My stomach growled. We walked past a couple packing up an outdoor flower stall. A man carrying a wooden crate held open a door with his foot for us.

"Uh-oh," Tess said when we stepped inside. "I think we missed the party."

Sure enough, the market stalls were empty, or in the process of being emptied.

"The market must open early in the morning and close in the early afternoon," Rosie said. "I didn't even think of that."

A woman walked by carrying a wicker basket holding bottles filled with salt and what looked like rose petals."

I squinted. "Were those rose petals?"

"I think so," Rosie said. "It's probably rose-flavored sea salt. You can make it with lavender, too. You could put lavender salt on grilled veggies. Or on a roast. Or use it to salt the rim of the glass for a margarita."

"You're killing me," Tess said.

"You could even put just a tiny bit on top of chocolate ice cream," Rosie said.

"Did you hear that, Ben & Jerry?" I said. "We could have done great things together."

We jumped out of the way of two women barreling in our direction, each carrying a towering pile of boxes.

"Oops," I said. "I have a sneaking suspicion we're not supposed to be in here."

"So what," Tess said. "Let's just do a quick walk through so we can at least say we've been to Avignon Les Halles."

We walked the length of the market and back out into the sunlight.

I blinked in the bright sun, unhooked my sunglasses from the front of my T-shirt, put them on again. "You know, that kind of reminded me of going to Pike's Place Market in Seattle last year.

"Yeah, a little bit," Tess said. "Except for the fact that it's hard to compare a closed market with one that's open."

"Come on," Rosie said. "Let's go eat our feast and drink that wine."

"Yay," I said as my Fitbit buzzed a few steps later. "Ten thousand steps."

Lavender Sea Salt

½ cup sea salt
2 teaspoons dried culinary quality lavender buds

Chop lavender with a knife. Mix with salt in clean 4 oz. Mason jar or saltshaker. (You can also empty out a sea salt grinder, mix the lavender and the sea salt together, then pour it all back into the grinder.)

As soon we got back to Rosie's and my room after our walk, we practically inhaled the food from our fridge.

Tess picked up her glass of wine. "I think I'll take this with me while I shower." She sighed. "And maybe I should have dinner with just Joy tonight. You know, make an effort to bond and all that crap."

"That's the spirit," I said.

Rosie and I took turns sipping our own wine and showering, savoring the L'Occitane bath products and the radiant-heated bathroom floor. The water pressure was fabulous, I was happy to note. Nothing ruins a vacation like mediocre water pressure.

We buckled up our life jackets and joined the other one hundred or so passengers in the lounge for a safety briefing. We all marched up the steps to the top deck for a safety drill. We checked out our fellow travelers. Mostly boomers, a few octogenarians and beyond, plenty of gen X's, some millennials traveling with their extended families. Couples, both gay and straight, groups of friends, solo travelers. A veritable boatload of Americans, but plenty of people from other countries as well. The dress code appeared to be nice casualwear for active travel. Now that we'd ditched our hats and taken showers and put on fresh clothes, we pretty much fit right in.

We stayed in our groups, waiting for the announcement that the safety drill was over. Tess broke ranks and sidled up to Rosie and me while we were checking out the deck-top organic herb garden. "Is this still the same day?"

We turned to watch Joy standing next to the deck-top putting green, laughing away at something someone had just said.

"Aloha," Tess whispered.

"Be nice," I said. "How's it going?"

"She told me I still have the same RBF I did in high school."

"RBF?" Rosie said.

Tess turned her back on Joy in case she was a long-distance lip reader. "Resting bitch face." She held her hand up like she was talking on a phone, thumb pointed at her ear and pinky at her mouth. "High school called and wants their mean girl back."

"Ohmigod," Rosie said. "I'm going to take her out."

I grabbed Rosie by one arm. "Come on, clumping together like this isn't going to help. Tess, go back over there so Joy doesn't think we're talking about her."

Once the safety drill ended, Rosie and I decided we were too tired to handle the welcome briefing in person. I uncorked a tall glass bottle of water that I hadn't noticed earlier, poured us each a glass. We watched the welcome announcements via in-room, closed circuit TV on the big flat-screen on the wall across from our beds.

"This is the life," Rosie said. "I can't believe all we have to do is stay awake until dinner."

I yawned. "How about we head to the restaurant now. You know, first in, first out, first to bed, long day tomorrow."

"Good thinking," Rosie said.

Tables of six filled the ship's main dining room. No reservations were allowed. Four people were just sitting down at a table on the far side, near the kitchen.

"Quick," Rosie said. "Go there."

We race-walked across the dining room.

"Hi," Rosie said. "May we join you?"

"Of course," a woman said.

We'd barely put our napkins on our laps when Andi arrived at our table, a bottle of white in one hand, a bottle of red in the other. Rosie and I greeted her like a long lost friend.

The restaurant managed to be both elegant and laid back, and it was filled with the buzz of friendly conversation. We chatted with our tablemates, a couple from Australia and a pair of lifelong friends, one from New Jersey and the other from Wisconsin. I devoured a salad with mango and asparagus and raspberry vinaigrette. I chowed down on sautéed beef and shrimp with an amazing Béarnaise sauce dotted with tiny flecks of lavender. I pigged out on chocolate mousse. I sipped my wine and tried to follow the conversation without keeling over on my plate from exhaustion. I twisted my twisty necklace. I looked around for Tess and Joy but didn't see them.

Just before Rosie and I patted our lips with our napkins and said thank you to Andi and goodnight to our tablemates, a moment of sadness passed over me. I couldn't help but wonder, just for a moment, what it might have been like to take a trip like this with Rick someday. If things had gone differently the night I'd spiralized zucchini for him.

Day 22

10,123 steps

We were on our way to dock at the village of Tarascon, which we'd been told was about fourteen miles south of Avignon. It was also about twelve miles north of Arles, where some of us would be traveling later today via motor coach, aka a fancy bus. Others would drive off to the marshes of the Mediterranean to see the wild horses in Carmague, and still others would head to Carrieres de Lumieres, an art installation space carved into an old quarry in the hamlet of Les Baux.

I'd felt a tiny jolt as our ship cast off about 5:30 this morning, but after that I couldn't even be sure we were moving. I'd dozed for a bit then tiptoed over to the slider. I opened the curtain just a crack to see the shoreline, still a dark gray, whizzing by as if it were moving and not us. I stepped out on the balcony and watched the sun rise over trees on the east bank of the Rhône River, rays of orange breaking through thick green trees and waking up the sky. Then I crawled back into bed.

From the other bed, Rosie let out an aggravating little snore that made me glad I'd hung on to my foam earplugs from the plane. I rooted around under my pillow until I found the earplug that had fallen out, tucked it back in my ear again.

Even without earplugs, our stateroom was incredibly quiet —definitely quieter than any hotel I'd ever stayed in, maybe even quieter than being at home. The room was small, but its contemporary design was both beautiful and efficient. It made me wonder if I could live a life like this someday: so stripped down to the essentials that I could actually see and appreciate everything around me.

My cellphone alarm went off, officially starting a new day.

Rosie and I clipped our lanyards and headphones into our fully charged audio receivers and looped them over our heads like the tourists we were. We walked across the dock in Tarascon and up a cement ramp to an embankment that gave way to a parking lot, where we matched the number on the cards we were holding with the numbers on the bus we were scheduled to take.

A smiling local guide with a silk scarf around her neck checked our numbers to make sure we were getting on the right white Mercedes-Benz bus.

"Can I tell you again how much I love this?" Rosie said. "My only worry is that I won't remember how to think anymore by the time we get home."

We grabbed a seat toward the front of the bus. Tess climbed on and slid into the seat across from us.

"Where's Joy?" I said.

Tess shrugged. "She signed up for a different excursion."

"Absence makes the heart grow fonder," Rosie said.

"Don't count on it," Tess said.

Our guide told us it would be a twenty-minute ride to Arles, but our driver would make a quick stop along the way because she had a surprise for us.

"Don't you love the way she says Arles?" Rosie said. "It's like a pirate's *arrrl*."

A few minutes later the driver put on his blinker and pulled over. And there by the side of the road was the most massive field of sunflowers I'd ever seen in my entire life. It was breathtaking—big saucer-like golden flowers bobbing under a cornflower blue sky as far as the eye could see.

We all climbed off the bus and snapped picture after picture as the occasional car whizzed by.

"Wow," I said. "Just wow." I could almost see Eva Cassidy standing with us and singing her stripped down version of Sting's "Fields of Gold," which always made me cry, no matter how many times I'd heard it.

"Beyond beautiful," Rosie. "I didn't expect to see sunflowers in Provence. I always think of Tuscany for sunflowers. Or even North and South Dakota. I came here for the lavender, but now I want to grow sunflowers when I get home, too."

I tried to imagine this field tucked in next to Rosie's lavender farm. "Do you have enough space?"

"We'd have to clear some land." Rosie held up her phone and took another picture. "It takes about 350 sunflower heads to fill a 25-pound bag of black oil sunflower seed. Once you know that, you can never look at a bag of bird food the same way."

I started counting sunflower heads to see how much space 350 of them took up, forgot which sunflowers I'd already counted, gave up.

"It is a bit sad," our guide said as we filed back on the bus, "when the farmers stop watering the sunflowers to prepare for the harvest. From smiling faces to so many droopy heads." She tilted her head, made pouty lips, and threw up her hands in a Gallic shrug. "*C'est la vie.*"

"That's life," I said before Tess could pull up her translation app.

Rosie, Tess and I had signed up for what was essentially a Vincent van Gogh day. We wandered the winding medieval streets of old town Arles. Our high-end headsets carried well and allowed us to wander a bit and still hear the tour narration. Our guide told us that Van Gogh had spent fifteen months in Arles, from 1888 to 1889. While there, he'd both descended into madness and finished 200 paintings.

We followed numbered and illustrated panels that displayed reproductions of Van Gogh paintings standing next to the scenes that had inspired them. We snapped photos at the outdoor café, now called the Vincent van Gogh Café, where he'd painted *The Café Terrace on the Place du Forum, Arles, at Night.*

We made our way to the spot, about a two-minute walk from the house he was renting at the time, where Van Gogh had painted *Starry Night Over the Rhône.*

"Unbelievable," Tess said. "I had that poster on my dorm room wall."

"Me, too," I said.

"Me three," Rosie said. "I thought the painting was called *Starry, Starry Night* though."

"I think that's probably because of the Don McLean song," Tess said. "You know, since the song was called 'Starry, Starry Night'."

"The title of the song," I said, "is actually 'Vincent'."

"I don't care what anything is called," Rosie said. "I can't believe we're standing here."

Our next step was a painting class at La Couverture Verte, which Tess and her app couldn't resist translating to The Green Blanket, at Arles's Siqueiros Fine Arts School.

As our small group followed our guide into the former schoolhouse, a few of us made nervous cracks about our lack of artistic talent. Since Rosie could draw landscape plans, I knew she'd be fine. As an elementary teacher, Tess certainly knew her way around an art class. She was looking for ideas to bring back to her classroom, as well as justification for the cultural enrichment grant she'd received.

I reassured myself that my goal for taking the class with them was to be a supportive friend. And to not embarrass myself too much. I went on to tell myself that if things got bad and I had an attack of extreme art anxiety, I could always excuse myself and go take a walk.

Philippe, our art class teacher, and his wife and young daughter, whose French names whizzed by so quickly I didn't catch them, gave us aprons and brushes. We took seats at rectangular tables covered with layer upon layer of paint splotches, a timeline of all the students who had spattered paint here through the years.

Philippe talked a bit about Van Gogh and the period during which he painted in Arles. "The light is always there in Arles," he said. "It is a unique and spectacular shade of blue. You see that blue in Van Gogh's work. The roof tiles are terra-cotta—you see that, too."

He flipped through a pile of Van Gogh prints, held them up so we could see. "But the walls of the buildings in the real landscape are pale limestone. Van Gogh made up that brilliant yellow color he is so famous for. He said it was the only way he could show the amazing sunlight of Provence."

We passed the prints around, wowed by the insider info that allowed us to see the famous paintings in a new way. Then Philippe held up enlarged sections taken from Van Gogh paintings and explained some of the brush techniques Van Gogh had used.

After that we took turns choosing a laminated enlargement of part of a Van Gogh painting. Philippe's daughter passed out tiny cardboard frames with two-inch square openings. Philippe's wife came around next. She checked our painting choice and made us a matching palette by dotting a row of several colors of acrylic paint on a square of paper. Then she gave us a smaller piece of paper with a two-inch square of coordinated background color painted in the center of it.

Philippe instructed us to place our frame over a section of our chosen painting. And to paint what we saw within the frame on our premade background.

I placed my tiny cardboard frame over the center of one of the swirly stars in *Starry Night*. A million years ago, I'd spent countless hours in my dorm room staring up at those stars on the poster hanging on my wall, as I tried to imagine what my life might be one day.

I dipped my brush into some yellow paint, gave it a try. Painting this small took the pressure off. Focusing in on one little section of the original painting kept the intimidation factor down, too. I was amazed at the power of that little cardboard frame.

By the end of our class, I'd painted pretty darn respectable pieces of a swirly star, a clump of irises, a sunflower, a wheat field. I couldn't wait to have them framed in tiny frames when I got home.

I leaned over to Tess. "These would be perfect in your tiny house."

"I can't wait to break out the school laminator and make my own materials so I can do this when school starts," Tess said. "The kids are going to love it."

Before we went on to our next stop, I copied down a quote from the classroom wall. It seemed like a message for my own life might be in there somewhere:

"Great things are done by a series of small things brought together."—*Vincent van Gogh*

We'd left our tiny paintings to dry at the art school, and our tour guide had whisked us off to a preordered lunch at a nearby restaurant. Good as his word, Philippe delivered our tiny masterpieces to us, carefully wrapped in brown paper bags, just as our dessert—a scrumptious chocolate fondant—was being served.

From there our guide escorted us to a lovely Van Gogh en Provence exhibit at the Arles Vincent van Gogh Foundation.

"I would have thought I'd be all Van Goghed out by now," Rosie whispered at one point while Tess shopped the museum bookshop for prints to bring back to her school. "But I'm still totally into it."

We rendezvoused with our fancy bus again and drove to St. Remy, our next stop on the Van Gogh circuit. We learned that many of the olive trees in the olive groves in the area had been killed by a frost. Some people dug them up and planted new trees. They waited twelve years for their first harvest. Others just cut the trees back. They had a new harvest in two years.

"Let that be a lesson," Rosie said. "Everything deserves a second chance."

I stared out the window, wondering if there was an olive tree equivalent to a life. Once you made a mess of it, rather than ditch the whole thing, how did you cut it back to encourage it to grow again?

Maybe half an hour later we pulled into Saint Paul de Mausole, a beautiful 12th-century monastery that had been converted into a mental asylum in the 19th century. Van Gogh voluntarily committed himself for treatment here and stayed for a year. Our guide told us that a part of the complex was still a working psychiatric clinic for women only.

At the entrance, we saw the olive trees that Van Gogh painted in *Les Oliviers*. Beside the monastery cloister was a bell tower and an amazing central garden of flowers surrounded by low hedges. Behind that were the back gardens, which Van

Gogh could see from the window of his room at the asylum, including a stunning field of lavender.

We stopped at an illustrated panel hanging on a tall stonewall. Beside a reproduction of *Les Irises*, a short explanation in English and French said that the blue bearded irises growing here were descendants of the ones Van Gogh could see from his room.

The irises that had inspired Van Gogh to paint one of his most famous paintings were past bloom, but it was still pretty amazing to see the juxtaposition of landscape and painting up close and personal.

"I wish we could have seen the irises in bloom," I said.

"If the irises were flowering," Rosie said, "the lavender wouldn't be."

"Good point." I pointed at masses of gnarled brown root-like things emerging from the ground at the base of the pointy green foliage. "So are those the iris bulbs?"

"Irises don't grow from bulbs," Rosie said. "They grow from rhizomes, which some people think are swollen root sections, but they're actually underground horizontally-growing stems. See the way the plants are so overcrowded the rhizomes are heaving out of the ground? Boyohboy, these irises really need to be divided so they'll produce more flowers."

"Is that something you have to do at a certain time of year?" I asked. If I hung around with Rosie long enough, maybe I'd actually turn into someone who knew something about plants.

"Irises are dormant right now during the heat of July and August so it's the perfect time to divide them," Rosie said. "It's easy—you just divide each healthy rhizome into a 3-to-4-inch piece that has at least one fan of leaves, and then you replant it."

"How long will it take?" Tess said. "Maybe we could do it fast since we're here anyway."

Rosie smiled. "I'd do it in a heartbeat if they'd let me take a single iris home with me to plant in my garden. They're just basic blue bearded irises, but still, what I wouldn't give for a teensy piece of a Van Gogh iris."

Tess darted a glance over her shoulder. "So take one."

"Tess," I said.

"Don't be ridiculous," Rosie said. "Can you imagine what they'd do to me if I got caught?"

Tess shrugged. "Just tell them you're a professional landscaper and the irises were in distress so you helped them out. I mean, come on, there are thousands and thousands of those gnarly brown things sticking out of the ground. And they might not even be the real Van Gogh irises. They could just be a tourist plant. Plus, we're already at a women's psychiatric clinic, so worst case scenario they'd probably just have you evaluated and/or make you give them their iris piece back."

"Tess," I said again.

"I couldn't," Rosie said. "It would be like all those tourists who chiseled off pieces of Plymouth Rock to take home with them because it was supposedly the first place the Pilgrims stepped. And eventually most of Plymouth Rock was gone and they had to put a big enclosure around this dinky little rock to keep people from chiseling away the rest of it."

"Totally different," Tess said. "Irises keep propagating themselves. Rocks don't have baby rocks."

Rosie shook her head. "Nope. Can't do it."

"I-ris you would," Tess said.

"Only a third grade teacher could make that joke," I said.

"Thank you very much," Tess said. "I take that as high praise indeed."

I caught up with Rosie, who had started walking in the direction of the rest of our group.

It was heartbreaking to climb up the steps to the recreation of Van Gogh's small, stark asylum bedroom. It was incredible to learn that he painted another 150 paintings while he was here, including a second version of *Starry Night Over the Rhône*.

Tess joined us and we stood for a moment looking out the tiny window with the big, beautiful views.

I blinked back tears. "It's just so incredibly sad that someone whose paintings are so full of life and color suffered so much."

"I wish we'd known him," Tess said. "Maybe we could have taken him under our wings."

Rosie sighed.

"But then again," Tess said, "if he was hanging out with us, he probably would have been having so much fun it might have done a number on his productivity."

While we'd been following Van Gogh's footsteps, our ship had traveled from Tarascon back to Avignon. So we climbed back into our shiny white motor coach at St. Remy and met our longboat at the same dock we'd been tethered to yesterday. The same Ferris wheel was doing its slow twirl across the street from us.

"Holy déjà vu all over again," Tess said. "It's like we're in *Groundhog Day* or maybe *Fifty First Dates*.

"I love it," Rosie said. "I'm completely losing track of time and place, and it doesn't matter because none of it is my responsibility."

"I know," I said. "It's like we're on a road trip, but instead of having to pack up all our stuff and move from hotel to hotel, we've got this great traveling hotel that always shows up exactly where we need it to be."

"I say we hit the lounge," Tess said. "I'm pretty sure it's wine o'clock."

I checked my Fitbit. "No can do. We still have over two thousand steps left today."

"Fine," Tess said. "I guess I can earn my wine if I have to."

We decided to drop our stuff in our rooms and walk until we hit 10,000 steps and then catch a more casual dinner from the bar menu at ship's terrace café.

We walked along Rue de la République, which cut through the center of old town Avignon, checking out the people we passed, walking in place while we window-shopped. We started weaving up and down the side streets, past displays of scarves and jewelry. A table filled with hats brought us to a complete stop.

"Bonjour, Madame," we said to the vendor.

We all pointed at the same hat at the same time. It was the color of straw and looked like it had been crocheted from raffia. It had a narrow ribbon of raffia wrapped around it and a loose, slightly rolled brim. It was both stylish and understated, everything the hats we'd brought with us weren't.

"It's perfect," I said. "You could wear it to walk or to go lavender picking."

"The original lavender picking hats," Rosie said, "were made of stiff straw, and they had these huge brims to shield you from the sun."

"Right," Tess said, "but I'd like to be able to fit through a doorway."

The vendor squished one of the hats to show that it bounced right back into shape, then handed us each our own hat.

We put them on, nodded approvingly at one another.

'Hmm," I said. "Is this weird, all of us buying the same hat?"

"Yeah, it's a little weird," Tess said. "So why don't you two pick something else."

"No way," Rosie said. "I saw it first."

"I'm pretty sure I saw it first," I said.

"Fine," Tess said. "Then we'll make it the official Wild-water Walking Club Provence hat."

We paid for our hats, put them right on, started working our way back to the ship. We hit 10,000 steps, one after the other, just as the Rhône came into view again.

We headed for the ship and piled our plates high with salad and grilled chicken and cheeses. Rather than sit at one of the terrace tables, we circled back to the deck to stretch out on lounge chairs.

We balanced our plates on our laps, sipped our wine, put our glasses down on little tables, dug into our dinner.

"Where's Joy anyway?" I said.

"Who cares?" Tess said.

The setting sun bathed the river in a pink glow.

We sat there until the sun dipped below the horizon and the sky turned dark and the stars appeared. And then we enjoyed our very own starry, starry night over the Rhône.

Day 23

10,019 steps

"I can't believe it's lavender day," Rosie actually sang when her phone alarm went off. "I'm soooo excited."

My phone alarm went off right behind hers, its cosmic digital chimes not any less annoying than Rosie's perky digital twinkle. No matter how pretty you make it, the purpose of an alarm is to jolt you out of sleep, so why even bother to try to make it likeable? Maybe I should start a business creating alarm sounds like fingernails on a blackboard or dental drills. I could even record Rosie's aggravating little snore from last night.

I groaned, retrieved the foam earplug that had rolled across my pillow, put both earplugs on my bedside table. "What I can't believe is that it's morning already. Why don't you jump in the shower first while I go grab us some coffee."

Rosie kicked off the covers and practically skipped to the bathroom. I pulled on a jogging bra and some yoga pants, put my sleep T-shirt back on, slid into a pair of flip-flops. I walked down the hallway and across the atrium.

I filled two takeout cups with coffee and cream at the

snack station, checked out the fresh pastries, decided I'd rather wait and have a full breakfast and thought Rosie probably would, too. I rubbed my eyes, yawned again, picked up the coffee cups.

As I turned to walk back to my stateroom, I noticed Joy seated in a corner of the little library area, typing away on her laptop. She was fully dressed, with makeup on and everything.

"Good morning," I said.

She looked up. "Aloha." Her flat voice that seemed at odds with the warm Hawaiian greeting. This was definitely not an invitation to come hang out with her at a luau someday.

I nodded at her laptop. "Good for you for keeping up with the real world. I've barely checked email."

Joy angled the top of her laptop down as if I might try to copy her work. She shrugged. "Satellite Internet—you've got to grab it when you can get it on a ship. Plus, I think the reception's better out here. And of course I wouldn't want to wake up Tess either."

Joy's eyes met mine. Then they darted behind me, like she might get lucky and someone more interesting would show up at any moment.

"Yeah, well." I shifted the coffee cups so they wouldn't burn my fingers. "So, are you going on the lavender excursion today?"

She shrugged. "Nope. Chateauneuf-du-Pape tour and wine tasting."

"Great," I said. "Well, have fun."

I walked back down the hallway. When I came to our stateroom door, I balanced one takeout cup on top of the other and held them in place with my chin. I reached into the waistband of my yoga pants where I'd tucked my key card.

I felt all around the waistband. I put the cups down on the floor. I gave a little jump, hoping the card might fall out of one of my pant legs.

"Damn," I said.

I picked up the cups again, retraced my steps.

Joy's laptop was sitting by itself on a table in the computer station. Its top was almost but not fully closed. I had a crazy urge to sneak over and open it fast. *Aha*, I'd yell when I figured out whatever it was that Joy had been hiding.

I kept walking. Joy was standing over by the coffee station. She saw me, opened the pastry case, grabbed a croissant with a pair of tongs, put it down on a small plate.

"Hey," I said. "You didn't happen to see my room key, did you?"

"Can't say that I did."

We crossed paths in the atrium, Joy heading back to her laptop.

I gave the coffee station a quick inspection, then turned around and walked back through the atrium again.

"Good luck," Joy said without looking up.

Rosie finally answered on my third set of knocks, wrapped in a fluffy white towel.

"Sorry," we both said at once.

"I must have forgotten my key card." I handed the full cup of coffee to Rosie, tossed the empty one in the wastebasket. "I was so sure I had it with me."

"I'll look for it while you shower," Rosie said.

As soon as we were dressed, we found Tess in the restaurant. We all chowed down a big breakfast—bacon, eggs, fruit, cheese—then grabbed our purses and hats and freshly charged audio headsets from our rooms.

"Do you think we should check to see if anyone has turned in your key?" Rosie said as the three of us passed the reception desk on the way to our awaiting bus. "Or even ask for new ones just to be on the safe side?"

"Nah," I said. "I'll look again when we get back to our room later. I'm sure it's around there somewhere. I do things like this all the time when I'm tired—you know, like leave my keys in the front door."

"I once found my keys in a book I was reading," Tess said. "I must have used them for a bookmark."

"I found my car keys in the dishwasher once," Rosie said. "Connor and Nick made fun of me, so I pretended I ran them through on purpose to sterilize them."

"Those car keys do get pretty germy," I said.

Our lavender excursion would take ten hours. Every seat on our fancy white Mercedes-Benz bus was filled.

Tess and Rosie sat next to each other. I shared a seat with a woman from Texas who said her husband had decided to tour the Pont du Gard aqueduct instead. "History makes that man happier'n all git-out," she said, "but I told him if I have to hear him salivate over one more ol' artifact, I won't be held responsible for the hissy fit I'll need to throw. Sometimes that husband of mine thinks the sun rose just to hear him talk."

"*Un, deux, trois, quatre, cinq . . .*" Today's local guide walked down the aisle of the bus doing a head count as if we were kindergarteners on a field trip. She double-checked her count on her way back, turned to face us. Like yesterday's guide, she was attractive in an understated, effortlessly well-dressed way. Although neither of the guides was conventionally beautiful, both had a certain French way of carrying themselves that was undeniable. If somebody could figure out a way to bottle this kind of self-confidence, *that* would be the souvenir I'd want to plunk down my euros for.

"*Alons-y!*" our guide said. "Let's go!" she translated before Tess had time to dig up her app.

We took a right onto Boulevard du Rhône and began our drive to the Musée de la Lavande, aka The Lavender Museum, in Coustellet. Along the way we saw apple trees espaliered under nets to protect them from birds and hail, and also from the mistral, a strong, cold northwesterly wind that blows through the Rhône valley and southern France and into the Mediterranean. We passed what Rosie identified as Queen Anne's lace sprouting proudly from irrigation systems along the side of the road.

Our guide explained the difference between lavender and lavendin (*lavendine* in French). She told us that fine lavender grows on the arid mountains of Provence, above an altitude of 800 meters, where it gets good drainage and doesn't have to deal with high humidity. Only a single flower grows on each stem. It takes 130 kilos of lavender flowers to make one liter of essential lavender oil. Lavender, with its more delicate, sweet floral scent, is considered the good stuff, and is used for perfumes and high end products.

Lavendin, on the other hand, grows in the lower altitudes as well as pretty much anywhere. It's a workhorse, a tall, sturdy plant that has multiple flowers on a stem and forms large clumps. It blooms a lot and has a strong camphor smell. You only need 40 kilos of flowers to get one liter of lavendin essential oil.

"Lavendin is used for cleaning products and detergents," our guide said as if it was all she could do not to hold her nose.

I leaned across the aisle to Rosie. "Poor lavendin. She's like Cinderella—I'm really starting to feel sorry for her."

"The Grosso we planted in your garden is a lavendin," Rosie said.

"I don't get it," I said. "I love my Grosso and its tall pointy spikes. I love the camphor smell, too."

Rosie smiled. "The Munstead and Hidcote in your garden are lavenders. The way that I look at it, we can appreciate the lavender while we're here in the fine lavender capitol of the world, but that doesn't mean we have to stop liking lavendin."

"Thank you," I said. "Grosso and I appreciate that."

Coustellet was an easy drive from Avignon. We piled out of the bus, wandered around the grounds of Musée de la

Lavande, stood in line for the bathroom. We toured the museum, learned about the process of lavender distilling. In the boutique, we sniffed lavender sachets and candles and incense sticks and soap. We tried samples of lavender massage oil, eau de toilette, body lotion, hand cream, face cream. Tess bought some things for her classroom. Rosie picked up a few product ideas for her lavender shop. I bought some lavender essential oil.

We wandered out of the boutique and decided to get some steps in before we took off for our next stop on the lavender tour. We circled around the building, taking in the sights. The scent of lavender was everywhere.

My seatmate from the bus was sitting at an outdoor table. She looked up from the paperback she was reading as we approached.

"Hi again," I said. "Would you like to walk?"

She looked over the top of her reading glasses. "I am fixin' to do just that one of these days. I'll let all y'all know when I'm ready to give it a whirl."

"I love that woman," Tess said as we walked away. "She just elevated blowing us off to an art form."

We walked up the road. A woman about our age was hanging laundry on a clothesline behind a beautiful old stone cottage. We waved but she didn't see us. Or maybe she just pretended not to see us because she didn't wave to strangers.

"What do you think her story is?" Tess said.

"Easy," I said. "Her name was Patty but she changed it to Sandrine. She moved here from Kansas City for the incomparable blue of the sky and the earthy smell of the lavender. And for her lover Didier—"

"Didier?" Rosie said. "I don't think so. Her lover's name is Guillaume and they met on Match.com. Guillaume loves good food and good wine and good sex, but he's got some nefarious secret—he disappears for months at a time. Sandrine only does his laundry when he's away. She washes his clothes and hangs them out to dry so the neighbors don't know he's gone."

"Sandrine needs to dump that zero ASAP," Tess said. "Come on, let's get her to walk with us. Maybe she can stow away on the ship and we can take her home with us."

"I think that was a no," I said as Sandrine walked quickly to the door with her laundry and disappeared inside the stone cottage. "Hey, speaking of nefarious secrets, what does Joy do for a living anyway?"

Tess adjusted the brim of her hat to keep the sun off her face. "Fundraising for a non-profit, I think she said."

"But then again," Rosie said, "you thought she said she lived in San Somewhere or Other and it turned out to be Austin."

"What do you think her deal is?" I said. "When I was getting coffee this morning, she was at the computer nook in the atrium, and she got all secretive with her laptop when she saw me."

Rosie did a little skip to catch up to our longer legs. "Maybe she didn't want you to steal her top-secret fundraising ideas? You know, like charity bungee jumping. Or that one where you put pink flamingoes in people's yards and then ask them for a donation to take them away."

"I'd just keep them," I said. "I love pink flamingoes."

"I am so over school fundraisers via product sales," Tess said. "Wrapping paper. Candles. Candy bars. The school makes such a small percentage, and it's the teachers and office staff who end up doing all the work to orchestrate it. I think we should just send home a note at the start of the school year telling all the parents how much it will cost them not to have to do any of it. And if they don't have the money, they can find another way to contribute. Or maybe we can do one big fundraiser a year, like a walkathon. That way the school gets one hundred percent of the pledges, and I get my steps in."

Tess took a deep breath. "Rant over. Anyway, I have absolutely no idea what Joy's thing is. She's a riddle wrapped in a mystery inside an enigma, as Winston Churchill once said."

"She's a donut hole wrapped in a fortune cookie inside a croissant," Rosie said. "And now I'm starving."

"She's a Ouija board wrapped in a Tarot card inside a Magic 8 ball," I said.

"A Ouija board is too big to be wrapped in a Tarot card," Tess said. "And I wouldn't give Joy that much credit anyway. But I agree, there's something off about her. Why would she want to come on this cruise and then completely avoid me? I mean, the two of us never got beyond small talk, and even that only lasted a few minutes before we hit a dead end."

"Ugh," I said. "I've had first dates like that. It takes about three minutes to realize you've got nothing in common and then you spend the rest of the date trying to figure out how soon you can go home semi-gracefully without being a total jerk."

"Just start talking to an imaginary friend," Tess said. "Either that or ask him to marry you and your cat."

"Brilliant," I said. "Why is it that other people's lives are always so much easier to figure out than your own?"

We turned around and retraced our steps, climbed back on our bus. We pulled off the road briefly in Simiane la Rotonde and Saint-Christol-d'Albion to take in sweeping views of vineyards and lavender fields.

"We are coming up on the spectacular Gorges de la Nesque," our guide announced from the front of the bus. "We will have largely a steady climb, with some exciting roller coaster ups and downs, as well as expansive vistas, drop-offs, and dramatic switchback turns."

The terrain changed. Cliffs rose up sharply on one side of the road. On the other side, steep canyons dropped into sheer nothingness. The barriers on the gorge side of the road were either shin-high or nonexistent.

As the road narrowed, our fancy white bus suddenly

seemed perilously oversized. The bus driver beeped his horn repeatedly as we entered each blind turn.

I leaned across the aisle to look past Tess and make sure Rosie was doing okay.

Tess grabbed my forearm in a death grip.

"Are you *kidding* me?" Tess said. Her breathing was shallow and she was making a funny dry-mouth sound.

Rosie looked over at me and smiled.

"This road doesn't bother you?" I said.

"Nope," Rosie said. "As long as the wheels are on the ground, I'm totally fine. How about you?"

I shrugged. "It's not my favorite, but as long as a snake doesn't fall down from the ceiling of the bus while we're driving, I can handle it."

"Did all y'all hear about the eight-foot cobra," the woman next to me said, "that came wigglin' out of someone's toilet? That'll wake you up in the morning. Anyway, the authorities were fixin' to catch it, but—"

I put my hands over my ears. "Please don't."

"Are you *kidding* me?" Tess said again.

We were heading straight for a low tunnel carved into the rock. Our bus driver began beeping the horn again.

"The driver beeps his horn," our guide said into her microphone, "so that automobiles traveling in the other direction will know we are coming, since there is little room for error on this road. It is what you call a balcony road, a lane cut into the side of sheer cliffs. It runs as a single track along the mountainside for some distance now, with space sufficient only for one vehicle."

"Holy shit," Tess said. "Make her shut up."

Our guide stood up and turned to face us. "We shall say a prayer that we have the road to ourselves until it widens again." She smiled and sat down again.

We were heading right for another low rock tunnel that

went immediately into a hairpin turn. We heard a loud gasp in front of us on the bus, echoing gasps behind us.

Tess dug her fingernails into my arm. "I need. To get off. This. Freakin'. Bus. Now."

"Rosie," I said. "I think this might be the perfect time to teach Tess to tap."

We tapped and we tapped. Some of the other passengers had taken our guide's prayer suggestion seriously, and the rhythmic chant of a Hail Mary or two accompanied us. My seatmate folded over a corner of the page she was reading. She pulled a silver flask out of her purse and took an enthusiastic gulp.

Finally our bus took the exit for Monieux. I pointed out the window. "See," I said to Tess. "We're fine now. Green trees, pretty countryside, no gorges in sight."

Tess buried her face in her hands and rocked back and forth. "All I know is there's no way in hell I'm going back that way. We're going to have to hire a plane to get us out of here."

"Just don't expect me to fly on it with you," Rosie said.

Two long tables were set and waiting for us on the umbrella and tree-studded terrace at Les Lavandes, The Lavender Restaurant, in Monieux. The trees were strung with twinkle lights. A gorgeous stone fountain took over one corner. On the other side of a squat stonewall, purple lavender fields stretched out below us. A warm breeze blew and the scent of lavender filled the air.

Rosie, Tess and I grabbed seats at the far end of one of the tables. Our guide told us that Monieux was a little hilltop village built in the 12th century, with a population of approximately 350. The mayor of the town also owned Monieux's only restaurant, the terrace of which we were now seated on.

As if on cue, the mayor strolled over to us, chatted in French with our guide, beamed at the rest of us.

We sipped our pink-hued wine, which our guide told us was a local rosé.

Rosie held up her glass and swirled the wine around. "Perfect for a long summer day in Provence. Elegantly balanced on the palate, yet easy-drinking with an underlying fresh acidity and a lingering and memorable aftertaste."

"Really?" I said.

"I have no idea," Rosie said. "I just made that up."

"It's delicious," I said. "I didn't know rosé could be dry and crisp like this. I think my rosé perception might have been colored by all that Mateus back in college—it tasted like fizzy watermelon."

"You have to admit those Mateus bottles made great doorstops though," Rosie said. "Maybe we can go to Portugal next and see if they still make Mateus. There's a lavender farm called Quinta das Lavandas in Portugal I'd love to see."

The mention of Mateus sent me traveling on a timeline of bad wine. "Remember Cold Duck? And Blue Nun?"

"My first child was conceived while drinking Boone's Farm Strawberry Hill," Rosie said. "Lesson learned: just because it tastes like strawberry Kool-Aid doesn't mean you can't get pregnant."

Tess took a long swallow of her local rosé. "All I can say is it's a damn good thing they have wine, since I'm going to have to live here for the rest of my life if we can't find a plane to rent. That ride was *brutal*."

We watched as three cyclists tucked their bicycles into a bike rack on the edge of the terrace and hung their helmets from the handlebars. They were wearing matching team bike shorts and tight shirts, and had numbers on their bikes as well as across their lower backs. They walked through the terrace and joined a table of other cyclists.

Tess perked up immediately. "Lycra bike shorts are *every-thing*," she said as she turned to watch them.

"Are you objectifying those poor bike riders?" I said.

Our guide circled around the tables to make sure we all knew that the cyclists were competing in the Tour de France.

"For real?" Rosie said. "Do you believe we're sitting at a restaurant in Provence during the Tour de France and the racers are sitting here with us?" She took out her phone and started taking pictures. "Even Connor and Nick are going to think I'm cool when they see these."

Tess kicked me under the table. "One of us is single. Why don't you mosey on over there and strike up a conversation? You know, start with small talk and see if somebody offers to take you for a ride."

"Right," I said. "Just what I need. Another man to take me for a ride."

But I had to admit a tiny part of me had an embarrassing urge to take Tess up on her suggestion. Or better still, I'd sit right here and one of the racers would catch my eye. I'd smile and he'd smile. I'd get up and wander over to the fountain to check it out and he'd wander over there, too. He'd be from somewhere exotic but speak great English with just the right amount of accent. He'd ask for my email so he could get in touch with me when the next leg of the race was over. With perfect serendipity, the race route would just so happen to be taking him past wherever our boat was going next. We'd have drinks at a sidewalk café. Tess and Rosie would lurk nearby just to make sure he wasn't a psychopath.

I turned and glanced casually at the Tour de France table. Nobody glanced casually back.

Rosie saw me do it. "Don't take it personally. It's probably the hats. Either that or the twisty necklaces."

"Note to self," I said. "Beyond the age of five, dressing like triplets may not be the wisest choice."

"You know," Tess said, "if we bought bikes and started

training as soon as we got home, maybe we could come back here and do the Tour de France ourselves in a year or two. I mean, how hard can it be? A couple of those guys are drinking *wine* over there."

"Tess," I said. "You do know that they race on gorge roads like the one we just came over, don't you? And I think some of the routes are even scarier."

"Are you sure?" Tess took another big gulp of wine. "Do they have any idea how dangerous that is? I don't think they should be doing it. We need to march right over there and tell them to find a safer sport."

Fortunately, our food arrived before we had to do any marching. In the center of a shiny white plate, something round and salmon-colored sat on a perfect circle of pureed tomatoes. A looser circle of pesto surrounded that. A single flowering stem of lavender had been stuck in the center of the round thing like a flag.

Our guide told us that it was the *plat du jour*, a dish featured by the restaurant on this particular day. Whatever it was, it was amazing—mousse-like and filled with the taste of cream and fresh summer vegetables and what our guide told us were local chanterelle mushrooms. Plates of fresh local greens and goat cheese followed. Dessert was crisp pastry rolled like a jellyroll filled with cream and topped with a fresh strawberry. A smudge of local jam garnished the dessert plate and a fresh local cherry was perfectly placed to make it look like an exclamation point.

"This is the best food I've ever tasted after almost being killed," Tess said. "If I have to be stuck here for the rest of my life, at least I'll eat well."

As we left the restaurant terrace, I followed Tess and Rosie while they made a slight detour for photos with and autographs from the Tour de France riders.

"My students are going to go crazy when they see these," Tess said.

One of the racers met my eye. I didn't even bother to smile. I just looked away. I mean, what was the point, really? You meet a guy, it doesn't work out. Whether he rides in the Tour de France or plays Pokémon Go, they were all basically the same. They pretended to be interested in you for a little while, and then they broke your heart.

I supposed it was possible that my compass was off and just kept pointing me to the kind of guy that wasn't relationship material. But maybe that was simply another way of saying that I was the one who wasn't relationship material.

I was fine alone. Better than fine really. I had friends. I did interesting things. I mean, I was in Provence—how many people are lucky enough to go to *Provence*? And I was about to have a fascinating encore career, as soon as I figured out what it was.

I turned, head held high, and followed the rest of our group to our fancy white bus.

Our guide announced that Sault was less than five miles from Monieux. Once Tess had triple-checked that it was a completely gorge-less route, we managed to get her to climb back on the bus.

Sault is an old fortified village with charming shops and cafés. It sits on a plateau bordered by mountains and overlooking a wide valley. It's surrounded by huge purple fields of lavender to the south and to the west as far as the eye can see. If you love lavender, you might want to add Sault to your bucket list.

After we drove around the village, the bus driver pulled over so we could all take pictures. I snapped photo after photo of purple lavender fields, hoping I might get lucky and one of them would somehow capture the magnificence of what we were seeing.

"Why are some of the lavender fields yellow?" someone in our group asked.

Our guide smiled. "That is Celtic wheat. It is the ancestor of modern wheat and considered the rice of Haute-Provence. It is sown in September and harvested eleven months later. The husk is removed before consumption and used as a stuffing for pillows."

Just outside Sault, our bus driver pulled into Arôma Plates Distillerie. Our guide told us it was situated on the slopes of Mont Ventoux at the perfect 800-meter height for lavender.

"*Allons-y!*" our guide said, and we all started filing off the bus. "You are spoiled for choice here."

"Spoiled for choice," Rosie said. "I love that."

I gave my twisty necklace a twist. "She said it like it's a good thing. Maybe that's my problem—I forget that having lots of choices has advantages. It always feels so overwhelming to me."

"Do me a favor," Tess said. "Hold off on getting all philosophical until after I find us a plane."

Some of our bus mates followed the signs to tour the distillery or take a class. Others went off to shop in the boutique or check out the café and juice shop. Tess went off to see about a plane.

Rosie and I walked down the road toward the lavender fields. The rustling of cicadas began to drown out the chattering of tourists. The sky surrounded us in that amazing blue of Provence. The air was hot and dry and breezy. I tried to drink it all in, to hang on to every detail so I could store it in my memory banks forever.

We turned a corner and a huge field of lavender stretched out in front of us, in all its glorious purpleness.

"Ohmigod," I said. "This is the most purple I've ever seen."

"Breathe," Rosie said. "Just breathe. It's sexy-sweet-spicy-soothing-earthy-exotic all rolled into one."

"I know," I said. "I'm pretty sure I can taste it. It's like sensory overload—I can't tell where sight, smell, and taste begin or end."

"There was a study," Rosie said. "I think it was done in the Netherlands. Anyway, people who smelled lavender became nicer—they picked up a dropped item from the floor instead of ignoring it, they shared money they were given. The researchers think it was because of lavender's calming property. And apparently the olfactory nerve is connected to the region of the prefrontal cortex that controls trust."

"Interesting," I said. "Maybe lavender could be used in negotiations. You know, you just sit everybody down and say, okay, sniff this, now make an offer. Okay, now you sniff and make a counter offer."

"If I were in charge of the world," Rosie said, "that's exactly the way it would work."

Rosie began walking in the tight space between the first two rows of lavender.

"I started to follow her, then stopped. "Whoa. Are these all bees?"

"Yup, thousands of them. They're busy pollinating the flowers and filling the larder for the queen and the colony. Don't worry, they hardly ever sting."

"I'll take your word for it," I said.

We walked the length of the lavender field, then moved one row over and walked between the next two long rows of lavender going in the opposite direction.

Back and forth we walked. Staying in the moment was usually a challenge for me, but I did it now. It felt like a lavender-wrapped walking mindfulness meditation. When we finished walking between all the rows, we sat on a big rock by the side of the road.

"You were right," I said. "We didn't get stung."

"They charge extra for bee stings," Rosie said. "It's part of the upgraded tour."

I turned to look at her. "That sounded like something Tess would say."

"Sorry, I didn't mean it to steal Tess's sarcasm. I was just thinking how much work it would be to make a place like this profitable. I've been on their website—they distill their own lavender plus do distillation for other lavender farms, they sell wholesale and retail essential oils, cosmetics, cold-processed soaps."

Rosie pointed. "And then there's all that."

A lavender field away, a group of tourists were gathered around.

"They're learning to cut lavender with a sickle," Rosie said. "And see, then they're putting the lavender in a small traditional bag called a *saquette* that you sling over your shoulder. They'll carry it to the distillery and be able to take home a small sample of lavender oil."

On the other side of the field, another group was sitting in a circle and weaving long strands of ribbon around bouquets of lavender they'd picked.

"Oh, look," I said. "They're making lavender wands like the ones we made last year in Sequim."

"I think they call them lavender spindles here," Rosie said. "But it's the same thing. You wrap ribbon around the lavender and then hang it in your closet or put it in a drawer or under your pillow."

Rosie sighed. "I know I've already told you this, but my mother used to make lavender wands for the store every year."

"Are you thinking of how much she would have loved it here?"

Rosie smiled. "She would have gone crazy. I've been doing kind of an interior dialog with her this whole trip."

"I think I know what you mean. Everything is starting to blur, so I can't remember exactly where it was, but we passed a sign for a hotel and golf resort, I think it was called Domaine de Manville. And the first thing that popped into my mind was that I had to write it down so I could tell my dad."

My eyes teared up. "And then I remembered he's dead. I can't believe that still happens to me."

Rosie gave her necklace another twist. "Me, too. All the time. And when I think of something I want to tell my mom, I'm not thinking of how things were at the end of her life. It's like I skip over the Alzheimer's part and just remember who she was before that."

"That must have been awful for all of you." I shook my head. "Sorry, understatement of the year."

"Yeah, it's a horrific disease. How did your dad die?"

"A heart attack. On a golf course. He was such a huge golfer—we all told each other that at least he died doing what he loved. But it was really hard not to get a chance to say goodbye to him. Sometimes I have these crazy dreams that he got to come back to life just for one more cookout."

Rosie rested her hand on my shoulder for a moment, pulled it away. "I used to read to my mom, sing to her, tell myself that a part of her understood what I was saying. And then one day she grabbed my hand and tried to use it to turn on the television—over and over again—she thought my hand was the remote control."

"I'm so sorry about your mom," I said.

"I'm so sorry about your dad," Rosie said.

A burst of laughter came from the group making lavender wands. I reached into my purse for the sunscreen, squirted a glob of it on the back of one hand, gave the tube to Rosie.

"Thanks," Rosie said. "Did your parents still love each other?"

"Yeah," I said. "I think they really did. Yours?"

Rosie nodded. "Ditto."

"My mother," I said, "was so dependent on my father. I have to admit I never thought she'd be able to function without him."

"Another ditto," Rosie said. "Only it was my mom who did everything for my dad. Even after the Alzheimer's started taking over, she did as much as she could. I mean, that's why we moved in—so my dad wouldn't completely fall apart without her."

I pictured Rosie's dad and my mom sitting at my kitchen table in their matching terrycloth robes, a distinct absence of falling apart going on between them.

I sighed. "I'm really happy our parents found each other, but does it ever feel to you like it's a little bit disloyal that they're having so much fun together?"

"Exactly!" Rosie picked up a pebble and threw it across the road. "Oh, thank you for saying that. Yeah, and a part of me feels like I'm being disloyal somehow, too, as if I'm not doing enough to keep my mother's memory alive."

I threw a pebble across the road, too. It released a little cloud of dry dirt when it landed.

"Yeah," I said. "I feel some of that, too. And I have to admit I'm a little bit thrown by the way my mother has managed to get past her grief and her survivor's guilt and whatever else she must have had to deal with and moved on. I mean, she's grown so much."

I blinked back tears. "My dad would be so proud of her."

"When my mom first got sick, she used to tell me to make sure I found my dad a new wife as soon as she was gone. I didn't even have to."

Rosie wiped her eyes. "And now you and I are framily."

"Ha," I said. "Framily. I love it. What happens if they break up?"

Rosie shrugged. "I guess we drop the amily and go back to being friends."

"And in the meantime, we just let them hop back and forth between our houses whenever the mood strikes?" I shook my head. "It's a good thing I don't have a life, because I have to tell you that might get a little bit challenging if I did."

Rosie put her sunglasses down on the rock and rubbed sunscreen all over her face and her ears. "I don't know what we're going to do. I mean, we sold our house to move in with my dad. His house is paid off so we've been paying all the bills and we renovated the basement for him. I guess we all thought we'd figure out the rest of the details as we went along. But now—"

"Maybe your dad will want to sell the house to you now that my mom's sold her condo. Maybe they'll want to buy a place that's new for both of them." I sighed. "Or maybe they'll think it's more romantic to keep flitting back and forth forever."

Rosie shook her head. "I have to say they are far more interested in sex than they should be in their seventies."

"I agree," I said. "It's totally embarrassing. And the worst part is I think there's a slight possibility that I'm a tiny bit jealous. They just seem to be having so much *fun* together, you know?"

Tess had tracked us down and was walking along the side of the road in our direction. We waved and she waved back.

Rosie leaned back on her elbows. Her freckles jumped out against the white film of sunscreen. "I guess what I've been trying to figure out while I'm here is that if my dad's ready to move on from the lavender farm, am I? Or do I want to commit to the farm as well as the house, really commit, and try to turn it into something? I mean, I started getting into the lavender store when we got back from Sequim last year, but after a while I kind of fizzled out."

Rosie waved her arms at the vast expanse of lavender fields in front of us. "You know, like this, but on a smaller scale."

I went into my long, slow pendulum nod without even planning to. "How would that look?"

"Well, I think it would have to be a destination like this place is. You know, a tourist stop on the way from Boston to

Cape Cod. Classes, events, lavender plants for sale. And products—not just lavender stuff, though there would have to be lots of that, but also the work of local artisans, maybe handmade signs and jewelry and pottery."

"And sunflowers," I said. "You'd have to grow sunflowers."

Rosie smiled. "And sunflowers. And maybe we could sell bird seed and locally made bird feeders and birdhouses."

"That's a great idea. You could do cross-promotion with the artisans via social networking and local media, and it would help everybody."

Rosie shook her head. "But it's so much work. And I'm not sure if I want to do it. A part of me feels that if my dad gets to walk away, then maybe I should, too."

"Why don't you two get a room." Tess wiggled her way in and sat between us on the rock. "Oh, wait, you already have one."

"Ignore her," I said to Rosie. "So the obstacle you're seeing is the amount of work. What kind of help would you need to change that?"

"Well," Rosie said. "I have to admit that one of my ideas is to get my dad and your mom to run the day-to-day operations. But even if they'd go for it, that still doesn't solve the problem of the two of them house hopping whenever the mood strikes, so I'm not sure what to do about that."

"Easy peasy," Tess said. "Just put a tiny house love shack for them on the lavender farm. And then change your locks fast."

Rosie and I both looked at Tess.

"Wowsa." Rosie punched Tess's shoulder. "I knew you'd come in handy for something one of these days."

"Total genius," I said. "If we can talk them into it, I think it might actually work."

"Of course it's genius," Tess said. "And not to get all opportunistic or anything, but this way I can try out their tiny house before I commit to one of my own. Maybe we can do an occasional house swap."

"Good thinking," I said. "So, how did it go with your plane search?"

"We don't need one!" Tess did a drum roll with her palms on her thighs. "So apparently that death-defying gorge road was a deliberate scenic detour. Can you believe that? I mean, talk about cruel. Anyway, there's another road that will take us straight back to Avignon."

"Crisis averted," Rosie said as she pushed herself up from our rock. "Come on, let's go make another lavender wand so we can do our part to support the local lavender economy."

Lavender Wands

15 fresh stems of freshly picked lavender, each at least 12 inches tall
3 yards of ¼ or ½-inch wide ribbon

Strip the leaves from the stems. Line up the base of the flower heads so that they're even. Tie them together tightly with one end of the ribbon.

Turn the flowers upside down and gently bend each stem down over the flower heads to make a cage. (You can use the side of a spoon or your fingernail to score the underside of the stem you're bending first to make this easier.)

Pull the long end of the ribbon out of the cage of stems. Leave the short end of the ribbon tucked inside. Line up all the stems of the cage evenly around the blossoms so that they don't overlap.

Beginning where the base of the flowers meets the stems, start to weave the ribbon under and over the stems, pulling carefully to make sure the weave is tight, and alternating under and over with each new row. (After the first couple of rows, it will get easier.)

Continue weaving until you have covered all the lavender flowers. Wrap the ribbon around the neck of the wand. Tie a knot. Continue to wrap the stems until you reach the end, then trim the stems to the same length.

Add a rubber band to secure the ribbon at the end. As the lavender dries out and shrinks, you can rewrap the ribbon to make it tighter if you need to.

Day 24

7,886 steps

We were docked in the sleepy little riverside town of Viviers.

Rosie and I stopped to ask Despina, the ship's concierge, for new key cards for our room.

"But of course," Despina said as she walked behind the reception desk. "It is always better to choose on the side of safety." She pulled up our information and ran two new key cards through a machine. "And now the original cards will no longer work in your door." She smiled and gave us our key cards.

"Thank you," Rosie and I said in tandem as we stepped away.

"I'm so glad we did that," Rosie said. "Last night when we opened the door to our stateroom, I had such a creepy feeling that someone besides housekeeping had been in there."

I looked at her. "Why didn't you say something?"

Rosie shrugged. "I didn't want to freak you out. Plus, it was just a feeling—nothing was out of place or missing or anything like that. I think it was probably exhaustion talking."

"It was definitely a long day," I said. "Actually, two long

days in a row. I wouldn't have missed those excursions for anything, but I'm really looking forward to spending some more time on the ship today."

Tess joined us in the atrium. We picked up takeout coffee in the snack station on our way out.

I looked at Tess. "Where's Joy?"

Tess rolled her eyes. "I asked if she wanted to come for a walk and she blew me off. And not with the flair of your bus seatmate from Texas, I might add."

"What did she say?" Rosie said.

"That she was going to make other plans," Tess said. "Which means she didn't actually have other plans, but would rather do anything else than be with us."

"Her loss," I said. "I just hope we didn't start it by making her feel excluded."

"She's the one who's been doing the excluding," Tess said. "From now on I'm going to try my best not to notice her so I can pretend I have a single room."

We sat on a bench near our dock to drink our coffee.

Out of the blue, Rosie started to sing "Under the Boardwalk." Tess and I joined in. We were sitting next to a river and not the sea. We were nowhere near a boardwalk. But we sang it anyway, just because we felt like it.

A man walking from the dock to his parked car turned to look at us. We waved and sang louder. He ignored us.

"Maybe we should sing it in French," Rosie said. "It might go over better with the locals."

Tess pulled up her app. "Under the boardwalk is *sous la promenade*."

We gave it a try.

"Well, that certainly doesn't fit the melody very well," Rosie said.

"We could switch to 'Frère Jacques,'" I said.

So we sang "Frère Jacques." And then we turned it into a round and sang it through a few more times.

"Not bad," Rosie said. "I think we might have to seriously consider that international tour."

"Right," Tess said. "Keep dreaming."

"I'd completely forgotten that expression," I said. "I don't think I realized how harsh it was back when we used to say it. You know, like keep dreaming and you'll never face reality."

"Rosie can take it," Tess says. "She has kids who are almost teenagers. What else did we used to say?"

"Catch you on the flip side," Rosie said.

"Keep your bellbottoms wide and your platforms high," Tess said.

"Can you dig it?" I said.

"Dynamite," Rosie said.

"Outtasite," I said.

"I was shitting bricks," Rosie said.

"What a space cadet," I said.

"Not too shabby," Rosie said.

"Far freakin' out," Tess said. "You know, I can't even remember if we really said those things or if we only think we did."

"I guess it doesn't really matter," I said. "I think we all rewrite our pasts anyway."

"Hea*vy*," Tess said.

We threw our cups in a trash barrel and took off on our own little self-guided walking tour along the cobblestone streets of old town.

"It's all too beautiful," Rosie said.

"It's all too beautiful," Tess and I started to sing at the same time. The lyrics to "Itchycoo Park" came back to us across the decades, at least some of them, and the rest of the words the three of us just made up as we went along.

"Psychedelic," Tess said when we finished. "Although I think we might be too young to remember that song."

"The Small Faces rereleased it again in the mid-'70s," I said, "so we don't have to pretend to be too young."

"As I was saying before 'Itchycoo Park' came over us," Rosie said, "it's like beauty overload. There's so much beauty I can't even take it in anymore."

"I'm sure there are history buffs who need to see every last town square and cathedral," Tess said, "but I'm ready to claim a lounge chair on the top deck of the ship and try not to get a tan for a few days. Geez Louise, remember when we used to be able to slather ourselves in baby oil with a few drops of iodine added and cover a double record album with aluminum foil to use as a reflector so we could bake ourselves to a crisp?"

"Aww, I used to cover my double albums with foil, too, and climb out a window to the tar roof on our porch," Rosie said. "That was so much fun, at least if you factor out all the sun damage we have now because of it."

"There's always a price," Tess said. "I hate that."

"Just don't start getting injectables and all that stuff, okay?" Rosie said. "Let's make a pact to grow wrinkly together. I mean, somebody has to look old, you know?"

"Agreed," I said. "Plus it's really distracting when someone's face doesn't work right or look like them anymore. It's wrinkle free, but it's kind of frozen, you know? I'd really hate to try to have a conversation with either of you and not be able to hear a word you're saying because I'm too busy checking out your face."

"I have to admit," Rosie said, "I couldn't stop staring at Joy's face last night at dinner trying to figure out what she's had done."

"Remember that old commercial?" I said. *Maybe she's born with it. Maybe it's Maybelline.*

"Even if she was born with it," Tess said. "It's definitely Botox now. I mean, it looks like somebody Photoshopped Joy's crows' feet away. Trust me, if we went to high school together, she's got a whole flock of crows' feet by now. Plus she has that startled expression I always think of as Celebrity Face. I think she's done injectables, too—her skin has a plumped-up look. Basically the way it works is that Botox is the gateway drug, and then they upsell you from there."

I raised my eyebrows just because I could. "You sure know a lot about all this for someone who's never going to do it."

Tess crossed her arms over her chest. "I most certainly do. I wanted to make sure I really don't like what that stuff does to your face, and that I'm not just being lazy. It's fine if someone else wants to do it. It's just not my thing. I think our smiles make us who we are, and we smile with our whole faces, so when you lose that, you've lost a big part of yourself."

"To Botox or not to Botox," Rosie said. "That is the question."

"What about this?" I said. "We get a little more wrinkly every year, and then we spend the money we save by not doing anything to our faces on taking another trip."

"Sunscreen and moisturizer," Rosie said, "are non-negotiables."

"Of course," Tess said. "I mean, we don't want to look like old hags—not unless hagdom comes with some sort of super power."

"A super power would be tempting," I said. "Or even a good haggy sorceress spell or two."

Tess ran her hands over her cheeks. "But I have to admit I did break down and buy a long strand mulberry silk pillowcase made with a traditional charmeuse weave, in case you were wondering why my skin and hair look so great."

"Of course we were," I said. "We were up half the night trying to figure out how you'd managed to look so great."

"Send us the link to that pillowcase ASAP," Rosie said. "If you want to hang out with Noreen and me, it's not okay to try to out-pillowcase us."

At the end of the cobblestone street our ship appeared again like a vision, just where we'd left it.

We stopped and checked our step count.

"Not bad for before breakfast," Tess said. "I'm going to eat and then lounge around on the sun deck all day slathered in sunscreen and under an umbrella."

"I'm going to eat and lounge around in the chair right next to you," Rosie said.

"Well, I'm definitely going to eat," I said. "And after that I'm going to catch up on my reading for class. Then I have to do a practice coaching session."

I curled up on my bed with my iPad and signed into my Skype account. I'd already added all my health coach classmates, as well as the health coach instructors, to my Skype contacts list. My mother and sister and brothers were on my contacts list, too, as were a few old friends and some former colleagues from Balancing Act.

To find out who was in my practice coaching triad this time around, I pulled up an email with my coaching schedule. I had to admit trying to keep up with health coach training while on a river cruise was more disorienting than I'd thought it would be. Time and place had started to lose meaning as we floated along on the river. There was probably a metaphor in there somewhere about the way my entire life was drifting by, but I wasn't going to think about it, especially while I was on vacation.

I found Karen and Ted's names next to today's date on my class schedule, started scrolling through my contacts list to find them.

About halfway down the list, Rick's face peered out of the tiny circle next to his Skype name: *Wizard on Board*.

"Oh, grow up," I said. I mean, come on, how about using your first and last name like an adult? Rick looked a little bit scruffy in his Skype photo, too. His hair was sticking up on one side. It was hard to tell since the photo was so small, but I was pretty sure his T-shirt was frayed around the neck, too.

There was a green check next to Rick's username, and beside that *Online.*

I blinked. One little tap of my finger and I could conjure him up. It would be so easy. We'd had some good times, hadn't we?

"Don't do it," I said.

I heard that little watery Skype ringing sound.

My heart skipped a beat, but it was only Karen from health coach class calling. I tapped *Answer with video,* and Karen's face appeared above mine in a square on my iPad screen.

"Hi," I said.

"Hi," Karen said. "I call Observer first."

"Then I call Client," I said. "I couldn't coach my way out of a paper bag right now."

From her little square, Karen smiled. "Vacation, right?"

"Yeah, a river cruise in France with some friends." I slid off the bed, walked over to the sliding glass doors to the balcony, held up my iPad so Karen could see the water behind me. "See?"

"Sort of," Karen said. "Good for you though."

An incoming call window from Ted opened on my screen. I clicked *Answer with video.*

"Hi," Karen said. "You're Coach first, Noreen's Client."

"I'm on to this," Ted said. "The third person who shows up always coaches first, right?"

"You got it," I said. "I think it's easier to start with the other roles and work up to Coach—I always struggle with who am I to try to help someone else, you know?"

"You figured out how to go to France on a vacation," Karen said. "Clearly you've got something going on."

"Good taste in walking partners," I said.

"Okay, let's get this show on the road," Coach Ted said. "What is your question, goal or problem, Noreen?"

I'd already pulled up a copy of **Noreen's Goals for Practice and Life**. I skimmed it: I'd been walking every day. Since I was on a river cruise, I obviously hadn't been cooking or grocery shopping, but it was easy to make healthy food choices here and I'd been doing a pretty good job of that.

I tried to glide right past the goals I'd written about working toward a healthy relationship with my boyfriend. Technically, I didn't think he was really even a boyfriend anymore anyway.

I glanced at my list of Skype contacts. Rick was still online.

I didn't plan to say it but it came out anyway. "I know healthy relationships with a significant other can be an important part of our health and wellbeing. So I'm thinking I'd like to try to have one. Either that or get over the idea completely. You know, I could adopt a dog from a shelter instead. Or maybe start with a Boston fern so I don't overshoot."

Coach Ted was already doing his pendulum nod. "So, you'd like to have a healthy relationship with a significant other."

I shrugged. "Or a fern. You know, a small step with a high probability of success?"

Observer Karen was scribbling away, probably writing *Client has deep-seated issues far beyond the scope of pretend health coaching.*

Coach Ted was still nodding. "So, assuming you went for the human relationship, how would that look?"

My eyes drifted back to Rick's tiny face on my contacts list. "Well, when I went to the trouble of spiralizing zucchini for him, he would definitely show up for dinner. I mean, you don't forget plans if the person you have them with is important to you."

Coach Ted did his pendulum nod.

Observer Karen was probably writing *Who actually spiralizes zucchini for a guy? And what the hell does that even mean anyway?*

"So," Coach Ted said. "What else would this relationship look like?"

I shrugged. "Well, besides remembering plans, I guess we'd sort of *have* a plan, you know, for our relationship."

Coach Ted tilted his head in his little video square. "So this is the Boston fern you're talking about, right?"

I tilted my head, too. "What do you mean?"

Coach Ted went back to his pendulum nod. "Well, with a Boston fern you could make a plan to give it a cool place with high humidity and indirect light. You'd agree to water it once a week, and it would agree not to turn brown and drop its leaves on your floor."

"Wow," I said. "You sure know a lot about Boston ferns."

"Yeah, I'm kind of a plant freak." Coach Ted launched back into his nod again. "So you could hold up your part of the plan? And you'd trust that the Boston fern would hold up its part?"

"Yeah," I said. "I could do that."

Observer Karen scribbled away.

"So," Coach Ted said, "what kind of plan did you have in place in this potential human relationship? I mean, did you have the zucchini spiralizing details worked out?"

"That's ridiculous," I said. "Everybody knows that if somebody is going to all the trouble of cooking for you and you don't show up, it's a deal breaker."

Coach Ted nodded some more. "How could *everybody* possibly know anything if you haven't had the conversation? You know what you know and feel what you feel. And the other person knows what he knows and feels what he feels."

The only thing I knew was where this was going. I sighed. "But what if you put yourself out there to have that conversation and you just get hurt again?"

Coach Ted shrugged. "Then maybe you could look at it as

an exit interview. Figure out what went wrong and how you could use that information moving forward. Sorry, I forgot I'm not supposed to give advice. I'm supposed to ask open-ended questions so you come up with things on your own."

"That's okay," I said. "I can use all the help I can get. I have a lifelong history of not exactly being brilliant at this relationship thing."

I heard that watery Skype ring again.

An incoming call window popped up on my screen. Rick's picture and screen name were on it.

I closed my eyes. I opened them again. Rick was still there. I didn't think he could have possibly overheard me talking about him. Although I supposed there was always the possibility that you had secret Internet eavesdropping tricks when your Skype name was *Wizard on Board*.

I could feel my cheeks turning bright red.

"Noreen?" Observer Karen said. "Are you okay?"

Rick's call window was giving me three choices: *Answer, Answer with video, Decline the call.*

What was Skype's problem anyway? Clearly they needed to offer more options. What about *Please try again later.* Or *Please send flowers and then try again later.*

"I'm fine," I said. I took a deep breath, tapped *Decline the call.* Watched Rick disappear.

"So," Coach Ted said. "From your perspective, what might a conversation in that potential healthy relationship with a human look like?"

I let out a puff of air. "You know, I think I'm just going to go with the Boston f—"

The tinkle-y sound of digital chimes broke in.

"Time's up," Observer Karen said. "I call Client next."

Day 25

22, 002 steps

Our ship had docked in Tournon-sur-Rhône sometime during the night. This morning we'd decided to skip the Train de l'Ardeche, a 21-mile steam train excursion. As soon as she heard viaducts, tunnels, and scenic gorges, Tess had gone ballistic.

So we'd lingered over coffee and breakfast at the terrace restaurant on the bow of the upper deck. Windshield-like glass partitions kept our croissants from blowing off our plates without obstructing our water views.

"This is the life," I said.

"It most certainly is," Tess said. "Don't even tell me how many days we have left—I don't want to get depressed yet."

We grabbed a map and the ship's daily newsletter, set off to explore on our own.

Right next to the spot where our ship was docked, we strolled through a charming park filled with plane trees. An adorable little girl wearing a sundress and a bow in her hair was running along a path.

The pint-sized child tripped and fell. Tess, Rosie and I all let out identical little gasps.

The mother stayed where she was, arms crossed over her chest. The little girl pushed herself back up to a standing position. Without even glancing at her mother, she brushed off her knees and started running again.

"Now that's not something you'd see at home," Tess said. "The mother would have helicoptered over and scooped up the daughter and made a big deal out of it. And the daughter would have started crying. And if it happened at school, I would have had to write an incident report. As if kids aren't supposed to fall. I mean, really, why else would they be built so close to the ground?"

"I get that the mom is trying to teach her daughter to be strong and independent," Rosie said, "but I'm not sure you should ever miss an opportunity for a hug, especially when they're little. I know it's a cliché, but kids really do grow up so fast."

I was busy strolling through the scraped knees of my own childhood. "Remember Mercurochrome? My mom and dad used to cover our cuts and scrapes in that mercury-laced stuff pretty much daily—our knees glowed orangey-pinkish-red for years. If you think about it, our entire childhoods could have killed us."

"Yeah," Tess said. "Whenever my parents hit the brake suddenly while they were driving, their idea of a seatbelt was flinging out one arm in front of us while blowing cigarette smoke in our faces and yelling *Whoa, Nellybelle.*"

"I just remembered," Rosie said, "my parents kicking us out the door on weekend mornings and telling us to go play and that they didn't want to see the whites of our eyes until the sun went down. We probably had more unsupervised time in a single weekend than my kids have had in their entire lives."

"It's such a crazy world now," I said.

"I think it's always been a crazy world," Tess said.

"Yeah," Rosie said. "Maybe it's just the brand of crazy that changes."

Talk of our hazardous childhoods faded away as we walked along the river. We swung our arms and picked up our pace, waiting for our endorphins, those great feel-good hormones, to kick in.

We cut inland, followed a maze of cobblestone streets meandering through the historic center. We passed Tournon Castle, which sat up on a rock overlooking the town and the river beyond. We stopped at the Church of Saint Julien to admire the gothic spires and the way the adjoining houses were built into the church walls.

We heard singing coming from inside the church. Tess opened the heavy wooden door and we all walked in. Light glowed through stained glass windows, hefty chandeliers hung from the ceiling, gorgeous frescoes decorated the walls.

Tourists filled the ancient church. Somewhere in the middle of it all a group was singing "Amazing Grace" in English. Shivers ran down my spine. Rosie and Tess and I joined in.

"Wow," Rosie said once we were out on the street again. "That was really beautiful. And I have to admit the three of us sure sound a lot better when we're singing with other people."

"What do you think that was all about anyway?" Tess said.

"Easy," I said. "They met at a photography Meetup group in Virginia, and then one day they discovered they all liked to sing 'Amazing Grace.' At first they only sang it locally, but now they travel around the world and sing it wherever they can."

"Not just at churches," Rosie said. "They like to sing it outdoors, too. But only in the middle of the night under a sky full of stars."

"I like it," Tess said. "I don't believe it for a minute, but I like it."

We walked along Grande Rue, a pedestrian area, winding our way through crowded cobblestone streets.

"What a pretty village," Rosie said. "I love all the shops and cafés and parks. And it's nice to see so many families out and about. For me, the timing of this trip was all about catching the lavender in bloom, but how cool that we're here for Bastille Day."

"That was part of my pitch to get the cultural grant," Tess said. She cleared her throat and went into recitation mode. "Bastille Day falls on July 14th every year. In France it's called *la fête nationale*. It's France's most popular holiday, and in modern times Bastille Day has turned into a big street celebration."

Rosie pulled the ship's daily newsletter out of her purse. "It says there'll be performers and brass bands and more and more parties as the day goes on, culminating in a big fireworks display over the river tonight."

We reconfigured into a single file to pass a clump of people, then managed to spread out side-by-side again. We smiled at cute babies in strollers and stopped to take turns petting a fluffy brown puppy while its owner beamed proudly.

A woman wearing leopard print shoes was walking a Chihuahua wearing a matching leopard print leash. When Tess held up her camera and gestured, the woman stopped and posed with pouty lips in front of an ancient stone building so we could take her picture. The Chihuahua might have made pouty lips, too.

"The French are definitely into their dogs," I said.

Rosie pointed downward and then jumped. "Yeah, but the pooper scooper thing doesn't seem to have quite caught on here yet."

"Now there's a business idea," I said. "Maybe I could stay here and start the movement. Pun intended. How do you say pooper scooper in French?"

Tess pulled up her app. "Poop is *caca*. That's the best I can do-do."

Rosie and I groaned.

We headed up a steep incline and stopped talking long enough to do some huffing and puffing. The sun was bright and it was getting hot enough that the fact that it was a dry heat mattered less and less. Eventually we managed to find Le Jardin d'Eden aka The Garden of Eden, a hillside garden surrounded by medieval ramparts and towers that was once a retreat for Jesuit monks.

The view from the garden was amazing—the village of Tournon-sur-Rhône and the river stretched out below us. We climbed steeply winding woodland paths past terraced areas and statues and fishponds and streams. Roses bloomed in the sunny spots.

"This garden is a work of art," I said. "Can you imagine what it takes to keep it up?"

"I know," Rosie said. "Every time I'm overwhelmed by the lavender farm, I'm going to think of this place. Plus it's giving me some great ideas for my own garden."

"What a workout," Tess said. "My thighs are screaming for mercy."

The owner, Eric, and his cat appeared and joined us as we walked. Neither Eric nor the cat spoke English, and Tess and her app were a little bit slow on the English-to-French translation, so mostly Eric pointed and the three of us *oohed* and *aahed*. The cat brought up the rear, occasionally stopping to hover over a fishpond and let its presence be known.

"*Merci beaucoup*," we all said once we'd finished our tour. Rosie, Tess and I wound our way back down the hill from the peaceful paradise.

We looped back through the village and out to the river, then we walked along the Quai Charles de Gaulle until we came to a pedestrian bridge. Closer to us, a group of men were setting up for the night's fireworks show. On the other side of the river, we could see vineyards sprouting from the hills.

"So," I said. "I'm not implying that phobias run through us like a river or anything. But is anybody in The Wildwater Walking Club afraid of bridges?"

"I'm good," Rosie said.

"I'm fine, too," Tess said. "And I'm okay with having a few phobias. The thing about getting to be our age is that on the one hand, you've got the courage of midlife, which in some ways makes you braver than you've ever been. And on the other hand, you've lived long enough to know all the scary things that can happen."

Bridges were nowhere on my anxiety hit parade either, so we walked across the footbridge to Tournon-sur-Rhône's twin city, Tain L'Hermitage.

Our first stop was the Valrhona chocolate factory. We toured the interactive exhibits and learned how chocolate is transformed from bean to bar. Then we made a beeline for the Cite du Chocolat Valrhona, the largest Valrhona boutique in the world, which turned out to be absolute chocolate heaven for any chocoholic.

Bowl after bowl of chocolate samples were laid out in rows across the length of long tables.

We dug in. "This is the best chocolate I've ever had," we said. And when we tried the next sample, we said it again. And again.

"I can't believe how many samples they're giving out," Rosie said.

"Now I understand the concept of death by chocolate," I said.

We dragged ourselves away from the sample tables and bought a few bags and bars of chocolate to take home as gifts.

"Make sure you buy some extras," Tess said. "We might need a little hair of the dog later on when our chocolate hangovers kick in."

Our next stop was the Chapoutier Tasting Room, which was a lovely place with beamed ceilings and what looked like outdoor streetlights lighting up the inside.

A very nice man welcomed us and gave us a tour of the vineyards high up on the hilly terraces of l'Hermitage, where we could see each grape vine growing on its own wooden pole. In perfect English he told us that the majority of the wines here are made from the Syrah grape. Some of the grapes are from very old vines, many more than 100 years old.

Tess handed him her camera and he took a picture of us standing in front of the grapevines in our matching straw hats and purple shoelaces and twisty necklaces we'd done our best to twist in the shape of wine bottles. We followed our host back to the tasting room, and he started pulling together a tasting for us while we wandered around the room.

"Do you believe we're in the actual place where they make Hermitage wine?" I said. "And look, their wine labels are also in braille—that's so cool."

"You know," Tess said, "I think we should have gone wine first, chocolate second. My taste buds might be permanently set in chocolate mode now."

"I'm having flashbacks to our tasting in Sequim last year," Rosie said. "Remember, we were wine tasting virgins then? I feel like an old pro now, even though I still don't really know anything about wine."

"We know how to drink it," Tess said. "That's all we need."

We sampled a 2010 Côte-Rôtie Les Bécasses, which our host told us tasted like spicy earth and bacon and violets.

I closed my eyes and tried to taste them all. I might have faked it a little, but I definitely enjoyed the wine.

We tasted Ermitage Le Pavillon and Ermitage l'Ermite. We tried Châteauneuf-du-Pape Barbe Rac and Côte-Rôtie La Mordorée.

"You might have to start a little vineyard next to the

sunflowers," I said to Rosie.

"I'll take that under advisement," Rosie said.

Our host kept pouring, so we kept tasting.

Finally, we looked at one another.

"Okay," Tess said. "Shut us off after this taste, or we're going to have to get jobs here to pay for all this."

Our host smiled and told us that there was no charge for the tasting.

"Seriously?" Rosie said. "Now you're never going to get rid of us."

But even given the diminutive size of wine-tasting portions, we knew it was time. So we moved on to the impossible job of each trying to decide on a single bottle to buy and take home with us.

"From a health perspective," I said, "I think we might need to up it to two bottles each. Just so we're balanced when we carry them back to the ship."

"Now you're thinking," Tess said.

"What if we can't fit two bottles in our suitcases?" Rosie said.

"No worries," Tess said. "If we can't fit them, we'll just throw some clothes away."

Joy came out of nowhere as we were leaving the restaurant after dinner and took a picture of us. And then she turned and walked away.

"Nice to see you, Joy," Rosie said.

Joy wiggled the fingers of one hand over her head and kept walking.

"That was weird," I said. I fingered my twisty necklace. The three of us had decided to twist them into identical bow ties for dinner. We'd also kept our straw hats on, since we all agreed that serious hat hair lurked underneath. We got a few looks when we walked into the restaurant, but when you're having fun with friends, who cares what anybody else thinks?

"Maybe we look particularly adorable this evening," Tess said.

"Doubtful," Rosie said. "Not with all that chocolate and wine still rattling around in our stomachs."

All three of us had ordered on the light side—green salads, broiled entrees—for dinner and stuck to water. Still, the earlier sample binge had taken its toll.

"So," Tess said. "Do you want to stake out some lounge chairs on the sun deck? I bet the fireworks will be amazing from up there."

"I definitely need to move some more today," I said. "Maybe if we walk off dinner, we'll manage to walk off the rest of this afternoon's free sample damage, too."

"Good idea," Rosie said.

Tess shrugged. "I suppose we can enjoy the fireworks from a vertical position just as easily as we can from a horizontal one."

So we walked and walked the streets of Tournon-sur-Rhône again. Bands were playing in the parks. It was hard to tell where the sidewalk cafés ended and the streets began. Laughter and dancing and the rhythmic exotic chattering of a language we couldn't understand surrounded us like a hug.

"Maybe we should be scattering baguette crumbs as we walk," Tess yelled above the noise, "so we can find our way back."

"As long as we know where the river is, we're fine," I yelled.

"How about that thing one of the guides said the other day?" Rosie yelled. "To find the bank of any river, stand facing the direction the river flows. The right bank will be on your right, the left bank on your left."

"We don't need to know which bank we're on," Tess yelled. "We just need to be able to find the ship."

225

Finding the river again turned out to be easy, because eventually everybody started surging in that direction. Parents pushed sleepy babies in strollers. Toddlers rode on their parents' shoulders. Teenagers clumped together. Couples walked with arms around each other. There were probably plenty of other tourists like us around, but the locals were out in force, the way at home just about everybody would turn out for the fireworks over Marshbury Harbor on the 4th of July.

The crowd gathered by the edge of the river. Tess, Rosie and I kept walking along Quai Charles de Gaulle until the fireworks started. And then we just stopped between two plane trees and looked straight up. It was like watching fireworks edged in lacy green foliage.

When our necks got stiff, we worked our way closer to the river for an easier view. I was certainly not a fireworks connoisseur, but it was an amazing show, filled with bursts of orange and magenta and green and red and blue and white. I loved the way each new explosion lit up the bridge and the river and all the happy people out for a night of Bastille Day celebration.

"Wow," Rosie said. "I can't believe we're actually here and seeing this."

"I know," Tess said. "Even I can't think of anything sarcastic to say."

When the grand finale blast was over, we worked our way through the crowd, staying as close to the river as we could, until we found our ship.

We stood under a streetlight and checked our step count.

"Wowza," I said. "That's some pretty good mileage today."

"Impressive," Rosie said. "We might have even worked off the chocolate."

"I can't believe it's 10:30 already," Tess said. "What a long freaking day—I don't know about you, but I'm heading straight to bed."

Day 26

22, 199 steps

I knew I was dreaming, but it was a really good dream. Rick and I were back in our Fresh Horizons small group outplacement counseling classes. Actually, we'd skipped class and instead we'd snuck into the senior center in the same building. We were sitting side-by-side in red faux-leather recliners holding our Wiimotes and trying to decide whether to play Wii bowling or Wii golf. Rick leaned over and we started kissing, and before I knew it the two of us were entwined in the same red faux-leather recliner. The kiss went on and on and on, slow, soft, deep, luxurious. The earthy sexy smell of lavender filled the air.

Suddenly somebody was knocking on the senior center door.

"Damn," Rick said. "I hate when that happens."

"Ignore it," I said. I ran my hand along his thigh.

"We could get arrested," Rick said. "Making out in a senior center is a felony."

The knocks grew louder.

"Wow," I heard Rosie say as she walked past my bed. "I want what you're dreaming."

I fought my way back to reality, or as close as I ever got to it. I sat up in bed, pulled my lavender wand out from under my pillow.

When Rosie opened the door, Tess burst into our room wearing her pajamas. "Hannah called the ship's emergency number because she couldn't get through to me. She knew we were in southern France but wasn't sure where. I just finished Skyping with her."

"Ohmigod," Rosie said. "Is she okay?"

"She's back at school for her internship," Tess said, "but she said she'd call her dad and let him know we're okay and tell him to get in touch with everybody else."

"*What* are you talking about?" I said.

Tess grabbed the remote for our television and sat on the bed beside me. Rosie sat down on my other side.

When Tess found CNN, a newscaster was recapping. At 10:30, just after the fireworks ended in Nice, a 19-ton cargo truck was deliberately driven into the crowd celebrating Bastille Day on the Promenade des Anglais.

We watched, horrified. The carnage. The stunned crowd. The people running. The woman in the white blouse stained red with blood, so much blood. Bodies in the street covered with sheets. Strollers abandoned.

Hot tears rolled down my cheeks. "Those poor people."

"I told Hannah," Tess said, "we're not even close to Nice. We just drove by the signs on the way from the airport."

"I'm pretty sure Nice is almost five hours away from where we are right now," Rosie said.

"Nice was a seaside celebration," I said. "Ours was on a river."

We stared at the television screen. A baby doll in a pink dress sprawling on the cobblestones like another dead body. Teenagers crossing a street with their hands on their heads as

French soldiers secured the area. The massive bullet-ridden truck. More bodies, so many more bodies.

I closed my eyes. "It was the exact same kind of Bastille Day celebration we just came from."

Rosie sniffed. "Our fireworks ended just before 10:30, too."

"Holy shit." Tess wiped her eyes with her pajama top. "It could have been us. I mean, it really could have been us."

I carried my iPad out to the balcony to give Rosie some privacy while she Skyped with her family in our room. It was almost 1 A.M. our time, which meant that back at home it was just before 7 P.M. the day before.

I pulled up Skype, found my mother's name on my contacts list, saw that she was online, probably waiting to hear from me. I held the cursor over her name, clicked on the video call icon.

My mom and Rosie's dad appeared on my screen, squished side-by-side in my desk chair at my computer.

"Hey," I said.

"So glad you girls are okay," my mother said. "It's all over the news here. Horrible, horrible tragedy."

"Horrible and senseless." Rosie's dad shook his head.

Tears ran down my cheeks like a river while they watched me.

I sniffed. "I don't know what to say."

"You don't have to say anything," my mother said.

"It's such a beautiful country," I said.

"It's a beautiful world," my mother said, "until it's not. So you just have to get out there and live your life while you can. Live and love, honey, just live and love."

"I love you," I said. "I'm going to hang up now."

"I love you, too," my mother said. "We'll see you soon."

I scrolled through my contacts list until I found Rick's photo and screen name. *Offline*, it said. I hovered over him anyway until the option to send a message popped up.

I'm in France and just wanted to let you know I'm okay, I wrote.

Rosie and I knocked softly on Tess's door.

Tess opened it right away. As soon as she saw our sneakers and our lavender wands, she knew what we were up to.

"We couldn't watch the news anymore," Rosie said.

"And it didn't seem right to try to sleep either," I said.

"Just give me a second," Tess said.

She came out dressed and ready to go, lavender wand in hand.

"Do you think you should invite Joy?" I said.

Tess shook her head. "I think Joy was relieved to see me go. I was in my bed zoning out in front of the television, and she was in her bed with her laptop. And let me tell you that room was feeling awfully small."

Without even talking about it first, we headed up to the deck-top track and started looping around and around. We circled our lavender wands like imaginary sparklers as we walked.

"Do you believe we haven't even walked this track yet?" Tess said.

"I know," Rosie said. "There's been so much else to do."

A sky full of stars twinkled above the sun deck. Off in the distance, some of the ship's crew had pulled lounge chairs into a circle. We heard the faint buzz of conversation.

"They work so hard," I said. "They probably have to be back on the job in a few hours."

Other than the crew, we had the deck to ourselves. We walked and walked, covering the small track over and over again.

"I wish we had candles," Rosie said. "We could light them for the people of Nice."

"After we finished lighting them for the people of Nice," I said, "I think I'd light a candle for my father. Just to let him know that I still think of him."

Rosie choked back a little sob. "I'd light one for my mother, too."

"Is it weird that your parents are dating?" Tess said. "I mean the parents that are alive. Although I suppose there's always the possibility that heaven exists and your other parents are dating up there, too."

"I kind of like that idea," Rosie said.

"I have to admit," I said, "that would make me feel a lot better about the whole thing. I guess it just seems unfair that some people get to go on with their lives and others don't."

"What else can you do?" Tess said. "Not getting on with your life doesn't bring anybody back. And I guess you could even look at it that the people who are lucky enough to still be alive are even obligated to actually live their lives instead of wasting them."

How would that look? I asked myself as we kept putting one foot in front of the other. In theory, I absolutely believed in living my life. In actuality, I had to admit things were still a bit vague.

"I can't stop thinking about Annalisa," Tess said.

Annalisa was a third-grade teacher from New Orleans. Hannah's class had adopted Annalisa's class after Hurricane Katrina, sending each year's new class letters and encouragement and classroom supplies they bought with their own money. Because Tess was also a third-grade teacher, she'd emailed Annalisa and sent supplies, too.

And because Tess was Tess, when she found out that Annalisa had cancer, she wanted us to bring this perfect stranger with us to the lavender festival in Sequim. Sad story short, instead of coming with us, Annalisa had died while we were in Sequim. Tess, Rosie and I had walked to the end of the Dungeness Spit and toasted her with lavender black currant champagne while we watched the sunset. We sang "Walk on By" and said goodbye.

"We'd light a candle for Annalisa, too," Rosie said.

"I still think of her all the time," I said. "Even though we never met her."

We walked another lap under the stars.

"Since we don't have candles," Tess said, "maybe we should toast them all instead."

Rosie and I offered up the bottles of wine we'd bought earlier in Tain L'Hermitage to the cause.

"Not necessary," Tess said. "I was a Girl Scout. Before we left I stashed some wine in my checked baggage just in case. Be right back."

"I don't know," I said as Rosie and I kept walking around and around. "Maybe we should go to bed instead."

"I'm not sure I could sleep yet," Rosie said.

Tess was back in a flash, a box of wine cradled in one arm and her iPad tucked under the other.

"Ohmigod," I said. "You brought a *box* of wine to *France*?"

"I can't believe they even let boxed wine into the country," Rosie said.

Tess handed out three takeout cups from the snack station. "Fine, then don't drink any. FYI, not only is boxed wine seriously cheaper, but it can be just as good as bottled wine. Every glass poured out of the box is like a fresh bottle because the bag inside it prevents oxygen from getting in. So boxed wine stays fresh for up to six weeks after opening."

"Like wine ever lasts up to six weeks after opening," Rosie said. "I mean, how would they even test that?"

"If you think about it," Tess said, "boxed wine is actually cutting edge. It's great for the environment—bottles have literally twice as big a carbon footprint as boxes. In fact, I'm thinking boxed wine might be our new clothesline. You know, we could start a boxed wine advocacy group when we get back home."

"I'm way too sad and tired to have this conversation right now," I said. "Let's make our toasts."

So we stood at the ship's railing and looked up at the sky full of stars. We toasted Annalisa and Rosie's dad and my mom and all the poor people in this beautiful country who just happened to be in the right place at the wrong time on Bastille Day.

And then we gave a toast to all the good people all around the world who'd had terrible, heart-wrenching things happen to them.

I pointed. "Look. The stars are twinkling just like diamonds."

"Oh," Rosie said. "That's the perfect song for us to sing for all of them."

And so we sang Rihanna's "Diamonds," about shining bright and how we're all beautiful like diamonds in the sky. We didn't really know the words, so we just made them up as we went along.

When we finished singing, we held our paper cups of boxed wine up to the sky full of stars.

"Shine on," we said.

We were stretched out on lounge chairs looking up at the stars.

"This boxed wine is actually really good," I said.

"Told you so," Tess said.

"Why did you bring your iPad out with you?" Rosie asked Tess.

"Please don't pull up the news sites," I said. "I don't think I can watch anymore right now."

"Ohmigod," Tess said. "I almost forgot." She leaned

forward, grabbed her iPad. Then she reached into the waist-band of her yoga pants and pulled out a piece of paper.

"When I went back to my room to get the wine, Joy was in the bathroom." Tess gave the paper a little shake, unhooked her reading glasses from the neck of her T-shirt. "Joy's laptop was on her bed and the top was almost but not quite closed, as if she was hiding something. I mean, if you're alone in your own stateroom and only going to the bathroom and then coming back to whatever you're doing, why not leave your laptop open, you know?"

I nodded. "That's exactly what she did at the computer station when I was looking for my key card."

"So," Tess said. "I dashed over to her laptop really fast and flipped it open."

"You didn't," Rosie said.

"I most certainly did," Tess said. "I mean, Joy already hates me, so what's the worst that could have happened? She must have just walked away from it, because I didn't have to wake up the laptop with a password—"

"Which you didn't have," I said.

"Exactly," Tess said. "Anyway, I only got a quick peek, but Joy was signed in as the administrator of a blog and it looked like she was in the middle of writing a blog post."

"Didn't you say she works as a fundraiser for a nonprofit?" I said.

"Yeah," Rosie said. "She probably has to blog for her job."

Tess leaned back in her lounge chair, took a slow sip of wine. She waved the little piece of paper back and forth like a flag. She took another leisurely sip of wine.

Under the soft deck lights, Rosie rolled her eyes at me.

"Fine," I said. "I'll bite. What's on the paper?"

Tess smiled. "I copied down the link to her blog so I could find it later. Guess what it's called."

"What?" Rosie and I said at the same time.

"*The Joy of Snark*," Tess said.

"Catchy," I said.

Tess typed the blog's address in her web browser.

Rosie and I slid our lounge chairs closer to Tess's so we could see.

I read a few lines. "Holy moly," I said. "No way."

"Way," Tess said. "I knew something wasn't right."

Rosie looked up from reading and shook her head. "I can't believe Joy would do this to us. It's just so vile and mean-spirited."

We scrolled through blog post after blog post, each one filled with nasty comments about the way Tess, Rosie and I looked and the things we said.

The photos were the worst part. Beyond unflattering images of us in our matching hats, our twisty necklaces, our purple Wildwater Walking Club shoelaces, shoveling down food, laughing like lunatics.

"I can't believe she calls us 'conjoined triplets in desperate need of a clothing intervention and some face work'," Rosie said.

"Look," Tess said. "Right there—she calls me a non-bloomer loser she went to high school with. And I can't believe she had the nerve to take those pictures of me while I was sleeping. Bitch."

"You've got to be kidding me," I said. "Look at this one."

A blog post titled "Breaking and Entering Just for Fun" consisted of a series of photos of Rosie's and my room. Clothes strewn all over our messy beds. My notes from health coaching practice. A close-up of a bra with the size showing on the tag. The plastic organizer hanging over the glass shower door in our bathroom, the clear pockets filled with our personal items.

"How the hell did she get those pictures?" Rosie said. "She's never even been in our room."

"Ohmigod," I said. "Joy stole my key card. I must have

dropped it on the way to get coffee that morning when I saw her and she scooped it up."

Rosie shivered. "Remember when I said I had a creepy feeling someone besides housekeeping had been in our room? It's like I could feel her bad vibes."

Tess was still scrolling through the posts. "It looks like she's written a whole series of scathing attacks on one of her coworkers. She calls her an incompetent idiot and makes fun of the way she dresses, and look, here's a photo of the coworker's secret candy stash."

"Oh, that's so mean," Rosie said. "I'd be mortified if Joy wrote something like that about me. Oh, wait, she did."

We all laughed.

"Here's the thing," Tess said. "We don't really care what Joy thinks about us. I mean, we don't care what anyone thinks about us, right? We have lives. We have each other. But this kind of thing could put someone else right over the edge. We can't let Joy get away with it."

"Let me see that for a minute." Tess handed me her iPad and I clicked through the rest of the website. On the About Me page was a generic shadowy photo of a mystery woman in dark glasses and a man's fedora, a trench coat with the collar up covering her hair. The bio said simply: *The Joy of Snark is everywhere. You could be next.*

"She's completely hidden," I said. "It's the anonymity that's fueling all her venom. It's like a protective shield for her nastiness."

"She's not anonymous anymore," Tess said. "But I know what you mean—it's so cowardly. If you want to get all malicious, at least have the courage to attach your name and face to it."

"Exactly," Rosie said. "It's like all the cyber-bullying at school. So much of that is anonymous and it can be so devastating to the kids. I just don't get why anyone would do it."

"I think," I said, "you have to be feeling really awful about yourself to write a blog like that."

"Oh, please," Tess said, "I'm so sick of people taking out their own problems on the rest of us. If everybody kept their deep-seated issues to themselves, the world would be a better place."

I handed Tess's iPad back to her. "So what are we going to do? Do you want to drag your mattress into our room and sleep there so you'll be safe?"

"No way," Tess said. "I'm not afraid of Joy. And if I drag my mattress into your room, how will I be able to take ugly pictures of her while she's sleeping?"

"Tess," I said. "We can't sink to her level. Even if she started it, if we act like Joy, we're really not any better than she is."

"Geez Louise," Tess said. "When did you get to be so mature? It's that freakin' health coach stuff."

"I think," Rosie said, "we need to march right into your room now and tell Joy we're on to her."

"I don't think so," I said. "I think we need to take our time and get a plan first."

"Fine," Tess said. "As long as it's a good one."

"Just so whatever our plan is doesn't get in the way of us having fun," Rosie said. "I mean, I'm totally pissed off at Joy, but I don't want to give her the satisfaction, you know?"

I felt a little jolt as our ship cast off for Lyon at 5 A.M. Rosie was snoring away, so I grabbed my foam ear buds off the bedside table.

I dreamed that Joy was driving a big white truck riddled with bullet holes and heading right for the three of us. We tried to jump out of her way, but our feet were glued to the street as if we were characters in an old *Looney Tunes* cartoon.

Just as Joy was about to hit us, the brakes screeched and she leaned out the window and took a picture of our horrified faces.

I woke up, my heart beating like crazy. I tossed and turned, fell back to sleep. I dreamed that Rick went to France to find me and ended up in Nice at the wrong Bastille Day celebration. Tess hired a plane to get him out, but Rosie was afraid to go up in the plane and we were afraid to leave Rosie alone in case something happened at our Bastille Day celebration, too. I kept sending Skype messages to Rick over and over, telling him to act like a wizard.

The smell of coffee woke me up at lunchtime. Rosie's bed was empty and the shower was running. There was a coffee cup on my bedside table. I reached for it—still warm.

I jumped in the shower as soon as Rosie got out. We met Tess in the restaurant and pigged out on an amazing bouillabaisse made with four types of fresh fish cooked in a stock with onions, tomatoes, garlic, and rouille, a spicy saffron garnish.

Joy actually sat down with us at our white tablecloth-covered table, as if she knew something was up. We smiled and chatted with her as if it wasn't.

We joined a walking tour of old Lyon. Our guide told us Lyon was France's second largest city and where the Rhône and Saône rivers meet with a kiss. We walked through secret passageways between buildings called *traboules*, built during the heyday of the Lyon silk industry to allow the silk workers to transport their delicate wares in all weather without them getting ruined.

We visited L'Atelier de Soierie, one of the old silk factories, and watched a demonstration of silk scarves being made. They kindly let Tess use their Wi-Fi so she could text the picture of a gorgeous 10-screen print of Lyon at night to Hannah, which Hannah approved almost immediately. Tess bought a silk scarf called *Van Gogh La Nuit Etoilée* (The Starry

Night) for herself. Rosie and I bought The Starry Night silk scarves, too.

"I can't wait till Joy sees us wearing these," Rosie said. "The more she makes fun of us, the more I want to dress alike."

"Just don't forget it's a vacation thing," Tess said. "We're going to have to tone it down once we get back to Marshbury. We do have to live there, you know."

We jumped in a motor coach for a tour of the walled medieval stone village of Pérouges, where the original *The Three Musketeers* movie was filmed. We wandered through streets so old that they were made of real stones instead of cobblestones. We admired the rows of geraniums in the unscreened windows, which our guide told us were placed there to keep the mosquitoes away.

And the whole time we walked, we talked.

By the time we got back to our ship, we had a plan.

Day 27

10,232 steps

We were on a goat cheese farm in the town of Lys, population 250. Our shiny white Mercedes motor coach was parked by the side of the unpaved road. Wildflowers sprouted from the dry dirt.

"Chickens!" Rosie said. "I can't believe we're seeing chickens."

I snapped away with the camera on my phone as one adorable French hen scaled the top of a little house, queen of the hill.

The chickens danced through the barn and back out to the yard like they were in a conga line.

"Wow," Rosie said. "The Supremes and Rod Stewart would love it here."

"They've got a pretty great life on the lavender farm," I said.

Rosie smiled. "It works both ways—chickens give back a lot. They eat bugs and weeds, and all their scratching and digging breaks up the soil for us. Plus their manure is the best, and they very kindly scratch that into the soil for us, too."

"Hmm," Tess said. "I once read that if 1000 households each raised three chickens, over 100 tons of waste would be recycled and kept out of the local landfills. Maybe chicken could be our new clothesline."

Rosie scooped up a chicken whose feathers were an exact match for Rosie's red hair. "Handling a chicken produces the same feel-good hormones you get from hugging a person or playing with a dog or cat."

"Or walking," I said. "And you have to admit sneakers are a lot less maintenance than chickens."

Inside the barn, the goats were playful and affectionate. We petted goat after goat, fed them handfuls of hay, obsessively snapped cute goat photos.

"I think you're going to have to get a few goats when we go home, too," I said to Rosie.

"Or maybe *you* should get the goats," Rosie said. "You could always rent them out on the side—they're great for clearing weeds and brush. Goat-renting is definitely a thing now."

I wondered if I'd look back a year from now and think *This was the day I decided to start a rent-a-goat business.*

Tess pointed to big branches of holly hanging from the ancient wood barn beams. "Do you think they have Christmas in July here?"

Our guide laughed. "No, no. It is a tradition. The holly is hung from the beams to protect the baby goats from disease and bugs as it dries."

We dragged ourselves away from the goats and chickens and hay and holly to visit the farm's shop, where a spread had been laid out for our tour group. We skipped the wine and stuck with water. We sampled fresh and mature goat cheeses, decided we liked them all.

We climbed back on our fancy bus and drove to a nearby truffle orchard. Our guide informed us that the black Périgod truffle is one of the world's most expensive and sought-after delicacies, a subterranean fungus often referred to as a black diamond.

The owner, Olivier, greeted us. He told us he and his wife were scientists. They'd bought his parents' house and planted the truffle orchard when they decided to "come back to earth."

"I love that," Rosie whispered. "It sounds so much better than 'back to the land'."

"I am absolutely going to come back to earth one of these days," Tess said, "but what's the rush, you know?"

Olivier's puppy Maestro galloped over to join us. Olivier told us that Maestro was a Lagotto Romagnolo, a breed of dog from Romagna, Italy that is universally considered to be the best truffle dog. Many dogs can be trained to hunt truffles, and Olivier's first truffle dog, a poodle, was a gifted truffle-hunter. But he was getting older, so Maestro had been brought in to eventually take over for him. Maestro, Olivier told us like a proud parent, had found his first truffle at ten weeks.

The best way to know when a truffle is ripe, Olivier continued, is from the aroma it gives off. Both pigs and dogs have keen senses of smell and can hunt truffles, and pigs have traditionally been used as truffle hunters. The problem is that the pigs like to eat the truffles, and when a 400-pound pig wants to eat a truffle, it's hard to convince it to give it up. With a dog, you simply tell it to drop the truffle and reward it with a treat.

Hearing his cue, Maestro ran over and sat. Olivier gave him a treat.

"Truffles," Olivier said, "are the result of a symbiosis between the tree and the truffle."

"I have no idea what that means," Tess whispered, "but it sure sounds sexy, especially with a French accent."

Olivier went on to tell us that truffle season is in the fall and winter, but even in July Maestro would entertain us by finding lesser truffles closer to the surface. Maestro ran off and began scratching away at the base of a nearby tree, his tail wagging like crazy. When Olivier followed Maestro to the tree, Maestro backed off. Olivier dug up something with his knife. He praised Maestro and passed the hard black walnut-like fungus around so we could all feel and smell it.

"Exactly how much do black truffles go for?" I asked Rosie.

"About a thousand dollars a pound," she said.

"I think you might need to cut back on the sunflowers," I said, "and consider adding a small truffle orchard."

We followed Olivier to a tasting cellar built of stone beneath his home. While Maestro dashed around like a puppy, Olivier served us bread with truffle-flecked butter as well as saffron flan and wine from his neighbor's vineyard.

The older truffle-hunting poodle came to join us, along with another dog, a Keeshond.

"Does this dog hunt truffles, too?" somebody asked.

"No," Olivier said. "This one refused to hunt. He simply wanted to be a dog."

I carried my iPad out to the tiny stateroom balcony and signed in to Skype.

Rick was online.

Our ship was docked on Quai Claude Bernard near the University of Lyon. I took a moment to watch a group of twenty-somethings laughing and talking as they walked by, wondered if their easy confidence was just a façade the way mine had been at their age.

When I looked at my screen again, Rick was offline.

I closed my eyes, shook my head.

When I opened my eyes again, the first of the evening's commuters were coming out of a nearby stop on the tramway. Maybe they were walking home or maybe they were walking toward their cars or to meet friends for dinner. Whatever they were doing, they moved with purpose through the charming, well-kept city. They had places to go, things to do, lives to live.

The watery Skype ring took me by surprise.

Rick's tiny Skype photo and username appeared with a message that I had an incoming call.

I gave my hair a quick fluff, checked myself out in the little box on my iPad screen, took a deep breath.

I tapped *Answer with video*. "Hey."

Rick appeared in a little box over mine, like we were both contestants on *Hollywood Squares*.

"Hey," he said. "I'm glad you're okay. Thanks for letting me know."

I swallowed. "I thought you disappeared again. When you saw me online. Just now."

"I went to change my clothes." Rick stood up so his computer camera could pan the length of his button-down dress shirt.

"Impressive," I said.

He smiled. "I only had time for the top half. I didn't want to lose you."

"So today," I said, "we were at this truffle orchard. And the truffle farmer had two truffle-hunting dogs, an older dog and a puppy. And then there was another dog. The third dog decided he didn't want to hunt truffles, that he simply wanted to be a dog instead. It really got to me. I mean, if a dog has the backbone to decide what it wants its life to be, what's *my* problem, you know?"

I took a deep breath. "I can't stop thinking about how with all this time I've had since taking my buyout, instead of actively creating a new life, I've been sitting around. Awash in indecision. Passively waiting to see where life takes me next. What business can I fall into? What life can I fall into? In a way, an embarrassing way, I think I've even been kind of waiting to be saved."

I looked up at the tiny camera on my iPad. "I could have spent this whole year deciding what I want—"

"Listen," Rick said. "There's something I need to tell you."

Dread came out of nowhere and sat on my chest like an elephant. My brain shut down. I felt a burst of adrenaline as my body went into fight or flight mode.

I'd been around the block enough to know that *there's something I need to tell you* rarely led to a happy ending. It was the kind of thing a guy said to you when he'd gone back to his ex-wife. Or found a new girlfriend ten years younger and fifty times more functional than you. Or had just become born again. Or realized he was gay. Or decided to move as far away from you as he could possibly get. Or didn't like the length of your hair or the way you dressed, which on the surface, might not sound as jolting as the rest, but was a sure sign of an emerging control freak.

I felt the sear of a blush as it climbed my cheeks. The best I could do was to try not to look as freaked out as I felt.

"Okay," I said, even though I knew it was probably anything but.

Rick cleared his throat. "So that night I didn't show up. I was in an accident."

It took every bit of my self-control not to say *Yeah, right.*

"I was playing Pokémon Go on the way to your house, driving five miles per hour, the perfect speed to catch virtual creatures out the window."

Rick shrugged. "I hit a fire hydrant—there was water everywhere. Somebody must have called 911 because two cops showed up in a cruiser. They arrested me and charged me with driving to endanger."

"Why didn't you call me?" I said.

In the little box on my screen, Rick shook his head. "To bail me out? I was too humiliated to call anyone. So I spent the night in jail and they arraigned me in the morning. The judge gave me community service—I'd never even had a speeding ticket."

"I'm sorry," I said.

"I could have killed someone. Somebody's kid or mother or girlfriend."

I nodded.

Rick ran one hand through his hair. "It was rock bottom. I didn't want to tell you. I was too embarrassed. Hell, I figured I'd blown it anyway, so what was the point?"

Sometimes you just have to keep quiet and listen. So that's what I did.

"And I spent a lot of time thinking, really thinking, which I know isn't always one of my strong suits . . ."

I smiled.

"And I remembered that health coach thing you said about the difference between a fixed mindset, when if you screw up, it means you're a screw-up, end of story. But a growth mindset is like being in beta, where your screw-ups give you the information you need so you can fix the bugs. And I realized that if you buy into that, you don't have to cut and run when you mess up. Or when somebody else does. You can take the lesson and grow."

I realized I'd fallen into my slow pendulum nod.

Rick matched his nod to mine. "And right after that I ran into my old metal sculpting teacher at the sub shop. He asked me if everything was okay, why I hadn't come back to class. So I told him the truth—that when somebody took my sculpture apart and threw it in the scrap pile, it seemed like maybe it was time to try something else I had a chance of being better at, you know? And he told me my metal sculpture fell apart by itself—nobody took it apart because they thought it was junk. The welds were faulty. I just needed to work on my welds."

"Life," I said, "is endlessly fascinating."

Rick smiled. "All by way of saying I realize my welds are not the only thing I need to work on. I did a really stupid thing that night, and I apologize. And if you can see your way to forgive me, I'd like us to get back on track."

A couple in jeans and sunglasses walked by the ship, so close I could almost touch them from the balcony. The man reached over and twirled a lock of the woman's long straight hair. She laughed and gave her head a flip, as if she were filming a shampoo commercial. As if he were the luckiest guy in the world to get to touch her hair. In my wildest dreams, I could never be that cool.

"So the thing is," I said, "I don't think we've ever really been on track. I think we've stayed in our own little corners where it's safe. And I don't want to do that anymore. I think we need to be either in or out, to figure out how to build a life together or let it go and move on."

Rick looked right at the camera. "I'm in."

"How would that look?" I said as I launched into my long slow pendulum nod again.

In his little rectangle, Rick leaned toward me. "I think we need to figure out what we'd like that life we build together to feel like. And once we have that, then we can figure out what we need to do for a living to support it."

"Yeah," I said. "And maybe then we just have to try some stuff and see what works. I'm pretty sure part of my problem has been that I've been thinking I have to pick that one perfect thing before my buyout package benefits run out. And what if it's the wrong thing, you know? What if the health coach thing is interesting, but I can't make a living at it? What if I put more time into the website for Rosie's lavender farm and it doesn't take off and I let her down?"

Rick grinned at me. "Growth mindset, just think beta and bugs."

I grinned back. If there were a way to kiss somebody on Skype without looking like an idiot, I would have totally gone for it.

"I have a question," Rick said. "Would now be a good

time to jump on a plane and meet you in France for a romantic interlude?"

It was tempting.

"Thanks," I finally said. "But I want to finish this trip with my friends. Maybe you and I could plan another trip though? You know, once we get things moving in the right direction?"

Rick nodded. "Deal. And this way I'll have more time to cook your welcome home dinner. Any requests?"

"I'm open," I said. "As long as it involves spiralizing zucchini."

Day 28

10,999 steps

The three of us were sitting at an umbrella-topped table out on the ship's terrace café eating salade Lyonnaise, which Tess and her app had proudly translated to Lyonnaise salad.

Our plates were filled with torn, bitter greens. The greens were topped with crispy bacon cooked in onion and garlic, sprinkled with croutons that had clearly come from a baguette and not from a box, and drizzled with warm Dijon mustard vinaigrette. A single perfectly poached egg graced the top of each salad.

"Enjoy," our waitress Andi said with a smile.

"I'm going to miss the ship's entire crew," Rosie said. "They're all so upbeat and positive. But I'm especially going to miss Andi."

"Maybe she can come with us on our next trip," Tess said.

"Let's get through this trip first," Rosie said.

When I pierced the egg with my fork, the yolk ran over the greens like liquid sunlight. "This salad is amazing," I said.

"I bet it was on the menu at all the little rustic bouchons we passed," Tess said. "I'm glad we're getting a chance to try it while we're in Lyon—it's got such a working class food vibe, like something the silk workers here might have eaten a century ago." Tess leaned back, took a picture of her plate. "At least that's the story I'm sticking to for my cultural grant report."

"I love that it's such a simple, everyday salad," Rosie said. "Sometimes people add a handful of chopped fresh tarragon to it, but you could definitely add lavender buds instead."

A few tables away, we had a perfect view of Joy chatting with a friendly couple from Canada. Joy was wearing makeup and jewelry with a white sundress that was so simple and perfectly fitted that it had to be really expensive. Her hair was twisted into the cute messy bun that Tess could never quite manage.

Joy caught us looking at her, stood up and took a picture of us and our matching Lyonnaise salads. We all gave her phony little waves with the hands not holding our forks.

"I've been thinking," Rosie said. "Maybe we should do something a little less confrontational. Like wait till we get home and then send Joy a letter. Or even just leave a comment on her blog so she knows we've seen it."

"No way," Tess said. "I didn't stay up half the night binge-watching *Intervention* episodes with you two for nothing. Plus, Noreen is almost a professional. She could practically hang out a shingle if she wanted to."

"Health coaches don't do interventions," I said. "They encourage their clients to come up with their own goals and then help them strategize to achieve them."

Tess took a long drink of water. "Fine. We'll wing it. Anyway, I took screen shots of some of the nastiest posts on Joy's blog, just so she can't take them down fast and try to tell us we were hallucinating. And I think it's important that we confront her in a public place with witnesses, so it doesn't turn into a screaming match. I mean, who needs the drama, you know?"

"Once we confront her," I said, "what's our goal? We want her to take down her blog, right? I mean, what's to prevent her from just starting another blog?"

"Nothing," Tess said. "But we want her to know that she's not anonymous anymore. We see who she is and what she's doing, and we're calling her on it. Maybe she'll be afraid I'll tell the rest of our high school class about it and that'll be enough to get her to knock it off."

"Maybe," Rosie said, "you should threaten to put Joy in charge of your next class reunion if she doesn't stop. That'll scare her straight."

"Funny," Tess said. "So funny I forgot to laugh."

Since it was our last night on the cruise, we ordered three different desserts and shared them—a flourless chocolate ganache cake topped with fresh raspberries, chocolate mousse, chocolate macarons.

"If it's not chocolate, why even bother," I said.

"*Absolument*," Tess said in a French accent that could use some serious work.

Rosie reached for another bite of chocolate cake.

We inhaled every last crumb of our desserts, drained our water glasses.

We dabbed our mouths with our cloth napkins. We picked up our lavender wands from the table. Tess reached for her roll of duct tape.

"Please tell me you're not planning to use that," I said.

Tess put the duct tape on her wrist like a bracelet. "Not unless I have to."

"Okay," Rosie said. "Let's do it."

"Ten-four, good buddy," Tess said.

"Be careful out there," I said.

"There she is!" Tess said in a perky voice I'd never heard before.

Tess swung one arm around Joy's shoulders. I squeezed in close on Joy's other side.

"I hope you don't mind us kidnapping Joy," Rosie said to the Canadian couple in a voice that was even perkier than Tess's. "We've got something extra-special planned for our final night."

Joy tried to slide out from under Tess's arm.

Tess squeezed Joy's shoulder.

I leaned in a little closer.

"Have a lovely night, eh?" one half of the Canadian couple said as we walked away.

"You, too," Rosie said. "Safe travels tomorrow."

"Let *go* of me," Joy said. "*Now.*"

We kept walking, waving our lavender wands with our free hands so we wouldn't look suspicious, until we got to the deck-top walking track.

"What the *f*— are those purple things?" Joy said. "Some kind of voodoo?"

"Yeah," Tess said. "We're going to magically turn you into a nice person. Here, sniff this."

"Isn't it a great track?" Rosie said. "I'm really going to miss it. Although it'll be nice to walk the beach again."

The rubberized track was way too narrow for us to walk four across, so Tess and Joy walked on it while Rosie and I walked along the deck on either side of them like bodyguards.

Tess gave her lavender wand a sniff, then held out it in front of Joy's nose.

"Get that thing away from me," Joy said. "I mean it."

"Listen," Tess said.

I cut Tess off. "So, Joy. We're sorry we didn't get to know you better on the cruise. Friendships are so central to our health and wellbeing."

Joy didn't say anything.

I went into my long slow pendulum nod anyway. "You always look and act so put together, but I know all of us have our challenges. That being said, what might a positive goal be for you in terms of friendship?"

Joy elbowed Tess. "Let go of me, you *psycho*."

Tess hung on tight. "Joy, Joy, Joy. We can do this the hard way or the easy way."

Rosie shook her head. "Somebody needs some better dialog."

"Who said that anyway?" I said.

"SpongeBob SquarePants," Rosie said. "Sadly, Connor and Nick were so obsessed with that show that I can still recite entire episodes. 'Now Gary, we can do this the hard way or the easy way. Or the medium way. Or the semi-medium easy-hard way. Or the sorta-hard-with-a-touch-of-awkward-difficult-challenging way.'"

Joy ducked out from under Tess's arm, turned and ran.

She was wearing high cork-wedge sandals, so we caught up to her easily between the two deck-top paisley-shaped Astroturf putting greens.

A man was just handing Joy his golf club. "Take it, sweetheart. The missus will have my head if I don't get downstairs and spiffed up for dinner pronto."

As soon as the man started to walk away, Joy held up the club like a weapon.

"No problem," Tess said. "We'll talk to you from here."

Joy started backing away.

"I don't get it, Joy," I said. "Why would you go to all the trouble of coming on this river cruise just to write mean things about us on your blog?"

Joy's eyes darted to Tess and back to me. "I can write anything I freakin' want to write. It's called freedom of speech."

"Sure you can," Rosie said. "But what we don't understand is why *would* you? What does making fun of other people do for you?"

"I didn't start it," Joy said.

"What do you mean, you didn't start it?" Tess said.

Joy shook her head. "Do you know what it's like to do fundraising for a living? To kiss up to rich people and beg for money? All day, all week, all year? How humiliating it is to kowtow like that? Do you have any idea what kind of sappy, idiotic stuff I have to write on my stupid work blog?"

Rosie started circling her lavender wand around like she was trying to smudge away the negative energy.

"So if you have to write a nasty, mean-spirited, anonymous blog," Tess said, "why not rip *them* apart? I mean, what did *we* ever do to you?"

Joy tapped the handle of the golf club on the deck a few times as she glared at Tess. "You don't remember me from high school, do you?"

"What do you mean?" Tess said.

Joy tapped the golf club again, harder. "Just what I said."

Tess tucked her lavender wand under her arm, pulled her hair elastic off her floppy ponytail, tried putting her hair back into a cute messy bun again. "High school was a long time ago. I have a hard time remembering whether or not I took my vitamins this morning."

Joy flipped her head back, and her cute messy bun got even cuter and messier. She ran a perfectly manicured fingernail around the handle of the golf club.

"I was Janice Robinson," Joy said. "Lumpy and bumpy and—"

"We were all a mess back in high school," Rosie said. "You should see my senior picture—totally tragic."

"Seriously?" Tess said. "You were Janice Robinson? Wow, I can't believe it. You look fabulous."

Joy glared at Tess. "And as for what you did to me? We were in the same homeroom, we had classes together. And one day there was an empty seat beside you in the cafeteria, so I walked up to you and your friends' table with my plastic tray and asked you if this seat was taken."

Joy paused, bit down on her lower lip. "And you looked right at me and said 'keep dreaming.' You got a great laugh, I'll give you that."

The color had drained out of Tess's face. "I don't remember that."

"I wish I could say the same thing," Joy said.

Tess crossed her arms over her chest. "I was probably trying to be cool in front of some guy or something. I remember every mean thing someone said to me in all four years of high school, but I don't remember that at all."

Joy just stared at her.

"Look," Tess said. "I am so sorry I did that to you. It was an awful thing to say, even for a teenager. Please forgive me."

"Do me a favor," Joy said. "Just stay out of my way."

We watched as Joy walked off, still carrying the golf club.

"Wow," I said. "So am I wrong or was Joy essentially saying that it wasn't her fault that she blogged awful things about us as an adult, because of what Tess did to her as a stupid teenager a gazillion years ago?"

"Seems about right," Rosie said. "So what do we do now?"

"I think we just stay out of her way," Tess said. "And the next time we take a trip, one of you gets to pick a roommate."

Day 29

10,501 steps

Disembarkation was as incredibly organized as the rest of our river cruise. Last night Rosie and I had found orange tags waiting for us in our room with our stateroom number on them. An accompanying note instructed us to put them on our luggage and leave the luggage in the hallway outside our rooms at 6:15 A.M.

When we opened our door this morning, Tess was rolling her own orange-tagged luggage into the hallway. We headed for the restaurant so we could chow down enough breakfast to last us for the day.

"So," I said as we sipped our coffee. "What time does Joy leave?"

"She's gone," Tess said. "3:30 A.M. Red tag, luggage in the hallway at 2:45."

"Painfully early," Rosie said. "Now there's some quick karma."

"Was last night awful?" I asked Tess.

"Not that bad." Tess shrugged. "We actually smoothed things over a bit. Joy told me she took down the blog. She gave me a big song and dance about how she's going through this nasty divorce and how much pressure she's been under because of that."

"It's always someone else's fault with Joy, isn't it?" I said.

"Seems like," Tess said. "Anyway, I told her to let me know if she wanted to go to our next class reunion together."

"Seriously?" Rosie said. "Did you say that to make sure she'd really take down the blog?"

"I don't think so. I mean, she'll take it down or she won't —it's not like anybody probably reads it anyway." Tess reached for her croissant. "And I did snap one really ugly picture of her while she was sleeping just in case we ever need it. Duct tape may or may not have been involved."

"Nice," Rosie said.

Tess shrugged. "Mostly I said the reunion thing because I just figured I kind of owed her. I know it was a long time ago, but I still can't believe I ever said that to her."

"We've all done stupid things," I said. "In a growth mind-set, you own the mistake, take the lesson, and move on. And part of that is letting yourself off the hook."

"Thanks," Tess said. "I really appreciate that. But can we save any additional health coaching until after my caffeine has kicked in?"

At 7:00 A.M. we strolled off the ship and watched our orange-tagged luggage being loaded onto yet another fancy white motor coach. A local guide met us at the Lyon airport, made sure we had our boarding passes, escorted us to security and watched to make sure we got through and were headed for the right gate.

"We've gotten so soft from this trip," Rosie said. "We'll never be able to think on our own again."

"Speak for yourself," I said. "I'm already trying to think of how we're going to keep our parents from hopping from house to house whenever the mood strikes them."

"I've already told you," Tess said. "A tiny house is the

perfect solution. I have a bunch of brochures—I'll drop them off when we walk tomorrow."

"We're actually going to walk tomorrow?" Rosie said.

"Of course we are," Tess said. "We're The Wildwater Walking Club."

We rolled our carry-ons back and forth along the length of the terminal so we could rack up some steps toward today's quota.

When our plane landed at Roissy Charles de Gaulle just before noon, we found our way through another security check and to our next gate like old pros. We hit the fancy restroom, grabbed some takeout coffee at a café, shared the nuts and cheese we'd packed up at the ship's restaurant this morning and brought with us for a snack. We got some more steps in.

"Okay," Tess said once we'd boarded our second flight. "If our flight to Boston takes off at 1:50 P.M. Central European Time and arrives in Boston at 5:15 P.M. Eastern Standard Time, which is six hours earlier, how long is the flight?"

"Oh, please don't make us do math," Rosie said.

"Yeah," I said. "Let's just say it's going to be a very long day."

So we drank water instead of wine to stay hydrated, circled our ankles, got up to move as often as we could make ourselves do it. We ate and watched movies and napped.

"I can't believe how exhausted I am," Rosie said once we'd made it through customs at Logan Airport's international terminal. "But that trip was so much fun. We definitely have to do another river cruise one of these days."

"Bathroom," Tess said.

"And then let's grab coffees on the way to baggage claim," Rosie said. "Dunkin' Donuts. Or Starbucks."

We followed a little girl and her mother into the distinctly unglamorous restroom, dragged our carry-ons into the stalls with us.

"Honey," we heard the mother say to her daughter behind their shared stall as we were washing our hands. "It's not okay to open the door until mommy finishes pulling up her pants, too."

"Like this?" the little girl said.

The stall door swung open. The mother let out a blood-curdling scream.

"Aww," Tess said. "There's no place like home."

We stopped outside the restroom and refilled our water bottles with filtered water. We rolled our carry-ons behind us as we followed the signs for baggage.

I checked the time. "Our flight landed early, so we might be able to get some more steps in before we have to meet our car. Hey, do either of you have any mints? I could really use one right about now."

Tess rolled her carry-on off to the side, unzipped its front pocket.

"Here you go." Tess handed me a tin of mints, reached back in to her carry-on pocket.

"And here *you* go," she said to Rosie. "A little present from me to you."

Rosie opened her eyes wide. "Where did you get this?"

Tess shrugged. "It's just one of those gnarly little iris pieces. I completely forgot I had it."

Rosie hid the iris rhizome under one armpit as she looked over both shoulders. "You *stole* a Van Gogh blue bearded iris and *smuggled* it into the country?"

A couple walking by turned to stare at us.

"You might want to consider keeping it down," I said.

"Talk about looking a gift horse in the mouth." Tess held out her hand. "Fine, give it back to me."

"What are you going to do with it?" Rosie said.

Tess shrugged. "I don't know. Throw it away. Learn how to garden. I'll think of something."

"Do you have any idea how illegal that was?" Rosie said. "Besides the fact that you *stole* it out of Van Gogh's garden—"

"S*hhh*," I said.

Rosie lowered her voice. "You're supposed to declare any kind of plant or food when you come into the country."

"Damn," Tess said. "I meant to declare those Goldfish crumbs that have been kicking around in my suitcase since the '80s. And we were also supposed to check Yes if we've been on a farm or in close proximity of livestock so that customs and border security could bring in an agricultural specialist to check our shoes for soil that could harbor foreign animal diseases. So unless you checked Yes on that form, don't get holier-than-though with me, girlfriend."

"Our shoes were clean," Rosie said.

"And the teensy weensy piece of iris that I rescued from an overcrowded garden where it was probably going to die of neglect was clean, too," Tess said. "If anybody said anything, I would have just pretended it was a piece of gingerroot and eaten it on the spot."

"You're certifiable," I said.

"So you admit it," Rosie said. "It *was* premeditated theft."

"Come on," Tess said. "Just give that fugly root back to me and I'll throw it in the trash. And then we can move on to getting the caffeine we so desperately need."

Rosie held out the iris rhizome to Tess.

Tess reached for it.

Rosie snatched it away again, tucked it under her arm. "I hate that you're putting me in this moral dilemma, *Tess*."

"You're really getting on my nerves, *Rosie*," Tess said.

I looked back and forth between my two friends. "Clearly we can come up with a compromise that will make everybody happy." I turned to Tess. "How might that look to you?"

"Fine," Tess said. "I'll march right back through security,

get in the customs line again and tell them I forgot to mention that I have this teensy weensy piece of iris and ask if it's okay if I bring it into the country."

"You can't go back through security," Rosie said. "You don't have a ticket."

I turned to Rosie. "So then, what might the solution look like to you?"

"Well," Rosie said. "Maybe Tess can write a letter of apology to the Van Gogh hospital and ask if they'd like her to mail them the iris rhizome."

"Right," Tess said. "And then what shall I say when they offer me a room *in* the hospital?"

I knew that as an emerging health coach I wasn't supposed to make suggestions, but I really needed a cup of coffee.

I started rolling my carry-on in the direction of the baggage claim.

"How about this," I said. "Rosie plants the iris rhizome in her garden and propagates it. Eventually she divides and sells the irises on the lavender farm, and every cent she makes has to be donated to a good cause. Beginning with a donation to the art therapy classes for women at the Van Gogh Hospital."

Rosie caught up to me. "I could work with that."

Tess was right behind us. "Sure. And after that we could use the money to support our box wine environmental advocacy campaign. What do you think of SCREW THE CORKSCREW for our first slogan?"

"Ooh," I said. "How about THINK OUT OF THE BOX TONIGHT?

"Chill," Rosie said. "And I'm not talking about the wine, you two."

We walked a few steps in silence.

"I think I'm going to take tomorrow off from walking," Rosie said. "I'll get my 10,000 steps in just playing catch-up after a week away."

"You know," I said, "that's actually a great idea. I wouldn't mind sleeping in tomorrow."

"Fine," Tess said. "You're both getting on my nerves, too. But after a day off, I'm sure we'll have passed the cluck off stage and be back in stride as The Wildwater Walking Club again."

Day 30

10,001 steps

The beach was filled with promise this morning. The sun was shining, the tide was rolling in, a sea breeze blew the summer heat away.

Couples and families and teenagers had already staked out a good chunk of the prime real estate by the time we got there, so we had to weave our way around their chairs and toys and towels to find sand to walk on. But it was still pretty great to walk the beach.

I took a deep breath. "Salt air is the best smell in the world."

Rick swung his arm around my shoulder. "I don't know, that pesto shrimp with spiralized zucchini I made last night smelled pretty good. If I do say so myself."

"And it tasted even better than it smelled," I said. "Don't think I'm going to forget for a minute that you can cook like that."

When the car service dropped me off at my house, I'd rolled my luggage inside to find Rick in my kitchen. A mountain of spiralized zucchini had taken over the counter.

"I might have overbought on the zucchini," Rick had said once we'd taken a break from kissing. "The recipe said four zucchini, but I didn't factor in that the only ones I'd be able to find were the size of baseball bats."

The leftovers had turned out to be the perfect breakfast.

We cut uphill through the hot dry sand, climbed the cement steps, took a seat on the seawall.

"So," Rick said. "What might a day in our life together look like?"

"Wow," I said. "How very health coach-y of you."

"I'd like to say I'm a quick study." His cat green eyes held mine. "But that hasn't always been true. I want you to know that I'm going to cut way back on video games. Maybe stick to mostly playing Wii sports with you, if you're up for it."

"My mom and Rosie's dad will be happy about that. Just to warn you, they're going to hit you up for some more Wii bowling tips."

"Yeah, I know. Lo and Kent were at your house when I got there yesterday. They said they want to turn us on to pickleball."

"Great," I said. "Whatever that is. So, our life together." I tilted my head until it rested on Rick's shoulder. "I'd like to be able to do this a lot. You know, not spend fifty or sixty hours a week at the office. I mean, I'm fine with working hard, I just want to have more of a life, you know? I'm hoping that once I get my health coach certificate, I can put together a corporate program and pitch it to some of the companies in the area. Maybe there would be an educational component, and I could try to get them to cover an intro one-on-one session for any employee who's interested. And if I get focused on Rosie's website, I think there's some good e-commerce potential there."

Rick nodded. "Sounds like the start of a great plan. I've been thinking maybe I'd do just enough IT contract work to make a living, and then use the rest of my time doing more creative things. Which may or may not bring in any money—"

"Ohmigod," I said. "I haven't even thanked you for the cement sculpture you made me. It's gorgeous. You know, I bet Rosie would love to sell them at the lavender farm shop. And even online."

"Really?" Vulnerability was written all over his face.

"Really," I said. "Not only do you have great taste in women, but you're pretty damn talented."

"Thank you. And not only do you have great taste in men, but you're going to make a terrific health coach."

I shrugged. "Who knows. But at the very least, I'm hoping the health coach training will help me get my own act together."

Rick leaped down from the seawall. It hit me with the force of a tidal wave that the reason Rick and I hadn't been able to truly connect as a couple was that we'd been floundering as individuals. We were still floundering, but maybe, just maybe, we were heading in the right direction now.

Rick reached up to hold my hand. I jumped.

"As long as we're putting one foot in front of the other," Rick said, "we don't have to have all the answers yet."

I leaned in for a kiss. "As one of our tour guides said, we're spoiled for choice."

Rick's Pesto Shrimp with Spiralized Zucchini

1 tablespoon olive oil
1 tablespoon butter
I pound large shrimp, peeled and deveined
4 garlic cloves, minced

1 ½ pounds (4 medium-sized or 2 baseball bat-sized) zucchini, spiralized
1 pint grape tomatoes, halved
½ cup prepared basil pesto
½ cup freshly grated parmesan cheese
salt and pepper to taste.

Heat oil and butter in skillet over medium-high heat. Add garlic cloves and shrimp. Sauté for 2 to 3 minutes.

Add spiralized zucchini and grape tomatoes. Stir until zucchini is al dente and shrimp is cooked through.

Stir in pesto until heated through. Sprinkle with parmesan cheese. Salt and pepper to taste. Dig in!

Thanks so much for reading **The Wildwater Walking Club: Back on Track**! If you enjoyed it, please take a moment to leave a kind review to help other readers like you find it.

Keep turning the page to read an excerpt of Noreen, Tess and Rosie's third adventure, **The Wildwater Walking Club: Step by Step**.

Excerpt WWC: Step by Step!

Day 1
10,002 steps

One year, three months and two days after I became redundant, I lurched awake as if I'd been electrocuted. I rolled over and tucked my vibrating wrist under my pillow so I wouldn't have to see the annoying flashes of light that came along with the vibrations.

Rick rolled in my direction, bringing a hint of yesterday's deodorant and sleep-seasoned morning breath. Tiny flecks of cement from his latest batch of garden sculptures added heft to the streaks of gray in his light brown hair. He let out a low frequency rumble of a snore that sounded vaguely like Darth Vader.

My Fitbit vibrated again, a gazillion buzzing insects attacking my wrist. I scrunched my eyes shut, opened them just long enough to poke the screen with an index finger to make it stop. ROCKSTAR, the screen read. I'd programmed it to greet me that way as a confidence booster, but right now I had to admit it felt more like my Fitbit was mocking me.

The sad truth was I'd thought that, even if it didn't quite reach rockstar magnitude, I'd have my life all figured out by now. I'd spent far too many years working for Balancing Act Shoes before they'd been gobbled up by another company. Most recently I'd been Senior Manager of Brand Identity, part of the team that created sneakers like Dream Walker (*You'll Swear You're Walking on Clouds*), Step Litely (*Do These Sneakers Make Me Look Thin?*), and Feng Shuoe (*New Sneakers for a New Age*).

A guy from the takeover company I never should have been fooling around with tricked me into accepting a buyout package. Eighteen months of full base salary and benefits seemed like plenty of time to get my act together. Who knew.

I dozed. My Fitbit vibrated. I poked it. It showed me an image of two feet and a big fat O, my step count for the day so far. And then it started vibrating again.

"Fine," I said. I rolled out of bed and paced around my bedroom, holding my stomach in just in case Rick happened to wake up and glance my way. It was a good thing I'd recently finished my health coach certification, because the average lay person might not even realize that the alarms on most fitness tracking devices turn off once you've walked fifty steps.

I'd met Rick at a series of small group outplacement counseling classes offered by a company called Fresh Horizons, another perk of my buyout package. Rick had recently taken a buyout, too. He'd been some kind of IT ethical hacking wizard at a company that helped financial institutions, as well as the occasional political party, identify their website vulnerabilities. Because the word *wizard* had actually been in his official job title, I always pictured him sitting at his computer behind a red velvet curtain, shirtless and wearing a pointy white wizard hat with Senior Overlord of Ethical Hacking emblazoned across the brim in gold letters. It was sexy, in a geeky kind of way.

For a while there, Rick had been even less together than I was, assuming that was possible. Eventually I realized that two people as screwed up as we were had absolutely no business attempting a relationship until they got their rebound career paths figured out.

So I called things off and sallied forth on another adventure with Tess and Rosie, the neighbors I'd bonded with because our lives had all imploded, each in a different way. Rick stepped it up and we found our way back to each other.

Now he seemed to be figuring out what he wanted the next chapter of his life to be. A big part of me was thrilled for him. The lesser part of me was pretty much seaweed green with envy.

I gave my teeth a quick brush and splashed some water on my face. Yanked on a pair of leggings and wiggled my way into a sports bra. Found the sleep T-shirt that had ended up on the floor last night during the throes of passion. The best thing about living in the golden age of athleisure wear was that you could pretty much wear anything anywhere. Either that or my post-buyout standards had really slipped.

When I opened my bedroom door, I heard giggles coming from the guestroom. My mother and Rosie's father were dividing their time between our houses. They had an irritating habit of hopping from house to house for romantic guestroom trysts whenever the mood struck. The upside was that they always made the bed and sometimes cooked breakfast.

I put on my sneakers and grabbed a jacket, pushed my door open and shivered. October had a way of really sneaking up on you. Just like the rest of life.

Under a sky full of stars, I stood in the dark making shiny loops with the flashlight on my phone. Then I walked in place to rack up some more mileage and to keep my toes from freezing. After that I breathed in the scent of pine trees—a stronger resin and just beneath that, a trace of what always smelled like lemon to me.

"Olly olly oxen free," I sang in a semi-whisper.

"Olly olly come in free," I tried. I was fairly sure that was the updated version, since oxen had basically gone the way of dinosaurs. At least in my front yard on Wildwater Way in Marshbury, Massachusetts.

While I waited for Tess and Rosie to appear at this ridiculous hour, I figured I might as well wish on some of the stars I was looking at. It couldn't hurt.

I thought for a minute. I was old enough to know that happily ever after was probably not going to happen, so I scrunched my eyes shut and whispered, "Happy-ish ever after. Star light, star bright, first stars I see this morning, just let me live happy-ish ever after."

How would that look? my inner certified health coach couldn't help asking.

"Well," I whispered. "Rick and I would get along most of the time, and I'd eat well and exercise regularly, and I'd make time for my family and friends, while setting healthy limits, especially with my mother . . ."

A cloud of impending doom came between the stars and me like an eclipse. I shivered some more, zipped up my jacket, flipped the hood over my head, tucked the hand not holding my phone up under one sleeve.

"And I'd actually figure out how to make enough money as a health coach to survive before my eighteen months of base salary and benefits run out. In less than three months. And I end up living in a tent pitched by the side of the road." I dug hard for some optimism. "Double wide, like the trailer."

I took a deep breath and began walking in the direction of the beach. With luck, the crisp air might turn out to be just cold enough to numb my fears. I waved my phone flashlight in front of me as I crossed the street, so I wouldn't get hit by some over-achieving early commuter and end up dead in a ditch. By the side of the road where my tent would eventually have been pitched if I'd lived.

"Wait up," Tess yelled behind me.

"Yeah," Rosie yelled. "Wait up."

I kept walking. "If you're going to make me get out of bed at this insane hour," I mumbled, "you could at least have the courtesy to show up on time."

"Don't whine," Tess said as she racewalked past me. "It's unbecoming." Tess was dressed for work as a third-grade teacher. Except for the fact that she was wearing her walking sneakers along with lavender fleece pajama bottoms with multi-colored coffee cups printed all over them.

Rosie racewalked past us both. Her red curls poked out from under a dark gray hat that looked similar to a mop and had a beard-like face mask attached to it. It clearly belonged to one of her sons.

"Nice hat," I said.

"Thanks," Rosie said. "It's called a barbarian. What can I say, it's really warm."

I jogged a few steps to catch up with them. "Cool. Maybe I can start making barbarian hats for a living. If I trimmed back the beards, they could pass as unisex."

"They look like artsy versions of the ski masks we wore during our crime spree," Tess said.

Just before we'd left on our first trip together to the Sequim Lavender Festival in Washington state, Tess had dragged me out of the house under the cover of darkness to protest Marshbury's official town clothesline ban. We'd covered poster boards with clothesline activism slogans like CLOTHESLINES ARE THE NEW COOL and FIGHT FOR THE RIGHT TO AIR DRY and THERE'S NOTHING LIKE THE SMELL OF YOUR SHEETS FRESH OFF THE LINE. We duct taped our signs to a clothesline stretched across the Marshbury town common.

Our final act of defiance had been to add bubbles to the elephant fountain. Perhaps a few too many bubbles, since overnight they'd multiplied and taken on a life of their own, overflowing the fountain and surging across the manicured grass.

When Tess, Rosie and I passed the common at the crack of dawn the next morning on the way to Logan Airport, the bubbles looked like a cross between a seriously late snowstorm and an effervescent tidal wave. And by the time we got to Sequim, a video of a hazy but identifiable me taking off my black ski mask and following a ski-masked and unidentifiable Tess and her laundry detergent over to the fountain had found its way to the Marshbury town website.

"It was *your* crime spree," I said now. "You just dragged me along for the ride. Which, as you well know, I didn't appreciate."

"Wuss," Tess said. "Okay, so then I'll take full credit for getting that Marshbury clothesline ban lifted."

I shook my head. "Like you haven't been doing that all along."

Rosie gave her mop top hat a shake. "*Caps for Sale*," she sang, possibly to change the subject. "Remember singing that on the jetway on our way to France?"

"The jetway on our way to France," Tess said. "How la-di-dah."

Rosie ignored her. "My kids loved that book. Actually, I used to love it, too."

"Everybody loves that book," Tess said, not for the first time. We'd been walking together just long enough that the edges of our conversations had a slight tendency to repeat.

Tess tucked a hunk of highlighted blond hair behind one ear and turned to me. "You wouldn't really become a cap peddler, would you? Spoiler alert: the monkeys steal them."

I tried to picture myself walking the beach with a pile of mustached barbarian hats on my head, monkeys scampering around behind me. Call me crazy, but I was pretty sure that wasn't the thing to take me from zero to hero.

Rosie, Tess and I walked three abreast on the street, ready to jump back to the sidewalk if we needed to. We found our rhythm almost immediately, swinging our arms, Rosie adding a hop and a skip every so often to catch up with Tess's and my longer legs.

"Before you start making hats for a living," Rosie said, "can you paint some more retractable clotheslines for the lavender farm store? We're completely sold out, and we could use some more of those lavender water spray bottles, too. How're the online sales going?"

"Sale," I said. "We've had exactly one."

"Who cares," Tess said. "You're a certified health coach now. That probably pays almost as much as being a third-grade teacher."

"I'm sure it would," I said, "if I had any actual clients."

We reached North Beach in no time, spectacular pre-sunrise streaks of pink greeting us. As much as I hated waking up this early so Tess would get to school on time and Rosie could be back to get her kids on the bus and then start work as a landscape designer-slash-lavender farm owner, I had to admit that the sky put on its most magical show in that half hour before the sun came up. I took it in, along with the briny tangy smell of the ocean.

We reconfigured to walk single file through the narrow opening in the seawall. Then we spread out again once we were on the beach. It was getting close to high tide, so Tess claimed what was left of the hard-packed sand, and Rosie and I had to walk on the loose, dry sand at the top of the beach, occasionally crunching over some dehydrated seaweed at the high tide line.

I had no intention of telling Tess because she'd only want to change places with us, but walking on dry sand was actually a better workout. Because your feet move around more on loose sand, the tendons and muscles of your legs have to work harder. My Fitbit might not register the difference, but I knew. I swung my arms a little harder, paid attention to the tempo of my breathing, putting my training to work so it didn't get stale. I might not have any clients, but I was one helluva health coach.

"*Allons-y!*" Rosie said. "You are spoiled for choice, Noreen."

"Aww," I said. "You sound exactly like that guide from our trip to Provence. The slopes of Mont Ventoux, right?" Just a couple of months ago, we'd taken our second trip together, the trip of a lifetime. A river cruise filled with Van Gogh and vineyards, wine and chocolate, lavender and more lavender. And Tess's twisted friend from high school, but we'd gotten through that part. I could still smell the lavender, feel my heart rate and blood pressure drop just thinking about it.

"Mont Ventoux is the perfect 800-meter height for lavender," Rosie said. "Which makes me feel grateful that my lavender does as well as it does here, given that it's basically growing at sea level."

"Our trip to Provence," Tess said. "That sounds so pretentious."

"Watch it," Rosie said, "or Noreen and I won't take you with us on our next pretentious trip."

"When did you get to be such a smart ass?" Tess said.

"It just takes me a while to warm up." Rosie shivered. "Especially on mornings like this."

I matched her shiver with my own, like echoing a yawn but colder. "Why exactly am I spoiled for choice?"

Rosie gave another little hop to catch up. "Think of all the options you have. You're not tied to a lavender farm you dragged your husband and sons to so your dad didn't have to be all alone. Only to have your father start gallivanting around with a certain someone's mother."

"Not my fault," I said. "It was Rod Stewart and The

Supremes breaking into my house that started the whole romance."

"Oh, cluck off," Rosie said. "And you're not tied down with the aforementioned chickens either."

"And," Tess said, "you're not trying to figure out how to get rid of all the stuff you've accumulated over the years so you can travel the country in one of those new retro electric microbuses which, by the way, will make my carbon footprint even smaller than my clothesline does. Not to mention the fact that my borderline adult kids will really have to work to track down my husband and me."

"Plus," Rosie said, "you're dating." She crossed her hands over her chest and pumped them forward and back like a heartbeat. "You're basically still in the lovey-dovey stage of life, before reality rears its ugly head."

"I'd like to date again on a part-time basis," Tess said for about the gazillionth time since we'd met. "Nothing personal against my husband, at least most of the time. I'd just like to divide my time between being married and single. You know, like maybe we'd have two retro electric microbuses, and each be in the same one sometimes and in different ones the rest of the time. We could wave to each other from separate lanes of the highway on road trips."

"I get that," Rosie said, like she always did. "Then when you saw each other, you'd actually see each other."

"Yeah," Tess said. "The scheduling might get complicated though. And by the time you paid for two microbuses, it's not like you'd have any money left for dates."

"Right," Rosie said. "And there'd be two sets of bills and two sets of dishes to wash in tiny sinks, assuming those minibuses have sinks."

"Microbuses," Tess said. "They'd better have sinks. Paper plates would completely screw up my carbon footprint."

I didn't say anything. There was nothing new to say.

I could feel them side-eyeing me as we walked.

"I pitched you for a teachers' health inservice at school," Tess said. "Maybe something will come of that."

"Thanks," I said.

"I pitched you to the parent group at Connor and Nick's school," Rosie said.

"Thanks," I said. "For what it's worth, I've got a few pitches in myself." It was a slight exaggeration, but it had the feel of truth.

All this pitch talk was really starting to impact my early morning zen. I considered proposing silent walking from now on, realized that would last for about three minutes.

Instead, I started belting out Carole King's "I Feel The Earth Move." Tess and Rosie joined right in. We knew most of the real lyrics, but we made up our own words anyway, because that's what The Wildwater Walking Club did.

"I'm not sure about the 'girlfriends' line," Tess said. "Beach babes might be stronger."

"Or boss babes," Rosie said.

"Just so it's not gals," I said. "Gals drives me crazy."

"And can everybody please stop calling women ladies," Tess said. "Unless they're drinking tea with their pinkies sticking out."

"We are women, hear us roar," Rosie said.

We all roared. Then we went back to our song. We sang louder and louder, scattering a flock of seagulls hanging out at the water's edge. A good-looking guy and his dog jogging in our direction turned the opposite way and broke into a run.

"Scaredy cats," Tess yelled.

"Well, that felt good," Rosie said once we finished our final chorus.

"Yeah," I said. "Now I just have to figure out what to do with the rest of the day."

"Clotheslines," Rosie said. "And lavender spray."

"You can go through all the crap up in my attic if you're looking for a project," Tess said. "If you sell it without letting me see it first so I can't keep it, I'll even give you a commission."

"Thanks so much for your interest in my career growth," I said. "I don't know what I'd do without you two."

Tess and Rosie raced off to start their days without even stopping to lift weights and stretch in the tiny gym we'd created in half of my garage. I opened the side door to the garage, peeked inside. It seemed a little sad, just like me. I closed the door again.

The smell of coffee summoned me to the kitchen. I poured a cup, took a solitary sip.

"I'm ba-ack," I said as I opened my bedroom door. The bed was empty.

I checked the guestroom. That bed was empty, too.

"Olly olly oxen free," I whispered.

Lovely Lavender Anti-Stress Aromatherapy Putty

¼ cup dried lavender buds
1 cup flour
1/2 cup salt
3 Tbsp. cream of tartar
1 Tbsp. coconut or olive oil
1/2 cup boiling water
20 drops of lavender essential oil
Purple food coloring (mix red and blue)

Combine lavender buds, flour, salt, cream of tartar, and oil in a big bowl. Add boiling water and stir. Add food coloring until you get the perfect purple. Once you've reached the desired consistency (add more water or flour as needed) add drops of lavender essential oil.

Squish and play to ease your worries away. (And I'm a poet and I don't even know it.)

Keep reading! Go to ClaireCook.com to find buy links for *The Wildwater Walking Club: Step by Step,* Book 3 of *The Wildwater Walking Club* series.

Have you read?

Time Flies

Two best friends. A high school reunion. And a rollicking road trip down memory lane.

Time Flies is an epic trip filled with fun, heartbreak and friendship that explores what it takes to conquer your worst fears so you can start living your future.

Wallflower in Bloom

Deirdre Griffin has a great life. It's just not her own. She's the round-the-clock personal assistant to her charismatic, high-maintenance, New Age guru brother Tag. While drowning her sorrows in Tag's expensive vodka, she decides to use his massive online following to get herself voted on as a last-minute *Dancing with the Stars* replacement. Deirdre's fifteen minutes of fame have begun.

Never Too Late: Your Roadmap to Reinvention (without getting lost along the way)

Wondering how to get to that life you really thought you'd be living by now? Claire Cook shares everything she's learned on her own journey— from writing her first book in her minivan at 45, to walking the red carpet at the Hollywood premiere of *Must Love Dogs* at 50, to becoming an international bestselling author and a sought after reinvention speaker.

You'll hop on a plane with Claire as you figure out the road to your own reinvention: getting a plan, staying on track, pulling together a support system, building your platform in the age of social networking, dealing with the inevitable ups and downs, overcoming perfectionism, and tuning in to your authentic self to propel you toward your goals.

Shine On: How To Grow Awesome Instead of Old

If you're a forty-to-forever woman who's interested in aging well, don't miss this motivating and inspiring book.

Join *New York Times* bestselling author Claire Cook on a transformative journey that will help you shake off all those worries about getting older and embrace what can be the most vibrant, creative and empowering chapter of your life.

Shine On: How To Grow Awesome Instead of Old speaks to midlife women everywhere and is filled with Claire's trademark humor, heart, honesty and encouragement.

Must Love Dogs , the series

Based on the bestselling novel-turned-romantic comedy movie starring Diane Lane and John Cusack!

Dogs, dating, adorable preschoolers, and meddling family in every book.

"Voluptuous, sensuous, alluring and fun. Barely 40 DWF seeks special man to share starlit nights. Must love dogs."

Must Love Dogs
Must Love Dogs: New Leash on Life
Must Love Dogs: Fetch You Later
Must Love Dogs: Bark & Roll Forever (#4)
Must Love Dogs: Who Let the Cats In? (#5)
Must Love Dogs: A Howliday Tail (#6)
Must Love Dogs: Hearts & Barks (#7)

Keep reading! Go to ClaireCook.com to find out more about all of Claire's books.

About Claire

I wrote my first novel in my minivan at 45. At 50, I walked the red carpet at the Hollywood premiere of the adaptation of my second novel, *Must Love Dogs*, starring Diane Lane and John Cusack, which is now a 7-book series.

I'm the *New York Times*, *USA Today*, and #1 Amazon best-selling author of 21 books. If you have a buried dream, take it from me, it's never too late!

I was born in Virginia and lived for many years in Scituate, Massachusetts, an awesome beach town between Boston and Cape Cod. My husband and I now live on St. Simons Island, Georgia, a magical snowless place to walk the beach, ride our bikes, and make new friends.

I have the world's most fabulous readers and I'm forever grateful to all of you for giving me the gift of my late-blooming career.

Get my free gift, *41 Essential Quotes To Get Your Glow On*, exclusively for newsletter subscribers. You'll also be the first to find out when my next book comes out and stay in the loop for giveaways and insider extras: ClaireCook.com/newsletter/

HANG OUT WITH ME:

ClaireCook.com
Facebook.com/ClaireCookauthorpage
Twitter.com/ClaireCookwrite
Instagram.com/ClaireCookwrite
Pinterest.com/ClaireCookwrite
BookBub.com/authors/claire-cook
Goodreads.com/ClaireCook
Linkedin.com/in/ClaireCookwrite